Praise for Bianca D'Arc's
Wolf Hills

"A truly fantastic read! With a page-turning plot, dynamic characters and plenty of heat, readers will devour every last delicious page."

~ *RT Book Reviews*

"...one of the hottest paranormal stories I have read in some time. The action is thrilling and the characters enthralling. I love the writing of Bianca D'Arc and Wolf Hills more than lives up to her reputation

~ *Coffee Time Romance*

"I love reading Bianca D'Arc! You can bet you are going to get a red hot read with memorable characters... just the right amount of chemistry, humor, and downright sass that makes for good reading."

~ *Night Owl Reviews*

"*Wolf Hills* has witty, amusing dialog. The interplay between good friends and lovers works well...definitely a must read, especially if you love protective, amusing, hot Alpha wolves and the strong willed wild women that love them back."

~ *Sizzling Hot Book Reviews*

Look for these titles by
Bianca D'Arc

Now Available:

Wolf Hills

Bianca D'Arc

SAMHAIN
PUBLISHING

Samhain Publishing, Ltd.
11821 Mason Montgomery Road, 4B
Cincinnati, OH 45249
www.samhainpublishing.com

Wolf Hills
Copyright © 2013 by Bianca D'Arc
Print ISBN: 978-1-60928-945-4
Digital ISBN: 978-1-60928-777-1

Editing by Amy Sherwood
Cover by Angela Waters

First Samhain Publishing, Ltd. electronic publication: April 2012
First Samhain Publishing, Ltd. print publication: March 2013

Dedication

This book is for the fans who have waited so patiently for new books from me. You've stood by me in my darkest hours and I will be forever thankful for that.

Prologue

Something was very wrong in the early dawn of the Rocky Mountain foothills. Wyoming was a place of big sky and endless wonder, and the forest was a haven for many of the goddess's beloved children, both magical and mundane.

But this day, evil stalked the woods. Evil that walked on two legs and hunted the most innocent of the Lady's creatures. Evil that carried shotguns and plotted ways to bring about the end of days for all beings of the Light.

Danger permeated the primeval forest, but hope fluttered among the leaves and pine boughs. Hope for the coming of a new blend of magic. Magic that was ancient in form but modern in delivery. Magic that could renew the woodland—if it finally accepted its birthright.

Hope was coming, but would it be in time?

Chapter One

"She's here! She's here!" Carly raced into the front room, glad the sun had gone down more than an hour before. She'd loved her house aboveground before she discovered the twin layout her new husband Dmitri had built beneath over a century ago. The home they now shared underground had all the same amenities with one major exception. No windows. And for good reason.

Carly had never been happier than she was with Dmitri, but she missed her friends. She'd moved out to Wyoming, thinking she'd only be there while doing an installation job at the local university. Dmitri's love had convinced her to stay. He was the Master Vampire of this region and, though only a novice vampire, Carly, for better or worse, was now its Mistress.

The wolves had been a big help. Befriending the Pack's Alpha, a hunk of a man named Jason Moore, had been a stroke of good luck. As it turned out, a number of his Pack members had the computer and office skills Carly needed to relocate her headquarters from California to Wyoming. The Pack had also had the carpentry expertise to expand the old farmhouse she'd purchased. There was a new wing of office space where the squad of werewolf geeks and their vampire boss could work.

"Calm, my love." Dmitri's hand landed on her shoulder a moment before he came up behind her. He cocooned her in his presence, his strength becoming hers as he watched with her out the window.

There was indeed a pickup truck moving down the lane. She'd sent one of the wolves to pick Sally up from the airport in the ranch's new truck. Now that she had the cooperation of the local wolf Pack, she'd opened up the unused farmland on which her home sat, for raising a few crops and animal herds. The wolves managed it all for her, of course. And they took a commensurate share of any profits. Together, the vampire Master and Mistress were forming a true alliance with the wolves. That was something, Dmitri told her, that hadn't been done in centuries.

Carly liked it. Working together, both supernatural races could achieve great things.

But politics would wait for a while. She had a friend to greet. An all-too-mortal friend who was about to be set among wolves. Carly had to stifle a giggle at the thought.

"From everything I see about Sally in your memories, my love..." Dmitri told her mind to mind, *"...I think she'll be more than able to hold her own."*

"I almost pity the wolves," Carly agreed with a rueful grin. Sally was, without a doubt, the most formidable of her college friends.

Dmitri chuckled as he walked with her to the door. The pickup pulled to a stop and Carly nearly dove down the porch steps to greet her friend.

Detective Sally Decker barely managed to get the pickup's door open before Carly was there, arms out, pulling her from the cab into a huge bear hug.

"Watch it, Carl! You're about to break ribs," Sally joked, returning the welcome. It'd been too long since they'd seen each other. Of the old college study group, Sally had always had a special place in her heart for Carly, the eternal geek.

"Sorry!" Carly pulled back, an odd sort of fear on her face. Sally was perplexed by the reaction, but then, Carly had always been an odd duck. It was endearing.

"No harm done. I was only joking." Sally held her at arm's length. "Let me get a good look at you. Man, Carl, you're looking good. Best I've seen you in years. No dark circles under your eyes and your skin glows, though you're a bit pale. You need to catch some rays."

Carly laughed and put her arm around Sally's waist, pulling her toward the stairs where a tall, dark, and too-good-to-be-true handsome man waited. The professor, no doubt. Damn, the geek had done good.

"You must be Dmitri," Sally said, holding her hand out as they mounted the three steps to the porch. "I've heard so much about you."

His grip was strong and his smile genuine as he shook her hand. "It is good to finally meet you, Sally." His slight accent was to die for as well. Carly really hadn't been exaggerating in her descriptions of this man. If anything, she'd been holding back. He was gorgeous and his gaze, when it turned to Carly, was filled with love.

Sally was a good judge of character and always knew when someone was faking emotion. It's part of what made her a good cop. She'd bet her last penny that the professor was every bit as in love with Carly as she was with him. One less thing for Sally to worry over. At least part of her trek out here had been to be certain that her geekiest, nicest, closest friend in the universe wasn't being taken advantage of. With just one look at them together, Sally could put those fears to rest. The professor had it bad for the geek, and that made Sally smile for the first time in a very long time.

"Please, come inside. Carly arranged a little welcome party for you." Dmitri's accent rolled over her again, sending a little shiver down her spine. She wasn't completely immune to his charm, but aside from the Greek god good looks and powerful air, he really wasn't her type.

Sally noted the young woman who stood on the porch, near the door.

"This is my top programmer, Amy," Carly introduced her, patting the woman's shoulder in a fond way. "She's been a godsend these past months as we set up the new headquarters."

"I was glad to be of help," Amy said, smiling at Carly then extending her hand to Sally in greeting. "Your friend here is a lot of fun to work for. Welcome to Wyoming."

Sally returned the woman's handshake with a grin. "Nice to meet you, Amy. Thanks for keeping my buddy, Carl, out of trouble in this strange and foreign land." Everyone chuckled at her little joke.

Sally was impressed by Amy's natural beauty. Sally had met more than a few of Carly's staff back in California and not a one of them looked like this budding supermodel. In fact, as she peeked in the doorway, everyone inside the house was tall, muscular and had nicely chiseled features—the men and women alike. They were all beautiful. Not a single balding fat guy in sight. Weird.

A random sample of people should have more variety than this. Maybe they were all related to some line of supermodels married to sports stars. Sally smiled at her train of thought but kept the wacky idea to herself as Carly introduced them all. Oddly enough, they were Carly's new staff of computer geeks and office gremlins.

And they definitely knew how to party. A drink was placed in her hand and platter after platter of absolutely scrumptious hors d'oevres were passed around as they chatted. Music played softly in the background and the mingling commenced. Carly rarely left her side, but Sally noted Dmitri holding court in one corner of the room, his eyes seldom leaving Carly as he sipped a glass of red wine. Good lord, the man could smolder. Sally felt warm just from the glances he kept throwing at her friend.

"Is he as good as he looks?" Sally asked in a whisper while she and Carly were alone for a moment.

Carly answered with a blush that told its own story. "Better."

"I'm so happy for you, Carl. You deserve every happiness and if I don't miss my guess, that man is it for you."

"He is. Oh, Sal, you have no idea."

Sally knew that look. The geek had a secret she was dying to tell.

"Spill," Sally dared her.

Carly bit the side of her bottom lip between her teeth. "I wish I could, but not here. Not now."

"All right." Sally let her off the hook for now. "But soon."

"Soon," Carly agreed.

Sally brightened as she turned her gaze to the gathered crowd. "So how did you find all these beautiful youngsters to work for you? I mean, there's not a plain one in the bunch."

Carly looked worried but smiled as best she could. Sally hadn't made detective by being unobservant. There was something going on here, but Carly was as straight an arrow as they came, so she doubted it was anything sinister. Still, something had her old friend on edge at Sally's question.

"They live nearby and had the skills I needed. The university computer program is top notch. Unfortunately, the local market for computer science grads isn't great, so I was lucky."

"Are they all related somehow? I mean, they're all tall, svelte and gorgeous. What happened to the stereotype of the computer geek that lives in his mom's basement until he's forty? These guys are buff." She took a good long look at some of the young men standing a few yards away sipping their drinks and talking to two girls about the same age. Pure beefcake, if much too young for a jaded cop like Sally Decker.

"Well, the athletics program is good too." Carly didn't sound convincing. No doubt she was trying to make up a story for some reason. Sally smelled a mystery and it got her Spidey Sense tingling, even though she was certain Sally could never be involved in something bad. Sally believed in her friend through and through. "In fact, Billy there is a senior and still plays on the school's basketball team. Ryan was on the football team. He graduated about three years ago. The girls they're talking to, Veronica and Jill, were a very successful volleyball duo. They graduated last year."

Sally had been introduced to everyone and had spent a few minutes chatting with almost all of them before she'd cornered her friend. She'd had a long trip here and had been at the point of exhaustion both physically and mentally before setting out on her journey. Seeing Carly so happy and in love, though, really helped. A vacation was just the thing to restore her energy and she could only kick herself for not taking it sooner. She'd been wanting to check on Carly for a while now.

Ever since the truth about their friend Christy's horribly abusive marriage had come out, Sally had felt a need to check on all of her old study group friends. She'd been able to spend a bit of time with each of the girls in California, but nobody had seen Carly since the wedding. The other girls were all married now and their husbands were hotter than hot. Each of the men in their lives had impressed Sally deeply and she'd seen the genuine love between the other couples. Seeing them all so happy had been the one bright spot in her increasingly burnt out existence back in California.

She still couldn't figure why nobody else seemed all that

worried about Carly, so she'd taken it on herself to make the journey and check on Carly. The other newlyweds were probably too caught up in their own happiness to worry. Sally had seen the brutality people were capable of in her years as a cop. She didn't trust easily and she'd had a niggling, nagging worry about Carly—the woman she'd been closer to than all the others during their years in school.

If Carly wouldn't come home to visit, Sally would have to get on a plane and go see how her friend fared for herself. And now, here she was. Her first impression was that the same incandescent love she'd seen between all their other friends and their new husbands blossomed between Carly and Dmitri.

Sally was relieved. She'd come here to see about her friend, but now that she was here, she realized more than ever how badly she needed some time away from the ball of stress her life had become. Of all their old college study group, she was the only one still single. She felt left out, though she didn't begrudge any of her friends the happiness they'd found.

But didn't she deserve a little joy of her own? Just a little? Sally tried not to dwell on it. She was a believer in karma and fate. If it was meant to be, she figured she'd find her Mr. Right. If not, she had a job she used to enjoy and lots of experience. If she couldn't face going back to the force, she could always try to find some kind of private security gig. Something. Anything.

"What's wrong?" Carly's soft voice penetrated the funk Sally had sunk into. Sally shook her head, surprised she'd let herself slip. It wasn't like her to let her mind wander.

"Sorry. I was woolgathering."

"Come on, Sal. This is me you're talking to. What's up with you? You don't seem very happy."

"Hey, just who's the detective here?" Sally tried to lighten the mood with humor.

"It won't work. I saw that look on your face. We're going to

16

talk about this again before you leave, but for now, why don't you let Seth pour you another drink?" Carly crooked her finger in a very regal way that almost made Sally laugh. Who knew her shy little geek friend would find her mojo in the middle of nowhere among a group of freakishly attractive nerds?

A very handsome young man sidled up to them at Carly's beckoning.

"What can I do for you, Mistress?"

Carly shot him a warning look that Sally didn't miss. Oh, yes, there was something funny going on here. Sally decided to be more amused than alarmed. The alcohol she'd already consumed could have something to do with her mellow mood, of course.

"Detective Decker needs another drink. Why don't you take her over to the bar and see what you can mix up?"

"As you wish." Seth turned a downright wolfish grin on Sally. It would have been exciting if he weren't so young. Too young for her, if truth be told, though he was one of the older folks in the room. It seemed like all of Carly's new employees were still wet behind the ears.

Still, she let him take her arm and lead her to the other side of the large living room, where a fully stocked bar was tucked into one corner. He was polite enough and handsome as sin, but he just didn't do anything for her. Although he was nice to look at. Definitely eye candy of the first order.

The selection of wines behind the bar was truly impressive. There was even a refrigerator-sized chiller with a frosted glass door just for the stuff. Sally recognized a few of the labels as coming from Atticus Maxwell's winery and thought fondly of her friend Lissa, who had married the vintner not too long ago. She'd been to their house for drinks a few weeks back and was amazed by the opulent manor house and extensive vineyard. Marc LaTour and her friend Kelly had dropped by as well and

17

the two blissfully happy couples had made Sally feel welcome. It had been a nice change from feeling like a third wheel among her police colleagues and their spouses.

Seth was good company. He teased her with a confidence you didn't often find in someone his age while he mixed her drink of choice like an old pro. Not one for wine, she'd opted for a piña colada when Seth had offered to make a frozen one for her. She'd agreed more or less just to see if he could do it and he'd surprised her, drawing a crowd when the blender switched on.

A few of the other women were lining up for a slushy drink of their own when Sally noticed the front door open. Carly was there, greeting the most brutally handsome man Sally had ever seen. He reached out and grabbed her attention simply by entering the room. She knew she was staring, but was powerless to stop herself.

"Who is that?" she asked as Seth deposited the frosty glass full of frozen drink in her hand.

At her side, Seth visibly gulped. "That's the Alpha."

The man's strong chin rose as he seemed to test the very air of the room. His gaze slid over everyone present before landing on Sally. Leaving a bemused Carly at the door, he strode forward.

"The what?" Sally's attention was focused on the man striding across the room toward her. His gaze was locked on hers like a heat-seeking missile and the rest of the room faded into the background. His grace, his gaze, his utterly devastating presence mesmerized her.

Seth melted away, as did everyone else. This man commanded authority. He looked only a little older than the others, but he was miles distant from their callow youth. He'd seen things. Done things. Some things he probably wasn't too proud of and some things that had changed him on a fundamental level. Sally didn't know how she knew it, but her instincts were something she'd learned to trust in her years as a cop.

"You're Sally." His gravelly voice touched something deep inside her and made it hum as he stopped in front of her.

"And you are?" Challenge seemed to be the best way to handle this man who reeked of authority. She'd learned not to back down while working the streets, and the strategy had kept her alive and made her the most effective officer in her division.

Some kind of fire lit behind his eyes and a crooked grin forced one corner of his mouth upward. He seemed both amused and enticed by her challenge. He held out one hand, a dare of his own. As if he were daring her to touch him.

He'd soon learn she wouldn't back down. Especially not from something as simple as a handshake. She reached out and took his hand in hers, giving him a firm grip, noting how he tempered his obvious strength so as not to hurt her. He was firm, but not hurtful. A coiled spring respectful of her more delicate flesh.

"Jason Moore, leader of this little Pack of wolves." She liked the humor in his words, even as she wondered at their meaning.

"Sally Decker," she returned his greeting automatically, enjoying the warm strength of his big hand enveloping hers.

"I know." His smile deepened. Drat. Of course he'd known who she was. And now he knew just how off-balance she was too. All thoughts of embarrassment fled as she noted the slight dimple on the left side of his face. Wow. She hadn't thought it was possible for him to get any more attractive. "Carly has talked about little else since she found out you were coming for a visit. You're the fuzz."

She laughed outright at one of the cutest of the nicknames for police officers. She'd always liked that one.

"Good thing you didn't say I was a pig. I've shot men for less." She was proud of her attempt at flirting. She didn't often get a chance to try out her rusty interpersonal skills.

"Pigs are prey. That nickname would never work for you." His words were oddly serious, his gaze intense, but the smile that hovered around his gorgeous lips made her heart beat faster.

"Glad you understand that." She felt like she was playing with fire, verbally sparring with this man. She'd never wanted more to feel the burn. "Of course, I've never really understood where 'fuzz' came from. It makes me sound like dryer lint."

He laughed at her small attempt at humor and she was glad she'd made the effort. His masculine chuckle sent shivers down her spine.

"Fuzz sounds furry and cute. Like a puppy. Small, but armed with sharp teeth and wild instincts."

"Small?" She raised one eyebrow.

"I suppose you're tall for a woman, but you're definitely small compared to me." He looked her up and down with a gaze that felt like a caress.

"Okay, I'll give you that." She glanced around the room, only just noticing that everyone was giving them a wide berth. There was an electricity in the air that hadn't been there before Jason had arrived. Of course, it could just be her perception. It wasn't often she was chatted up by an amazingly attractive man. And she still couldn't figure out why everyone she'd met here was so fit and good looking.

"The same could be said for all the men in this room," she observed. "Even the young, pimply ones. Are there steroids in the water here or something?"

"Or something." He took the hand he was still holding and turned it over so that her hand rested on top of his. Tugging lightly, he pulled her toward a padded barstool that stood only a few feet away.

She sat at his urging, still holding his hand. The space was a little awkward. He hadn't moved the stool far enough away from the bar's edge and she had to move her knees apart a bit to catch her balance. The next thing she knew, he had moved to stand a bit closer, his muscular thighs touching the inside of her knee. It wasn't completely improper. Not really. But he was a little too close for comfort. At least in a room full of strangers.

Make that a room full of strangers except for one close friend. Who was on her way over with a worried look on her face.

"Don't look now, but the cavalry is on its way," she whispered as she turned her gaze back to Jason. Man. He took her breath away every time she looked at him. She couldn't ever remember having such an extreme reaction to a guy.

Surprisingly, Jason straightened and moved a few millimeters away, apparently waiting for Carly to arrive. The smile on his face was polite but the set of his jaw was predatory. An interesting, enticing combination.

"Mistress Belakov," he began politely as Carly reached them. "It was good of you to invite us to your party."

"I wasn't sure you'd come, Alpha. Thanks for taking the time. It's always nice to see you."

Carly's words were strange but polite. Still, there was an edge to her voice and a look in her eyes as she shot a glance toward Sally. Something was up. Then again, Sally had felt something was a little off from the moment she arrived. Carly was too much on edge.

"Okay, you two." Sally tugged her hand free from Jason's, hoping to clear her head a bit. He backed off, thankfully. "What's going on here? You've been acting strange since the moment I got here, Carl. And why do you call him Alpha? What is that, a title or something? And why are people calling you Mistress? Has your new hubby gotten you into a BDSM community or something? What gives?"

"And what exactly do you know about BDSM, Sally?" Jason posed the question with a definite devilish gleam in his eye.

"I'm a cop, Jason. Not a nun." She tapped him on the shoulder, pushing him another few millimeters away. She needed the space if she was going to think clearly. "Nice attempt at distraction, by the way, but I'm not giving up. I want answers."

"And I have a lot to tell you," Carly inserted, drawing her attention. "This isn't the best time for it, however. A lot has happened since I last saw you. Some of it, you're going to have a hard time accepting."

"Dude! You can't say something like that and then tell me I have to wait to hear your big, mysterious explanation."

"She's got you there, Mistress." Jason tipped his drink to Carly with a saucy grin.

"You're not helping, Jason," Carly shot back.

"Perhaps I can assist." Dmitri had arrived soundlessly, putting one brawny arm around his wife's shoulders from behind, pulling her back to his front lovingly.

Carly rolled her eyes. "I wanted to talk to her alone. You know that."

"I know, my love." He bent his head to place a kiss on the crown of Carly's head. "But the more I think about it, the more I believe it would be better if she were presented with proof of your claims right away rather than spend unnecessary time thinking you had lost your mind."

"It's like pulling off a Band-Aid. All at once is better than a little at a time," Jason agreed.

"Figures you men would stick together," Carly sighed. "How

do you want to do this?"

"I could always strip and shift for her." Jason's hands went to his belt buckle as his smile went up another notch.

"Don't you dare." Carly stopped him with her tone.

"Just trying to be helpful." Jason held up his hands, palms outward. His innocent act was almost humorous. Sally would have laughed if she wasn't so ticked by the idea that Carly and this new crowd of hers were hiding things from her.

"The Alpha is right about one thing. Quick is better," Dmitri agreed. "Sally, I am a vampire, as is Carly, now. I had to change her in order to save her life, but I knew she was my mate from the moment we made love. It is our way." He shrugged his elegant shoulders. "I can see you don't believe me, but you will." He closed his mouth then opened it again. Where before he'd had normal teeth, he now had fangs. Sharp, dangerous looking fangs.

"Holy shit," Sally whispered into the sudden silence around them.

Chapter Two

"It's all right, Sal," Carly lisped through a set of fangs of her own. Sally did a double take. No shit, they both had fangs. Ohmigod. Was this some kind of joke? "You're safe with us. We are mates and that means we only like to bite each other now." Carly actually giggled, gazing up at her husband mischievously. Damn.

Sally looked around at the rest of the partygoers. None of them had sprouted fangs yet. Thank goodness.

"What about them?" Sally motioned to the room in general.

"Members of my Pack," Jason added, drawing her attention. He tipped his imaginary hat to her. "I'm the Alpha wolf of this Pack. When Carly moved her computer business here, she was good enough to employ a few of our more educated youngsters."

"Wolf Pack? Is that like a club or something?"

Dmitri tried and failed to stifle his laughter.

"Perhaps I should clarify. I'm the leader of the local *werewolf* Pack." He emphasized the word.

"You've got to be kidding. Vampires and werewolves? Nice practical joke, Carl. Now knock it off." She said it with a smile, mostly because she didn't know what to think. Could they really be telling the truth?

"It's not a joke, Sal." Carly's whispered words and worried look made Sally's stomach clench. She wasn't kidding around. Before her eyes, Carly's fangs shrank back to normal teeth. "Dmitri is the Master Vampire of this area and since we mated,

I've become the Mistress. That's why the kids who work for me keep calling me that. They still haven't broken the habit, even though I keep telling them not to stand on formality with me."

"Formality helps keep frisky young wolves in order, Mistress," Jason cut in. "The hierarchy of the Pack is important. Isn't it just as important among your kind, Dmitri?"

Dmitri bowed his head but didn't lower his eyes. "You are correct, Alpha. Without the hierarchy, there is chaos. I have been Master here for a long time. There have been challenges through the years, but I have always prevailed to maintain the order."

"I've been Alpha long enough to face a few challenges of my own," Jason agreed. "Someday the challenger will win and I will either die or accept my new role as elder in the Pack." Jason shrugged as if he weren't discussing his own death with such a casual air. "It's the way of things. The way it needs to be among predatory races like ours."

"You really believe you turn into a werewolf at the full moon?" Sally asked. Her analytical mind needed proof.

"Not just on the night of the full moon. We become wolves, not just the half form you're thinking of from bad, old movies. Our combat form is something only the strongest of us can maintain for any length of time." Jason snapped his fingers and her temporary bartender stepped forward. "Show her, Seth. Drop your jeans behind the couch. She wasn't raised among wolves."

The phrase took on a whole new meaning if what Jason was saying was true, Sally realized. The young man took off his shirt and dropped his pants. The high back of the couch hid his private parts from view, but he had an amazingly muscular chest and equally bulky arms.

"Combat form," Jason ordered succinctly.

Before her disbelieving eyes, the young man's body began

to morph and change. He went from a relatively clean-cut, six-foot tall dude with a shock of blonde hair to a seven-and-a-half-foot hairy beast. He was trembling as he came out from behind the couch. A quick look downward told her that he was hairy enough that the more sensitive bits were mostly hidden. The way his newly formed legs crouched hid the rest.

"Holy Moses..." Sally breathed the words, in shock at what she was seeing. Seth walked closer on legs that were jointed oddly and ended in huge, sharp claws. His hands were clawed too, but his eyes were the same innocent blue she'd seen when they'd been introduced. His limbs trembled. "Does it hurt?"

"Seth is young. He is still growing into his true strength. The more he practices the battle form, the easier it will become, but to answer your question, yes, it can be quite painful to hold the shift at this point." Jason turned his attention back to Seth, who now stood a few feet in front of her. "Take it to completion, Seth. Show her your wolf."

The transformation began again. Or perhaps it was more accurate to say it continued. Muscles shifted under the skin, bones realigned and changed shape. Still, the eyes remained that clear, sweet blue. A moment later, the young man who'd become the scary creature had turned into a fluffy blond wolf.

Bigger than any natural wolf had a right to be, of course, but he definitely looked like a wolf. Seth walked right up to her and bowed his head, as if awaiting further instruction. Then she remembered Jason. He was in charge of these wolves, if all this was real. Seth was waiting for Jason's instructions.

"You can touch him, if it will help you believe." Jason's words sounded in her ear. He'd moved closer without her realizing it. The heat of his breath on her skin made those shivers return.

To get some space, Sally hopped off the stool, careful to move away from Jason, though she had to move closer to get away, the way he'd positioned her. Standing on her own two feet, she faced the light-colored wolf, considering him.

"You really are Seth?" she asked the wolf directly. His head tilted sideways, then nodded. "I guess that answers that question. Wow." She walked closer, moving around the wolf, who sat patiently while she inspected him.

She came back around to face him, marveling at the change. If she hadn't seen it with her own eyes, she never would have believed it. The men were right in that respect.

"Go ahead and scratch his ears. We have at least that much in common with dogs. Not much else, but in this form, our paws kind of limit our reach." Jason had once again moved silently closer to her. The man had an uncanny knack for sneaking into her personal space.

"I guess I can understand that," she agreed wryly as she bent to touch the wolf's head. Seth arched into her touch when she did as Jason had suggested and she couldn't help but be charmed by the way Seth's tongue hung out of his mouth as he panted in happiness.

"Don't spoil him," Jason said. She could hear the humor in his dark velvet voice and she drew back her hand, standing from her crouch. He was at her side, but she didn't mind. She was moving rapidly from disbelief to fascination.

"You can do this too?" she asked Jason. "You all can?" She glanced around the room. Everyone was watching her and the small group by the bar. They all, no doubt, realized that something special was happening.

"Indeed I can, and I'll show you at the first opportunity." He moved closer. "But since I get naked when I shift, I thought I'd save the demonstration until we know each other a little better."

She felt the blush rising to her cheeks at the thought of him stripping for her. Hoo boy, now that would be a show worth watching.

"Is that why everyone here is so tall and good-looking? Is that a side effect of being a werewolf?"

"Good genetics," Jason agreed.

"So you breed? You don't become a werewolf by being bitten, like in the movies?"

"Well, we can make someone a werewolf in very special circumstances, but mostly we expand our population the old-fashioned way. It's more fun, don't you think?" He winked at her and she couldn't help the little fire that lit in her middle at his roundabout mention of sex. She was fairly certain sex with Jason would be memorable, to say the least.

"Why are you telling me all this?" Sally got a sinking feeling in her stomach that replaced the heat in a flash. She turned her gaze to Carly. "What are you going to do with me?"

"Nothing you don't want, sweetheart," Jason was quick to reassure her, but she wanted to hear it from Carly. She knew Carly better than anyone in this room. Better than anyone in the state, for that matter.

"I discussed this with the other girls, and our husbands have talked among themselves. It's their world and their rules, but considering all of us have proven to be vampire mates, it was likely you were special too. For that reason, and because it would be hard to hide from you forever, we decided you should be let in on the secret that could destroy us all. Normally, you understand, no normal human is allowed to know anything about any of this."

"Wait a minute. The other girls?" Sally feared she knew what was coming.

"It started with Lissa. Her husband is second in command to Marc LaTour, Kelly's husband. Marc is the Master of his region, like Dmitri is Master here. When Christy was in the hospital that last time, Sebastian turned her to save her life. That's when Jenna found out about all of this and she had to be watched. Ian is an enforcer of sorts and it was his job to watch over Jenna. One by one, they all discovered they were mates. That means something special among their kind. These men have waited centuries to find the one woman who is their perfect match. Like Dmitri is my perfect match." Carly reached up to place one palm over her husband's cheek in an obvious sign of affection.

"You're the only one left unmated from the original study group," Dmitri picked up the thread of the conversation. "We are all wondering if you could be another woman with special traits, able to mate with one of our kind."

"Or one of my kind," Jason interrupted challengingly.

"What's this?" Dmitri demanded.

"Can't you detect it? In her scent?" Jason spoke to Dmitri alone though everyone could hear.

Dmitri stepped out from behind Carly and sniffed. He sniffed her!

Sally pulled back, but Jason was behind her, having outflanked her. She felt suddenly threatened.

"Subtle," Dmitri's eyes scrunched up as he thought aloud. "Magical. Wild. Predatory. Not like us." He looked up toward Jason, his eyes widening. "Like you."

"What is he talking about?" Sally demanded.

"Somewhere in your family tree, maybe centuries back, there was a wolf," Jason said in a low, intimate tone near her ear.

She stepped out of the space between the two men, needing room to think.

"You're saying you can *smell* something like that?" She was scandalized by the thought. Nobody had ever accused her of hiding a werewolf in her ancestry before. Not that she knew much about where she came from.

29

"Haven't you ever noticed your senses are a bit sharper than other people's?" Jason prodded.

Now that he mentioned it, she had noticed. She could hear things others didn't seem to. She could smell things others didn't. And she had instincts only a few other cops of her acquaintance had developed over many years on the beat.

"I see I struck a chord." Jason was smug about being right.

"So what if I can hear better than some other guys? That doesn't mean I howl at the full moon."

"No, you wouldn't. You don't have quite enough wolf in you for that. Or maybe it just hasn't been awakened yet." Jason moved into her personal space again. "Of course, it would be my pleasure to try to help you find your inner bitch."

"Call me that again and you won't have to look far," she promised with a snap of her teeth.

The other wolves in the room grew even more silent, holding their collective breath, but Jason only laughed. He looked like he took her words as a challenge, and this man seemed to really enjoy a challenge. Oh, great. As if she didn't have enough to deal with at the moment.

Her best friends were all married to vampires. She wondered if...

"Have all the other girls become vampires too?" Sally shot her question toward Carly, who looked concerned.

"Yes, we've all been turned. You're the odd man out, Sal. As usual." Carly tried for humor, but Sally could read the worry in her eyes.

"Odd *wolf*, if these guys are to be believed." Sally sipped her drink, tempted to chug it for the alcohol if it wasn't for the slushy ice. Chugging anything ice cold would give her brain freeze and she didn't want to deal with that on top of everything else.

"Whoa there, pretty lady." Jason took the glass out of her hands and placed it back on the bar. She wasn't happy about it, but she let him. She had learned early on to pick her battles. "Level heads are best for this kind of conversation."

"Give me a little credit." She shot him an exasperated look but argued no further. "So when were you all planning to tell me the big news?" Sally asked Carly accusingly. "I can't believe you hid this from me for so long."

"It wasn't really by choice. There is a strict edict about telling regular folks about all this. Punishable by death, Sal. None of us wanted to take that chance. But now that we're all..." She made a helpless gesture with her hands, at a loss for words, apparently.

"Now that you're all immortal," Sally supplied. "You are immortal, right? That part of the legend is true?"

"Yes, Detective," Dmitri answered with a nod. "I've searched for Carly for hundreds of years. Now that we are together, I hope we can share centuries of wedded bliss together."

"Hope? You don't know for certain?" Worry edged into her mind. Worry for her friend.

"There are a few things that can end us. We have some vulnerabilities. Especially the newly turned. It is my duty and pleasure to teach my mate how to protect herself and to keep her close to my heart and under my wing." Dmitri looked down at Carly with such love, Sally had to look away. Would anybody ever look at her like that? She doubted it. She wasn't lovable. Her youth had taught her that.

"Sunlight? A wooden stake through the heart?" she asked, wondering aloud.

"And silver," Jason added. "Silver isn't very good to either of our races."

"Why?" Sally turned her questioning gaze on the werewolf

leader.

"It's poison," he answered simply. "Shuts our systems down."

"Wine can reverse the effects for us," Dmitri added. "Wine is one of our few ties to the sunlit world. Grapes flourish in the sun and capture some of that energy in their essence."

"Which is why Lissa's husband owns a vineyard, I suppose." Sally was making interesting connections. The idea of such creatures existing alongside humanity was both shocking and tantalizing.

"Carly always said you were quick." Dmitri bowed his head as he complimented her.

"So you really can't go out in the sun anymore, Carl?" Sally moved a step closer to her friend.

Carly shook her head, placing her hand over Dmitri's. "I don't really miss it. Not when I've got Dmitri. He's showing me all kinds of things about the night."

"I bet." Sally couldn't help the lascivious wink she gave her friend. It was so easy to accept all this because of the undeniable happiness she could see on Carly's face.

For that matter, all their newly wedded friends were blissfully happy. Sally had seen it for herself during their monthly get-togethers. Sure, none of them really ate anymore and the dinners had turned into outings for drinks, but they were the same old girls she'd gone to college with. Same senses of humor, same love of laughter.

"I can't believe you all hid this so well. And here I pride myself on my investigative skills." Sally shook her head.

"It was for your protection, Sal," Carly said earnestly. "Besides, we knew we couldn't keep it from you forever. We'd all reached the decision to tell you. We figured this trip would be the perfect time, since you're on leave from work and have time to assimilate the information. I just hadn't figured on telling you tonight."

"Sorry, Mistress," Jason offered sheepishly. "But the moment I caught her scent, I knew she belonged among us. As you know, wolves can be...impetuous, at times." His charming grin did a lot to alleviate her annoyance. This Alpha wolf really had a way with women.

"I've still got two weeks of vacation," Sally broke in. "What were you planning to do with me during the day? You can't go out in the sun, right?"

"That's part of the reason I had planned to break it to you quickly," Carly agreed. "I'm still so new to this, I'm not functional at all during the daylight hours. My employees," she gestured to the crowd, which was still watching unabashedly, "have been kind enough to adjust their hours to mine somewhat. They start work in the afternoon and continue until I get up at sundown. We work together for a few hours and then call it a night. You'd be amazed how well the business is going with them on board. We're getting so much done."

Sally could see her friend's enthusiasm. Carly had always been passionate about her work. At least at first. In recent years, she'd been a little burnt out, if Sally were being honest. It was good to see that energy back in Carly's expression. Dmitri and the werewolves had done that, so maybe there was more to this than met the eye.

"We all get up late, compared to normal folks," Jason cut in. "It's safest for us to run at night, even way out here in the middle of nowhere. We tend to stay up late and sleep in during the morning hours. Not because we have to, but because it's more fun that way." He winked and that devilish charm that was never far came to the fore once more. "I'll be honest and say that our arrangement with the Master and Mistress here is unique. Most of the Other races don't get along all that well, but

Dmitri and I have had an understanding for many years. Carly and her willingness to help our Pack with jobs and friendship has helped even more. I doubt there's a Pack or Master closer in all the States." He shrugged. "It works for us. Just don't ever expect other bloodletters to be as accepting of your wolf heritage."

"Except for our friends, of course," Carly put in. "Though I'm not sure anybody ever realized you had werewolf blood before. I wonder what the boys will make of that." She grinned as she stroked Dmitri's hand where it rested over her arm. "They've been hatching all kinds of theories about why we'd all gravitated toward each other in the first place. Apparently we're quite the oddity."

"Not the first time I've been called that," Sally quipped. "And probably not the last."

"It would be my honor, Detective, to show you around during the day when your friends must rest," Jason offered. "I could help you learn a bit about your forgotten heritage and show you the local sights. I offer you the hospitality of my Pack."

From the way the others in the room went utterly still, Sally figured there was something more to his words than a simple offer of a tour guide. She had a lot to learn about werewolf and vampire culture if she was going to keep her friends. To put it simply, the women she'd bonded with during college were as close to her as sisters. They were the only ones who had always accepted her for who she was and never tried to change her to fit some other expectation. She loved them like family. They *were* her family—the only family she'd ever known—and she didn't want to lose them. Not ever. She'd do whatever it took to keep them as close as they were. If that meant embracing the werewolf lifestyle, then so be it. The least she could do was learn what it was all about.

"I accept your offer of hospitality," she said formally, noting the reaction of the others. A collective sigh was released around the room and she thought maybe something significant had just occurred. She'd have to learn more about them before she could fully understand.

"Excellent." Jason grinned and winked at her. "Then we'll leave you to talk these momentous events over with your friends for the remainder of the night." He straightened from his casual lean against the bar. The other wolves began to gather themselves as well. "Thank you for inviting us to your party, Mistress. We had a great time." He leaned down to kiss Carly on the cheek, seeming to enjoy the way Dmitri bristled as he drew near. They might be friends, but the wolf seemed to like tweaking the vampire when he could.

"Thank you for coming, Jason," Carly replied with a chastising smile for the werewolf. She turned away from him to say goodbye to her staff, the lesser wolves who worked for her. Dmitri followed suit, leaving Sally alone for a moment with Jason.

He wasted no time, moving right into her personal space. His head dipped closer to hers and she read his intention to kiss her clear in his expression, which was hot enough to melt glass. Sally gave in to temptation and allowed it. She wanted to know what he would feel like, closer to her, his lips on her skin, and a room full of people should have been a safe enough place to test the waters.

But what she'd expected to be a simple kiss on the cheek, like the one he'd given Carly, turned into a full-on lips-to-lips meeting. How he managed to counter the deliberate turn of her head she'd never know, but that was the last thought she had for some time as his lips claimed hers.

Forget glass. His kiss was hot enough to melt steel. Hot lava raced through her body as his strong lips met her softer ones. Damn. The man could kiss. And as far as kisses went, this one was pretty tame. He kept his tongue to himself until the last minute, leaving her with a last lick over her pursed lips, making her want more. And more. And more.

She wasn't sure she'd ever get enough. Her body followed his as he drew back, just an inch or two, but it was enough to make her snap out of the trance he'd put her in with a simple kiss. She drew back and tried to reclaim her composure. For all that had been thrown at her in the last half hour, she thought she'd been handling things rather well. Until a minute ago. And that killer kiss.

Damn. She'd have to watch herself around Jason. He was too charming for his own good in a rough and tumble way that really appealed to her. He wasn't urbane like Dmitri, but he had that same coiled power that made her belly clench with need.

"I'll come for you around lunchtime," Jason promised as he drew away from her.

All she could do was nod, still reeling from that kiss. Had Carly seen? She'd find out as soon as the rest of the party left. If so, chances were Carly would never let her live it down. Sally wasn't the type to give a strange guy free reign.

Dmitri and Carly saw the last of their guests out. The moment the door closed, Carly turned around and leaned against it, her gaze pinning Sally in place near the couch. She'd begun to pick up some of the trash left behind, though the wolves were remarkably neat. It had been an attempt at derailing the coming inquisition that had died before it even began. Sally sighed and dropped the napkins in a small trashcan under an end table, then flopped on the couch in defeat.

"So..." Carly began, leaving her post by the door and walking toward Sally in a slow stalk. "You and the Alpha?"

"Jason?" Sally tried to inject just the right note of scoffing surprise into her tone. She knew she had failed when Carly just kept staring at her, one eyebrow raised in challenge. "All right, so I think he's cute. It's not unheard of, you know. Every man in here tonight was a ten on the scale. You know that."

"Cute? Your friend thinks an Alpha wolf is *cute*?" Dmitri seemed unable to help himself from interjecting. Carly shot him a glare and he backed away, out of the room, still chuckling to himself.

"He does have a point, you know." Carly gestured toward the retreating back of her husband as she sat on the opposite end of the wide couch from Sally. "Werewolves are dangerous. Oh, they were on their best behavior tonight, but some wild things go on out in those woods. And Jason didn't get to be Alpha of a Pack that size without shedding blood in the process. They fight to decide who leads. He's not the cuddly puppy he tried to make you think he is. Seth is one of the younger wolves, still fuzzy and soft. He'll probably be an Alpha one day, if what Dmitri tells me is true, so he was strong enough to show you the battle form, but those baby blues are deceptively adorable in his wolf face. He can run and hunt with the best of them. All in all, he was a good choice to demonstrate the change to a newcomer they didn't want to scare off, but you should see Jason change."

"You've seen it?" Sally was immediately curious and a little jealous.

"He was the first werewolf I ever met. He came to the house to see Dmitri and I think he saw us...um...through the window. We were...uh...in the middle of...something." Carly's blush was a dead giveaway and Sally started to laugh.

"He saw you having sex?" Carly's blush only got deeper at Sally's words. "Why, the little Peeping Tom," Sally marveled with a grin. "So you got to see him shift? Was he naked?" Sally sounded just a little too eager to her own ears, but Carly didn't seem to notice, still caught in her own embarrassment.

"Dmitri knew what would happen, of course. He brought a towel out with him to the yard, where Jason was waiting for us in wolf form. I got an eyeful as he shifted shape. He took his time bending down to retrieve the towel and wrap it around his hips. Trust me when I say, that man is huge all over." The blush reasserted itself on Carly's cheeks. "And when he's a wolf, he isn't nearly as cuddly as Seth. Jason is the kind of wolf you back away from slowly. He's fierce."

"Says the woman whose husband is a vampire. Seriously, Carl," Sally leaned toward her friend, her concern edging out over her dazed, all too female reaction to the werewolf. "Are you okay with this? Really?"

Carly touched her hand where it rested along the back of the couch. "Definitely. I love him, Sal. More than I've ever loved anyone or anything. He's it for me. And I know he feels the same about me."

"Are you sure?"

"As sure as I know my own mind. You see, there's something different about vampire mates." She shifted, a little uncomfortable. "We actually share our minds. I know exactly what he's thinking and he knows what I'm thinking."

Sally sat back, nonplussed. She thought about the ramifications of such an arrangement. It would probably be both reassuring and a little annoying.

"He hears what you think? Like all the time? Is he listening in right now?"

"No. It's controllable. Except during times of great stress or distraction." Carly blushed again and Sally had a pretty good idea what she meant. "It wasn't at first, of course. We learned how to deal with it as we went along. We're still learning. But we've gotten to the point where we can shut the connection to a slow trickle instead of a flood. It was really overwhelming at first—especially for me. Dmitri has lived a very long time and has some amazing memories to prove it."

"I bet." Frankly, Sally was having a hard time wrapping her head around the idea that Dmitri had been alive for many of the events she thought of as history. It would take awhile to come to terms with that.

"You know, you're taking this a lot better than I would have expected." Carly watched her as if she was studying her. Sally didn't like it.

"Hey, it's not like I haven't seen some weird stuff on the job. I even have a few secrets of my own."

"Really?" Carly sat forward, playful in an instant. "Do tell."

Sally laughed. She'd always enjoyed Carly's zest for life. That energy had been missing from her friend for a long time. It was good to see her as she used to be.

"You look happy, Carl. And full of life, which is weird, considering you're undead," Sally joked.

Carly slapped at her arm. "I'm not undead. Sheesh! That word gives me the shivers."

"So what really happened? How'd you end up a vampire?" Sally really wanted to know. It seemed so incredible, yet the proof was sitting there on the couch, opposite her.

"Well, I'd already met Dmitri. I knew pretty soon after meeting him what he was. There was really no way to hide it from me after we'd become lovers. And I was okay with it. I knew he'd want me to change eventually, but we both figured we had plenty of time to make those decisions. Possibly years. Then I got into a car accident and almost died. I still am not used to driving on ice and snow. I was a goner, but Dmitri stepped in and saved my life. He made me into a vampire a bit sooner than I would have chosen, but it really doesn't matter. In the end, I know I would have chosen to stay with him forever.

The wreck just sped up my decision. And it *was* a decision. Even as I lay in that hospital bed, Dmitri asked me first before acting. If I had said no, he would have let nature take its course. And then he would have followed me. I know this with certainty because I know his thoughts and his heart. We are One now."

"Wow." Sally sat back in her seat, impressed by the seriousness of Carly's words. Finally, Sally broke the silence. "I'm just glad to see your old spark back. Carl, you were heading for a meltdown. You hadn't taken a vacation in years and you seemed to have lost your zest for living. I'm glad Dmitri brought that back to you."

"You have no idea. He's been good for me and I know in my heart I've done the same for him. He wasn't the smiling guy you met before. He was...I guess brooding is the best word. Quiet, dark, handsome as sin and *brooding*. All the co-eds were worshiping at his feet. They still do, of course, but he barely notices. He only has eyes for me." Carly batted her eyelashes playfully as she said the words, but Sally knew there was more than a grain of truth in them. Lucky girl. "Now that you've distracted me enough, let's get back to you and the Alpha. I was serious before, Sal. That guy is dangerous."

"I'm not a fool, Carl. I can handle him. I've handled worse in my time as a cop."

"Maybe bad-guy-wise, but I don't think you've ever dealt with an Alpha wolf who wants, without a doubt, to get into your pants. Even I could see that."

Sally thought about it for a minute. "Would that be so bad?" she wondered aloud, daring to share her innermost thoughts with one of her oldest friends.

"Detective Decker, I'm appalled," Carly teased. "And maybe a little jealous. Or I would be, if I didn't have such a fantastic man of my own. To be honest, I don't know enough about

40

wolves and their mating habits. I could ask some of the girls who work for me, but the overall impression I got is that they're pretty free with their favors until they find their mate. The first time I met Amy, she'd just come from a tryst in the woods with Jason and counted it as a favor. She said he'd taken pity on her and that after that night she'd be a lot more popular with the more attractive males in the Pack."

"You're kidding." Sally was shocked by the idea and jealous as hell.

"Afraid not. They hold these parties called howls and sometimes host mate hunts that spill over into my back pasture. That's why Jason came here that first day. He wanted to warn Dmitri that they were holding a hunt that night and some of his Pack members might stray onto our land. When Dmitri introduced me as his mate, Jason extended the hospitality of his Pack to me and invited us to the after party at the Pack house. That's when I met Amy and a lot of the other programmers who now work for me."

"Pack house?" Sally asked, trying to sidetrack herself from the almost unreasonable fury of jealousy that rose in her at the mention of the other woman's name. Why she was so possessive of Jason after a single kiss, she had no idea, but if she'd had hackles, they'd have risen in irritation.

"It's sort of the communal building where they all gather and a few of them live. There's a patch of land out back that they farm for vegetables, though I have the impression their diet consists mostly of meat. Wolves are carnivores, after all." Carly paused to chuckle. "The parties all sort of begin and end there. It seems to be their gathering place. The house certainly is big enough. It's really pretty. Maybe Jason will show it to you—if you decide to take him up on his offer of being a tour guide."

Sally thought about it. "I plan to. There's something about him…"

"Yeah, I can see by that faraway look in your eye that he's gotten to you. Just promise me you won't roll over and play dead when he snaps his fingers. At least put up a little fight." Carly's cajoling words made Sally laugh.

"Yes, ma'am, Mistress, ma'am." Sally saluted her, going along with the joke. "I'll do my best."

But as Sally said good night and went down the hall to the guest room she'd been given, she wondered if she had enough strength of will to hold out for long. Jason was potent. Even that one small kiss had set her senses reeling. And they'd been in the middle of a crowded room. She could only wonder what he'd be like when they were alone. Would she be able to hold out against his charm? She had the sneaking suspicion that she wouldn't.

And did she care? No, not really. She wanted to know what it was like to be the center of that man's attention. She wanted to take a walk on the wild side. She'd tread the straight and narrow all her life. Wasn't it about time she let her hair down and learned what it felt like to be daring and bold? Wasn't it about time she let herself have a vacation fling?

She was only going to be here for two weeks. The fling—if fling there was—had a built-in expiration date, after which she would return to her nice, comfortable life. She'd go back to hunting bad guys and Jason could go back to his horny Pack bitches.

But she could have him for a couple of weeks, maybe. She almost feared those two weeks could change her outlook forever. Did she dare?

Even if it meant heartache, she couldn't pass up her chance to be with a guy who made her mouth water. She'd never been so attracted to a man before and somehow, she doubted she ever would be again. If not now, then when? Time to let her hair down and be wild. Just once.

Well, more than *once*, she amended her thoughts. She'd let him get wild with her as many times as she could manage in the two weeks allotted. That ought to be enough to tide her over...for the rest of her depressing, lonely life.

Sally determined not to think about the future now. It would come when it did. All she could do was live each day, one at a time. Her job and her past had taught her that. She couldn't help it if there was a little spring in her step knowing that the next few days would hopefully be spent with a gorgeous man who seemed to genuinely be attracted to her. And here she'd thought there'd be nothing to do in the country during her vacation. Boy, had she been wrong. Not only was there something to do—there was some*one* to do—and she hadn't had that kind of fun in much too long.

Chapter Three

Good as his word, Jason pulled up around noon the next day. Sally had woken early, her internal clock still a little off due to jetlag. She'd followed the scent of brewing coffee not to the kitchen, but rather to the office wing that had been added on to the main house. How she'd smelled the coffee through three closed doors she didn't know, but she'd done things like that often enough in the past.

Maybe her heightened senses were because she had a werewolf in the family. She hadn't questioned it before, though it had been clear she could smell things other cops couldn't. Like the life-giving brown juice of the coffee bean that began flowing into her system, waking her up.

The majority of the office staff had gotten in around ten a.m. and one or two rolled in around eleven. By then, Sally had chugged her usual two cups of black coffee and nibbled on a croissant one of the wolves had brought with them. Apparently it was their habit to bring a tray of pastries with them each morning.

Sally renewed acquaintances from the party the night before. She even saw Seth and thanked him for showing her how he could become a wolf. She asked a few questions, but she got the distinct impression that they were all a little nervous around her. She wasn't sure why.

Sally was used to either respect or outright challenge from the people she met on the job, but these folks didn't see her as a police detective. At least they shouldn't. Maybe it was her bearing. She'd been told a few times that she was kind of imposing, but she'd attributed that to her height. Five foot eight was a little taller than average, but these men all had at least half a foot on her and even the women were a couple of inches taller than her.

When Jason arrived, she saw the same wary respect in their eyes, tempered with genuine affection. They loved him and followed his lead in all things, it was easy to see. She liked that. It said good things about him. She thought she could read these people well enough to know that they wouldn't follow just anyone blindly. Jason had earned their respect and their love. That meant a great deal.

When he'd walked in, Sally had registered his presence immediately. A tingle of energy brushed across her skin and she'd turned to find him strolling in, his gaze meeting hers with heated intensity. For a moment, the rest of the room faded around them. Damn. He really was as good-looking as she remembered.

Overnight, she'd almost convinced herself that maybe she'd been glamorizing him in her mind, but no. He was lickably handsome and built for sin. And Sally, the good girl turned upholder of the law, suddenly wanted to sin like never before.

"Are you up for a little sightseeing? I think I promised you a tour." He stopped a few feet shy of her, perching one hip on the corner of someone's desk. Sally had been standing in the office area, chatting, when he'd come in. Suddenly she remembered they had an audience and time started up again.

"Sure. I do have one request though. I'd like to stop at a garden center or someplace I can buy plant seeds."

His head cocked at a questioning angle for a moment, then he shrugged. "Sure. I know a few places we could try. But if you want to buy plants, I'll have to borrow a car. I drove my Harley today. Are you okay with riding behind me on the motorcycle?"

Hoo boy, was she ever! Her palms tingled at the idea of

holding onto his muscular torso.

"That's fine. I just want seeds. They'll fit in my pocket. We don't need the car and I'm okay with motorcycles. I own one myself, in fact."

"Really?" He stood, leading the way out of the office by the main office door that Sally hadn't yet seen. Last night she'd used the house entrance on the other side of the building. "What kind of ride do you favor?"

"A Harley Sportster, actually. I got a new model Nightster just last year."

"A girl after my own heart." He clutched his chest theatrically as he ushered her out the door and into the light. There, in all its flame-painted glory, was a giant Harley Dyna model. It was one of the largest of the newer models, built like the man who rode it—tough, sleek and on the large side.

"Wow. I saw some of these in the showroom but they're too big for me. Impressive."

"Thanks. It fits me pretty well. Plenty of room for you on the back though. And I don't let just any girl ride bitch on my saddle." He winked, probably waiting for her to react to that word again. She didn't like it, but she knew it probably had other connotations when talking in terms of a wolf Pack, so she let it go. Wouldn't do to be too predictable now, would it?

He went ahead to reach around the other side of the bike and came up with two helmets. Good. He was safety conscious. Too many guys cracked their skulls riding without a helmet. She'd seen enough bike-meets-car wrecks when she'd first joined the force to know that the bike rider seldom won that kind of duel.

He handed her the smaller of the two helmets. "Hope it fits. I borrowed it from one of the female Pack members who looked about your size."

She looked at the clean, practically new helmet in surprise. The name Heidi was stenciled on it in pink at the base of the neck. If he'd had to borrow the girl's helmet, maybe he was telling the truth about not letting a lot of women ride behind him. She didn't know why it mattered. She knew he was a stud of some kind among his Pack. Carly had seen it firsthand, for goodness' sake.

All Sally wanted was a fling. She had to keep that in mind and tamp down the possessive streak that suddenly reared its ugly head where this man was concerned. He wasn't hers. He couldn't be hers. Not long term. He was a werewolf, for cripes sake!

Get a grip, Sal, she counseled herself. All she wanted was to jump his bones a few times before she had to go back home to her nice, normal life. Was that too much to ask? The man practically oozed sex appeal and he didn't seem to have trouble spreading it around among his harem of werewolf girls. If she was lucky, he wouldn't mind giving a little to a human. She could be a curiosity—no matter that he seemed to think she was some kind of long-lost relative. She knew for a fact that she'd never turned furry on the night of the full moon.

She pulled on the helmet and tested it for size. "It fits well," she told him, carefully keeping her more lascivious thoughts to herself. There'd be time for that later this afternoon, she hoped.

"Great, then let's saddle up. I know a garden place on the edge of town that we'll go to first. If they don't have what you want there are a few other places we can try. We can get some lunch near there, then I want to show you around Pack territory a bit, if you like."

"Sounds like a plan. I'm on vacation, after all. Nowhere else I need to be, except back here by nightfall when Carly comes out to play."

It felt weird to acknowledge her friend's new state, but

Jason seemed to understand. He winked at her while he adjusted his helmet and watched to make sure hers was fastened tightly, then he threw his leg over the metal beast and waited while she did the same, snuggling up behind him.

When she would have held on to the edge of the seat, he stopped her, taking her hands in his and tucking her arms around his torso.

"Hold on to me, sweetheart. I won't let you fall off."

She wanted to come up with a witty reply, but her mouth had gone so dry, she couldn't speak. Damn, the man was built. His body was warm under her hands, and hard. She could feel the muscles shifting under her touch and it made her breath catch. This was a male animal in his prime.

Between his heat and the thrum of the machine between her legs, Sally was in a state when he finally throttled back as they neared the edges of town. She saw his destination, a sprawling lawn and garden place that even had some small animals for sale. Bunnies, chicks and such. It was a mom and pop operation—a charming change from the giant chain stores that dominated where she lived.

She got off the bike and her legs still vibrated for the first few steps. She'd felt safe with Jason driving, even when he pushed the speed limit a bit.

"Think they'll have what you need?" he asked as he took her helmet and stowed it on the bike.

"Probably. This place is so cute. Do you think they'll let me pet the bunnies before we leave?"

Jason laughed at the question. She looked at him with as innocent an expression as she could manage.

"What? I don't look like the cute, fuzzy animal type?" She gestured to her jeans-clad body and well-worn boots.

"Honey, you have no idea how much I'm *hoping* you're the

animal type. I just didn't expect a city-hardened detective to have a soft spot for prey."

Her eyes widened, realizing he was a wolf. And wolves *ate* bunnies. At least she thought they did.

"Maybe we'll skip the bunnies."

He laughed outright at the look on her face and she decided retreat was the better part of valor. Sally headed toward the store, leaving him to follow behind. A quick scan of the layout told her where everything was. She walked over to the seed racks, quickly locating what she had in mind.

Within ten minutes they were out of the garden shop and on their way again. Jason took her on a short ride farther into town. He stopped in front of a restaurant that had a neon sign, unlit at this hour of the day, proclaiming it to be Wild Bob's Steakhouse. She should have known a wolf would want meat for lunch.

"You're not a vegetarian or anything?" Jason asked belatedly as he stowed their helmets for a second time.

"Nope. I like a good steak as much as the next carnivore." She smiled as he opened the door for her to precede him into the restaurant. It was busy, filled with bustling noise that died down perceptibly as Jason walked in behind her.

He nodded to a few people and the noise resumed its normal level. The small pause told her a few things. For one, Jason was known here. She suspected more than a few of the patrons were shifters who knew damn well that Jason was the Alpha of the local wolf Pack. Some of them were probably part of his Pack.

She thought it significant that he'd taken her someplace where his people would see them together. She wasn't sure what that meant in shifter circles, but she knew what it meant when a human man wanted his friends and colleagues to see you together. He was staking a claim.

49

Warmth flooded her at the thought. Even if it was only temporary, it was a nice, pseudo-Neanderthal touch. Sally was strong enough to admit there was a little bit of the cavewoman in her that enjoyed such a public declaration.

They were seated in a prime location near the rear of the restaurant, not too close to the kitchen, but along a wall where they had a view of almost the entire dining room. Judging by the clothing of the patrons, there was a sort of loose hierarchical order to the way they were seated. The men and a few women seated near their table all had a polished look about them. Many were visibly older than Jason, though still in good shape with the tall, lithe form she'd come to expect from the wolves she'd met the night before.

"Welcome, Mr. Moore," said the hostess. She hesitated long enough before using Jason's name that Sally would bet the girl had been about to call him Alpha—before Sally's presence made her rethink which title to use.

"It's okay, Cindy. This is Mistress Belakov's friend from California. She knows about us."

"Oh." The girl's face lit up as she smiled at Sally. "Welcome, Detective. My sister works for the Mistress. She told me about the party last night. Said the Mistress was really looking forward to your visit."

Sally was surprised by the girl's candor, but Jason's indulgent smile set her at ease. Still, it wasn't quite normal for Sally to have everyone know her business. As a police detective, she usually kept a much lower profile.

"Thanks," Sally answered as Jason politely held her chair.

"Can I put in your drink order?" Cindy was all smiles for the Alpha as Jason seated himself. She handed each of them a menu. They ordered soft drinks and Cindy left.

Sally noted that Jason didn't even glance at his menu before pushing it to the side of the table. Sally looked through
50

hers, surprised to see there were no prices next to the selections. *Un*surprisingly, almost every choice was meat of some kind. Chicken, veal, mutton, even buffalo and ostrich meat was listed in various dishes.

"I had a buffalo burger once. They say the meat is leaner than beef and therefore better for you," she observed, trying to make conversation. Jason was staring at her. She could feel it. Along with half of the other patrons of the restaurant.

"Do you like steak? How about filet mignon? Bob wraps it in bacon. Very tasty."

"Sounds good, but..." She closed the menu and placed it on the table. "...there are no prices on this menu. And I know filet mignon is expensive in any restaurant."

"Don't worry. I invited you out, I chose the place. I'm paying for lunch. Have what you like. I can afford it." She didn't know what to say to that. "Besides, a Pack member owns this place. I eat here all the time. You won't find a better filet mignon this side of the Mississippi."

Outmaneuvered, she gave in. "All right. You've convinced me."

"How do you want it cooked?" he asked, placing her menu atop his.

"Would it be rude to ask for well done?"

He laughed, catching her wry tone. "Not at all. Just because we're wolves doesn't mean we always eat our food raw. There are some compensations to this form. Opposable thumbs and the ability to manipulate a spatula are among them." He opened and closed his hand, staring at it with humor before he turned that mischievous gaze back to her. "And we may have better senses of smell and hearing in our fur, but human taste buds are a bit different."

When the waiter arrived, Jason placed their order. Sally

marveled at the respect Jason commanded and his easy acceptance of the way the other Pack members treated him. Because she was with him, and the odd human in the place, she was getting some strange looks herself. She tried to ignore it, but the sense of being watched never quite faded all through their meal.

The filet mignon was everything Jason had promised and she turned out to be hungrier than she expected. They ate, enjoying each other's company and talking about their respective lives. Mostly, she answered Jason's questions about her work as a detective.

"You're very good at interrogation," she commented after a while, realizing that she was talking way more than he was.

"I can't help it. You intrigue me." He met her gaze over his glass as he took a sip.

"Now it's your turn. Tell me about you and your Pack, if you can talk here." She looked around, trying to gauge how private they were. Jason followed her gaze.

"Everyone in here is a shifter. Mostly wolves. A few other species over by the bar."

"Other species?" Sally tried to glance at the bar unobtrusively.

"There are more than just wolves in the forest, sweetheart. Big cats, a few raptor breeds...many of the animal predators have shifter counterparts. Some are rarer than others. There are only a few bear shifters in this part of the country, for example. A family of them are sitting near the door, as it happens."

Sally looked at the table he gestured toward and saw a very normal-looking man and woman with a small child sitting in a booster seat. The kid was eating with his hands and as she watched, one hand partially shifted to a furry paw complete with sharp claws. The mother noticed and corrected the child with a smile, and the hand returned to human shape and color, the claws retracting into human nails.

"The children shift at such a young age? Must be hard to keep track of the little buggers."

Jason laughed outright at her calm observation. "You've got that right. But only a few species start shifting that young. Bears are among the most magical of shifters. Their kids go furry from almost the very beginning, according to what I've heard. Among wolves, the first shift usually coincides with puberty. All those raging hormones seem to trigger our inner wolf. Or not." He shrugged and took another sip of his drink. "Occasionally a child born of the Pack won't have the ability to shift. It happens. We try to keep those members in the Pack now, whereas in the past, many Alphas demanded such children be shunned." He frowned at that idea. "I don't hold with that. If you're born to the Pack, you shouldn't be forced to leave it for any reason. Not to mention the fact that even a non-shifting child carries the genes and could potentially have a child with the ability." He gestured toward her as he picked up his fork again. "You might've picked up your shifter blood from just such a circumstance."

There was a collective breath taken by most of those around them, clearly listening in. Wolf hearing was as good as he'd claimed. She made a point to remember that their conversation could be heard several tables away.

"Thanks for sharing that little tidbit. But you might want to say it louder next time. I don't think the people sitting at the bar heard you." She saluted him with her fork before digging in for the last remaining bits of beef on her plate. Jason chuckled again as he finished his steak. "Glad you find this amusing."

"Oh, honey, you have no idea." He wiped his mouth with the napkin and sat back in his chair, watching her.

Uncomfortable with his regard, she looked around the

room. "Nice place. Do you bring all the tourists here?"

"I picked this place for lunch because the food is good, I knew we could talk relatively freely, and I like to throw business Bob's way."

"How come?"

"Wild Bob really used to be wild. He ran up in the hills with the timber wolves. Real wolves, not shifters," he clarified. "His mate died and he sought solace in the hills. Sometimes it helps to get away from it all for a while and stay in our fur. Bob came back to us a few years ago and it was rough for him at first. He's doing well now though, and I like to drop in when I'm in town. A good Alpha supports his Pack members." Jason rose as he looked toward the kitchen door. "Speak of the devil. Here comes Bob."

Jason shook hands with a giant of a man who wore a spotless white apron around his waist. It seemed a little incongruous with the idea that he'd been cooking in the back, but Sally saw how respectful Wild Bob was toward his Alpha. He'd probably put on a new apron before coming out to greet Jason.

Sally smiled when Jason introduced her and shook hands with the big man. He had that wounded look in his eyes that she equated with many victims of violent crimes where loved ones had been killed. She'd seen it before. That look that said something was broken deep inside that would never be whole again and her heart went out to them every time, though she did her best to maintain a professional distance.

She wasn't on the job now. She returned Bob's greeting with more warmth than she could have shown to a victim back home. She complimented his cooking and his establishment as effusively as she could. Bob responded to her overture and chatted in friendly tones for a few minutes before heading back to the kitchen after thanking her and the Alpha for dropping by.

Jason settled the bill and they were on their way a few minutes later. She'd learned a lot from the stop and had an absolutely delicious meal in the process. She climbed behind Jason and snuggled up to his back with a drowsy sort of satisfaction. After only two trips riding behind him, she already felt as if she belonged there, putting her life in his hands, trusting his skill and wrapping her body around his from behind.

"Comfortable?" he asked before he started the engine.

"Mmm. Food coma is setting in. I never eat such a big lunch back home."

"Ah. I think I know just what you need." He took off without further ado and headed out of the city.

They rode along, the wind whipping at her face and around her body, except for where she was shielded by his big, warm frame. He was her safe harbor in the maelstrom. She was mellow enough from the good meal to relax and enjoy the speed and skill he demonstrated on the back country roads as they climbed higher into the foothills. She recognized most of the roads from the trip out but where he should probably have turned to take her back to Dmitri and Carly's, he took another path.

She noted the scenery flying past with interest but not alarm. He would keep her safe. She didn't know why she trusted this man so completely on such short acquaintance, she only knew she could. Perhaps it was the way he treated and was respected by his Pack members. Perhaps it was some innate instinct of her own that told her, after watching him interact with people last night and again this morning, that he could be trusted not to harm her. It might be a cop thing. Or it might be some sort of instinctual werewolf thing she'd been born with—though she still wasn't sure she believed him about that.

He slowed the bike and turned off road, creeping along the grass at a slow pace until he entered a wooded area and slowed even more. They continued along for a few moments until the woods suddenly gave way to an enchanted glade, complete with a small waterfall that was only a few feet high, but absolutely lovely.

Jason stopped the bike and waited while she hopped off first. Sally was enthusiastically looking around at the scenery, her breath almost taken away by the natural beauty of the place. A brook leapt over an outcropping of rocks, tinkling merrily as it sped away downhill after collecting in a small pool beneath the waterfall.

"What do you think?" Jason asked in a hushed voice as he came up beside her on silent feet.

"It's gorgeous," she replied without taking her eyes off the beauty of nature.

"I'm glad you like it. Thought you might." She turned at his softly spoken words to catch the look of satisfaction on his face as he watched her watching the waterfall.

"Did you? Take a lot of *chiquitas* up here, eh?" She was suddenly in a playful mood and felt like teasing him.

"Would you believe me if I said you were the first?" His eyes crinkled at the corners as he smiled.

"That innocent look may work on some people, but not on a hardened police detective like me." She rolled her eyes at his expression, smiling all the while.

"Are you absolutely certain?" He tried one more time for the earnest look, but she wasn't buying it.

"Sorry." She shook her head in the negative. "You'll have to do better than that."

"Oh, I can do better. Question is, can you handle it?"

He moved closer to her, dropping the helmets on the soft

grass beneath their feet. Suddenly she felt like she was being stalked by a wild predator. A thrill ran down her spine as she thought about avenues of escape. Did she want to run? It might be fun to lead him on a short chase, though ultimately, she really wanted to be caught.

Giving in to temptation, she stood her ground as he reached her. It wouldn't be right to start this relationship by playing games. She decided she would meet him as an equal or not at all.

Wordlessly, he reached out, one hand just barely touching the sensitive skin of her cheek. When she didn't move away, he deepened the contact, cupping her cheek in his warm, rough palm. Her pulse rate leapt higher as he moved even closer, right into her personal space.

His head dipped toward hers. She closed the space between them, stretching upward to meet his kiss. And then she was lost.

The kiss the night before was nothing compared to the full, intimate heat of him. His tongue invaded, plundered, staked his claim, and she loved every second of it. She met his challenge and returned it, reaching up to drag him downward, moving her body into his, daring him to take it further.

He didn't disappoint. His hands roamed her back, sliding downward to cup her ass and lift her into full contact. She could feel the hard rod of his excitement against her belly and it made her want more. More of his kiss. More of him.

She didn't know how long the kiss lasted. She only knew that when he drew away from her, she tried to follow. She was firmly under his spell and didn't want to stop. Not for anything.

Somehow—and it shamed her to realize she'd been so far gone—Jason pulled back and cooled things down. His forehead rested against hers, his breathing harsh. That was some consolation, at least. She could feel the trembling of his upper thighs against hers. She knew a little of what it cost him to stop. She felt it too.

"Why?" The word escaped before she could stop it.

"Too fast," he replied through ragged breaths. "You're human." He let her go and stepped back as if forcing himself to do so. "Mostly human, at any rate. Were mating can be…kind of rough on the uninitiated. I'm trying not to scare you off." He shot her a rueful expression, his grin catching her off guard, but charming her just the same. "Is it working?"

"Why don't you come back over here and find out?" she challenged.

He stepped back another pace. "Later," he promised. "First, I want to show you something." He held one hand out to his side, inviting her to take it.

Like teenagers on a first date, she held his hand as they walked together toward the small waterfall. He stopped for a moment beside it and she listened to the trickling water, appreciating its peaceful bounty as the cool, moist air helped bank the fire he had started within her.

"My mother used to come up here all the time when we were kids. We used to bring a picnic lunch and she'd let us play in the water and in the woods nearby. It was our special place."

Touched by his words, Sally looked up at him. "She sounds like a special lady."

"She was." Sally sensed a wealth of pain in his simple words. "The year I became Alpha, she was killed in the violence. There was a bit of a clan war brewing until I stepped forward to claim leadership and broker peace. It was her death that finally turned me into the Alpha I am today. It was a harsh way to discover my own inner strength, but our world is like that sometimes. You should know this before you get in any deeper." He turned to her, his expression earnest. "Right now, you're on the periphery. Your friends are fully in our world, but you might get away with simply being watched by one of the vamp enforcers for the rest of your life. You could go on with your normal, totally human life. Only you would know what really goes on in the dark. And it wouldn't affect you much, other than having to swear yourself to secrecy about your friends. Those ladies and their mates are powerful enough to allow you that freedom."

"Carly mentioned something like that last night."

"Or..." he went on, "...you could choose to fully embrace the small part of you that has always been different. Like your friends, you could become part of the bigger world—the world where shifters and bloodletters and even magic users share the Earth with regular folk. The world where we live in secret among them. You could join my world, Sally. You could join with your wolf."

His words were so stirring, she felt in that moment, almost anything was possible. For a split second, she was ready to throw caution to the wind. She wanted to be with him, to embrace all that he was, and all that she could be. Then sanity interrupted.

"I'm not sure."

Sally thought about her life to this point. Her hard-won career was waiting for her back home, along with a beautiful apartment she had spent the last three years decorating until she got it just so. Her life was somewhat empty, now that all her friends were married and they saw each other less frequently, but it was still her life. The one she had created for herself.

"It's okay." Jason dropped her hand and tucked both of his into his jeans pockets. His shoulders hunched a bit as he began walking toward the woods. She followed. "You don't have to make any decisions today. You're on vacation, right? We'll just see where things lead. But I figured I should draw your attention to the facts at least once before we do some serious sightseeing."

His smile was easy, but she could feel the undercurrent of tension in his voice. Her response mattered to him more than he was letting on, for some reason. She liked that he wasn't pushing her too hard. She had things to think over and she needed to learn more about Carly's new existence. She needed to learn a lot more about shapeshifters too, for that matter. This world was completely new to her, though not as unsettling as she would've expected. Somehow, she had always suspected there was something more to the odd things that happened to her as a cop.

She'd felt the pull of the full moon and chalked it up to coincidence, or perhaps superstition. She'd always been able to hear things others couldn't and see things in greater detail than her colleagues. She had gained a reputation as a sort of super cop among her peers and enjoyed the way they treated her with increasing respect as she rose through the ranks.

Hers was a sometimes violent job. It could be rewarding as well. Catching bad guys before they could harm anyone else had been her passion for a long time, though lately she had found herself more than once simply going through the motions. She hadn't felt the same elation that she had when she was younger. Justice had become her goal in both work and life, and sometimes, it was hard to achieve. She'd become disillusioned with the system over the years and now that she was away from home for the first time in a long time, she realized she was at a crossroads. She could either continue the way she was going, or choose a new path.

Jason had just laid a tantalizing new possibility before her. The question was, did she dare pursue it?

"Jason..." She trailed off, uncertain how to ask all the questions in her mind.

He turned toward her. They stood facing each other in the

whispering woods. Suddenly the tension was back. The yearning. The need.

"I had such good intentions." His hand rose to touch her hair, tucking a loose strand behind her ear. His eyes honed in on her lips, parted...ready...willing. "I think I know how Adam must've felt in the Garden of Eden. You are temptation itself, my Eve."

"Sally," she reminded him playfully, though she was touched by his words beyond bearing. No man had ever given her such verbal tribute. And no man had ever looked at her like Jason did. As if she were special, though that was too mild a word. As if she held his world in the palm of her hands.

She knew she was being fanciful, but it didn't matter. All that mattered was Jason and this moment—and how much she'd wanted him from almost the first time she'd seen him. There would be time to worry about everything else later. Right now, all she wanted was him.

His head dipped, and his lips found hers. She had a sensation of weightlessness and then she felt the cool grass beneath her back, tickling her neck as Jason pressed her into the thick green mat. A fresh scent rose from the crushed fronds, enveloping her in its delicious aroma. Never before had anything felt so right.

Jason's hard body bracketed her, his long, jeans-clad legs slipping between hers as if they belonged there. The only problem was, they were wearing too much fabric. Skin on skin would feel so much better.

As if her thought conjured his action, Sally felt her jacket slide down her shoulders. Jason paused, breaking the kiss as he encountered the shoulder holster for her service revolver. He gazed down at her, one eyebrow raised in question, a faint smile on his lips.

"I keep forgetting you're a cop."

"That's the nicest thing a guy has ever said to me," she joked, shrugging out of the holster as he made room between them. He took the firearm from her, placing it delicately at her side, within reach, but safely away from where they lay entangled together. Her jacket went on top of it, hiding it from view.

He resumed the kiss, bringing her back to the sharp edged excitement only Jason had ever shown her. She felt the hem of her T-shirt rise, Jason's strong hands skimming it over her heated skin as their kiss went on and on. She wriggled under him, helping his progress, wanting the fabric gone. She wanted to feel the tickling grass beneath her bare back and Jason's skin above.

And most of all, she wanted to feel what it would be like to have him inside her, as close as two beings could be. She wanted to know how he looked when he came and how he made her feel when he sent her over the edge into a bliss she could only imagine.

Everything felt new and oh-so-right with Jason. She was sure being with him would be very different from her past experiences with men. Not just because he wasn't entirely human. Mostly it was because she sensed something in him that called out to a hidden part of her own soul that she hadn't known existed—until she met Jason.

When those two sparks met, she wondered if either one of them would survive the explosion. Wanting more than anything to know, she pushed at his clothing, trying to touch skin. She wanted to feel him, touch him, *know* him.

Wordlessly, he ended their soul-shattering kiss and helped. His shirt and hers flew away somewhere. She didn't care where. All that mattered was his warm skin, the slightly hairy chest, and the massive size of him that made her feel small and feminine for the first time in her life.

His lips returned to her skin, skimming down her neck and into the curve where her shoulder began. His teeth nipped at one bra strap, sliding it down her arm while his hand slid the other away, pulling the triangles of stretchy fabric down as well, effectively imprisoning her inside the fastened garment, but baring the important bits.

The bits that craved his touch, his tongue, his teasing. Jason obliged without being asked, lowering his mouth to her breasts, teasing the nipples with his hands and lips, making her writhe on the cool grass in heightened pleasure.

"Jason," she whispered, feeling things no other man had made her feel from such simple contact.

He didn't answer, but seemed to take her exclamation as permission to go farther. He rolled to her side, giving himself room to maneuver. One of his hands lowered to the waistband of her jeans and something inside her rejoiced. She wanted more. So much more.

Sally toed off her shoes while Jason expertly unclasped and unzipped her jeans. She lifted her hips, helping as he stripped them down her legs, taking her panties with them. The grass tickled the backs of her knees, adding new sensations to the overload of pleasure. She'd never lain naked in the grass before. Only this man and this moment could have made her do so, and she momentarily regretted having never felt these delicious sensations before. The leaves sang a song of joy through the surrounding forest. The soft murmur of the waterfall added a counter harmony to the magical tune nature played in this secluded glen. Sunshine dripped through the leafy canopy to tickle her skin where it wasn't covered by the deliciously warm and hard man above her. The scent of grass and leaves, flowing water and clean earth mixed with the heady aroma of aroused male.

The combination made her head spin in the most delicious

way. Lying naked in a patch of grass in the middle of a forest with a half naked man poised above her was something she'd never imagined. Yet it was perfect in every way.

It only became more perfect when one of Jason's large hands slid between her bare thighs, spreading them, making way for his possession. Thick fingers slid through the arousal she couldn't hide, seeking entrance. She not only allowed it, she encouraged him, spreading her knees wide and pushing up into his hand.

One thick finger found its way inside, making her gasp. He was a little rough, but she found she liked the way he handled her body. As if he owned it. As if he knew just how much she could take. He pushed her to her limits and a little beyond, until she was swimming in a sea of pleasure that only Jason could bring her.

A second finger joined the first. This time she cried out his name, bucking her hips as he took control of her body, her pleasure...her soul. Or at least, that's what it felt like.

Surrounded by fragrant grass and covered by Jason's hard body, her mind spun away as Jason's skilled touch brought her to a quick, hard climax. She was panting when she cried out his name again, drinking in his answering satisfied chuckle. She opened her eyes to meet his gaze and found herself warmed all over again by the knowing look in his eyes.

He'd just played her body like a virtuoso and she was ready for more. She stretched upward to entice him into a kiss, hoping to show him she was ready—and willing—for more.

"Don't let me interrupt." The strange male voice came to her from a few feet away.

Sally jumped but her arms were still pinned by her bra straps and her legs remained splayed, Jason's fingers still inside her body, pulsing lightly. She was trapped.

Chapter Four

"Jason?" Sally knew her voice held fear. She was in a vulnerable position. The most vulnerable position a woman could be in. Jason remained calm, his eyes sparkling with a mix of irritation and excitement, if she was any judge.

She was freaking out and he was excited? This could be bad. Really bad.

Sally lifted her head to look at the man standing near her feet, knowing he could see all of her there was to see and Jason wasn't making the slightest move to prevent it. The guy was naked. And hard. And huge. All over.

His cock was in his hand and he rubbed it as she watched, drawing her gaze. He was blond. A golden god from the sun-kissed thatch of hair on his head to the light bush around his heavy sac. His looks and size reminded her of the werewolves she'd met. He must be a shapeshifter too.

One thing was clear in her jumbled mind. If he was part of Jason's Pack, he would follow Jason's orders to the letter. She wasn't in any danger if she trusted Jason to keep her safe. Oddly enough, she discovered she did. Somewhere along the line, she'd decided to trust him—at least in this.

Jason must've sensed the tension ease in her body because his fingers began stroking again and his lips lowered to hers, blocking her view of the stranger.

"It's okay, Sally. He's a friend. Let him watch. I won't let anything or anyone hurt you. Ever." His words whispered against her lips, seducing her.

It was a hell of a time to discover she had exhibitionist tendencies, but Sally found her hips moving almost involuntarily as Jason's fingers increased their stroking pace in her pussy. The adrenaline rush faded into a sexual high increased by the knowledge that the strange man had a really good view of Jason's fingers pushing in and out of her far too excited body.

Clenched knees relaxed and opened, giving him an even better look at what Jason did to her. Sally heard a moan, belatedly realizing it came from her own mouth as Jason kissed and licked his way down her body, pausing at her breasts, biting lightly, playfully, enough to arouse but not enough to hurt.

She could see the blond man when Jason's head moved out of her line of sight, and what she saw made her breath catch. His gaze focused on her pussy and the fingers filling her wet hole.

She came with a keening cry as she watched the stranger's cock erupt, ropes of thick come spilling out onto the grass near her feet. Jason swallowed her cries with his lips, muffling her screams of pleasure, seeming to want to keep them all for himself.

The thought amused her as much as it aroused. Poor Jason. She'd come more than once, and his golden friend had gotten off too. What about the author of the feast? She'd have to make sure he found some relief before much more time had passed.

Unfortunately she was too wrung out to move at the moment. Jason slid his fingers from her body as her climax died down to magnificent aftershocks and left her side. He didn't go far and the sun was warm enough to keep her comfortable for the moment.

She watched idly as he walked up to the naked man and

they spoke in hushed tones even she couldn't hear. After a few minutes, and not a few heated glances in her direction, their conversation ended when she sat up and started looking for her clothes.

The sex kitten was starting to shiver and it was time to cover up. Sally had discovered a hidden facet of her sexuality in the heat of the moment. Apparently she really got off on being watched. But in the cooler light of day, being naked in front of a perfect stranger made her feel a wee bit shy.

"Don't cover up on my account," the golden man said as he and Jason approached. He had a killer smile to go along with his gorgeous body.

"It's a little chilly."

"We can tell." A pointed look at her pointed nipples made her cheeks heat in a blush. She didn't know why she was blushing now. The man had seen things she never would have imagined letting anyone watch, much less someone she didn't even know.

"Knock it off, Redstone." There wasn't much fire behind Jason's words and he seemed not to notice that the man he spoke to was completely naked.

"You can't blame a guy for noticing something so enticing." He sniffed the air around her from a few feet away as she pulled up her bra and shrugged into her shirt. "You smell *good*, little girl. Sure you want to hang around with the dog? I have it on good authority that cats are more fun." His wink was as outrageous as his words.

It was all Sally could do not to stare. Michelangelo's David had nothing on this guy.

"Cat?" she repeated, her mind still in a fog from the intensity of her orgasm.

"I'm a werecougar, to be precise. Steve Redstone's my

name." He nodded his head with a jaunty grin. "Thanks for the show, by the way. I needed that more than you'll ever know. If you really want to take a walk on the wild side, I'd love to get inside that tight pussy of yours. It looked awfully fine to me. I bet it felt even better, eh Jason?"

"Better watch your step, cat. This is Sally. She's got powerful friends." Sally heard the repressed rumble of a growl in his voice, though the cougar seemed to ignore the implied threat.

"Do tell? Since when have we been letting humans—even part-blooded humans—into our little club?" Steve stood casually. Apparently he was completely comfortable in the nude.

"Smelled that, did you? She's got a wolf somewhere back in her bloodlines, I think. But to answer your question, she's the new Mistress's friend. Seems every woman in their old college study group married a bloodletter. I bet there's a bunch of vamp historians trying to figure out why they would cluster together like that, even now. Sally here is the odd one out. Shifter blood, but way back, and so far, not attached to any bloodsuckers."

"I don't think she was meant for them." The cat sobered, straightening his posture. "She smells like one of us. And something more." His eyes narrowed. He gazed at her as if measuring her against some scale in his mind.

"I'm a cop. A detective," she clarified, more than a little uncomfortable with the way they had been discussing her, as if she weren't sitting right in front of them—albeit half naked. "Maybe that's what you smell." She tried for sarcasm and felt a little thrill when his eyes widened and he looked *at* her, not *through* her.

"She has teeth," Steve admitted. "Forgive me, Detective. I didn't mean to talk over your head. It's kind of a rarity to meet someone like you—one foot in our world, but living and working among non-magic folk."

"She only learned about all this yesterday," Jason supplied. "You're the first non-wolf shifter she's met." He casually scooped up her jeans and panties, handing them back to her as she stood.

Her T-shirt covered the most important bits as she bent to dress. It looked like their interlude was over for the moment, even though the bulge in Jason's jeans was still hard as a rock. Her mouth watered just glancing at it, but Jason seemed to be able to ignore his rather blatant need.

"I'm doubly honored." Steve nodded toward her, then his expression grew more serious. "I'm glad I ran across you, Alpha. Not only for the obvious reasons." He gave her an almost comical leer as she finished dressing. "But also because I saw more sign of hunters up on Yellowtail Ridge. You might want to warn your Pack to steer clear. Something is going on up there and my instincts tell me it's nothing good."

Jason was instantly alert, his gaze narrowed in concern. "This isn't the first I've heard about hunters up there. The bear clan saw something a few weeks ago, but since then, nothing. I'd hoped whoever it was had given up and left for the season. But if you saw them recently, they might've been in the area all along, gathering intelligence. Not good."

"What did the bears see?" Steve asked, both men all business now.

"One of their cubs got out on his own and knew enough to hide up a tree when he smelled men approaching. He was too young to really know what he was looking at but from what he described, it sounded like a high tech operation. Night vision, laser scopes and darts. Regular ammo too, but it's the darts that really concern me."

"You think these hunters know what you are?" Sally asked, joining the conversation now that she was fully dressed, except for her jacket and firearm, which lay at her feet. Her cop instincts were taking over as she listened to their conversation. There was a mystery here and though she didn't quite have the lay of the land yet, she might be able to help in some way.

"If they've got darts they're either collecting for the private trade or a zoo—illegally, of course—or they want specifically to bag a werewolf or some other kind of shifter. We're the best known in the media, of course, so we get the occasional nutcase who wants to catch a werewolf or even be bitten by one. Occasionally, some of the other shifter clans will be targeted." Jason was revealing a whole new level of danger to being in his world that she hadn't even considered.

"There's an ancient organization called the *Altor Custodis* that supposedly watches us and keeps records of our kind. I'm still not clear on why." He went on, shaking his head. "There's also a truly dangerous bunch called the *Venifucus* who want to kill us all and impose their own kind of rule over humanity. I've had reports of run-ins with both groups in the past few months among other groups of shifters and bloodletters. So far, we've been on the winning side but there's a sense the bad guys are gearing up for an all-out assault. The recent skirmishes may have only been a test of our strength."

"I had no idea." Sally was really surprised by his words. She hadn't considered that shifter society might have villains all its own. And he seemed to indicate that her friends could be in danger, even with their powerful and experienced mates to protect them. This was something she needed to know more about.

"It's not something we advertise, but there are certain dangers in our world," Jason admitted.

She liked that he was leveling with her. He wasn't trying to shield her from the truth or hide the nastiness of life from her. He treated her as an equal—in this, at least—and her respect for him went up another notch. She'd had to fight long and hard for that kind of respect from her fellow detectives. It meant a lot to her that Jason had treated her fairly from the moment they'd met.

"Can the sightseeing wait a bit? Or can we incorporate a look around Yellowtail Ridge into the tour?" she asked. "I have a feeling you probably want to check things out and I might be able to help. I am a detective, after all. Finding things out is my job."

Jason's visible relief was answer enough. "I won't put you at risk, Sally, but I do really need to take a look around up there. I dare not go in my fur if someone's hunting in the area. In fact, having a police escort might be just the thing. If you don't mind, of course."

"Not a bit. In fact, it'll be fun. Usually, I track suspects in a concrete jungle. I'm sure I could learn a thing or two from you about tracking in the woods. And if we run into trouble, I am armed."

"You are?" Steve's eyebrows rose as he regarded her.

Sally reached down and deliberately pulled her service revolver out from under her jacket, shrugging into the holster and checking its security before shrugging into her jacket. Her gaze rose to meet Steve's in challenge.

"Do you have a pair of handcuffs too, detective?" the cat purred.

Sally laughed at the question. Oh, yeah, she had cuffs. They were in her jacket pocket. But it wouldn't be the cat she'd be using them on. No, if she wasn't using the cuffs on bad guys, her first choice for fun would be the wolf. Woof.

"I never leave home without restraints of some kind, Steve. You never know who you might run into on a dark night."

That she felt comfortable enough to joke around with these

guys in such a blatant way was kind of fascinating. Too often in the past she'd been accused of being cold until she got to know someone. She barely knew either one of them but they'd both been witness to some incredibly intimate moments and she didn't feel the least bit threatened.

"A woman after my own heart." The cat shifter clutched his hard-muscled chest.

"Keep dreaming, Redstone." Jason cut short the cougar's teasing. "Get your own girl. This one's mine." Jason put one arm around her waist and hauled her close to his side.

Sally didn't resist. She'd already decided on a fling with Jason and had gotten a taste of his incredible passion. It was just a matter of getting him in the right place at the right time so they could seal the deal. Given half a chance, she'd jump his bones and leave his head spinning. Her mouth watered at the idea. But it was clear now was not the time. Jason's Pack might be in danger and even on such short acquaintance, she knew his Pack's safety came first before his own desires. He was that kind of Alpha. That kind of leader. And she respected him even more for it.

"Are you sure I can't tempt you, sweet Sally?" Steve raised one eyebrow looking from her to Jason and back again.

"Sorry, Steve." Sally felt rather than heard the growl of triumph coming from deep in Jason's chest. He liked her answer.

That hearty sound set off some answering ripples of pleasure in her mid-section. Oh, yeah. There was no shortage of attraction between them and now she knew what he could give her, she wanted to fuck him for real—his cock inside her straining body—all that much more.

"Thanks for the warning, Redstone." Jason offered his hand and the other man took it, being a good sport about her rejection. She liked the cat. She just liked the wolf more.

"No problem, Alpha." He turned his gaze to her. "Thanks for...everything, Sally." Steve paused long enough between the words to make his point. "I won't soon forget this lovely afternoon interlude."

She knew she'd never forget it. Not as long as she lived. But she wasn't saying that out loud. Not where Steve could hear. He seemed overconfident enough as it was. She gave him a nod of acknowledgement and a smile instead.

The air shimmered and where Steve had stood, suddenly a tawny furred mountain lion sat on his haunches. The shift was slightly different than what she'd seen when Seth had become a wolf for her. It was quicker for one thing. More of a blur. Maybe Seth had gone slow to show her the various stages. Or maybe he was just young and inexperienced. This shift from man to cougar looked seamless and almost instantaneous.

"That is so amazing," she said without thinking.

Steve loped over to her, sniffing at her hand, and then her torso. When he tried to put that big cat nose between her legs, she scooted away, laughing.

"Be on your way, you mangy cat," Jason said with laughter in his voice.

Steve put his nose in the air as if offended and walked away, tail swishing like a flag behind him.

Sally watched with rapt fascination as Steve Redstone walked back into the woods. He paused on the edge of the clearing to stretch, digging his claws into a tree, then he took off at a lope. Within seconds, he was gone.

"I was going to show you around up here but something is telling me to check out Yellowtail Ridge as quickly as possible. You don't mind, do you?" Jason looked torn.

"Not at all. I, of all people, understand the necessity of keeping people safe from bad guys. Though I really feel like you got cheated here." She stepped close enough to place her hand on his chest, moving it slowly downward. He stopped her midway, before she could get to the really interesting parts.

"Can I take a raincheck?"

"Most definitely." She smiled at him, leaning up to place a little kiss on his strong jaw. "Now let's go check out that ridge. I'll feel better after we have, and I'm pretty sure you will too."

Jason leaned down to place a smacking kiss on her lips. She wanted more, but she understood his urgency. Her cop instinct was telling her they needed to get up to that ridge before somebody got hurt.

Jason led her back past the waterfall and they mounted the bike in short order. The drive up to the ridge took about a half hour considering they had to follow winding mountain roads. Time enough to cool down a bit. Her head cleared and she wondered who the wanton of the past hour was and where she'd come from. Sally had never encountered that part of herself before. It was disturbing, but also very freeing.

Only with Jason had she ever felt so alive, so daring. He brought out the bad girl inside and invited her to play. She'd never been so brazen or climaxed so hard. Jason had given her that, without taking anything in return. Poor guy. She vowed to make it up to him as soon as possible. As soon as they took a look around and were sure everyone was safe and there was no danger to Jason's Pack.

She'd bet it was a lot easier to get to the ridge if you could climb straight through the forest. That was probably why Jason was so worried about one of his Pack members running around up there. There was little doubt in her mind that this ridge was part of their regular territory. If not, Jason wouldn't be so worried and his worry wouldn't be communicating itself to her so strongly.

As they approached, even the trees felt anxious to her.

74

Sally didn't know why, but she'd always been sensitive to green, growing things. Her garden was her place of solace and she had some peculiar talents when it came to plants. Trees sometimes spoke to her. Not in words, of course, but they communicated nonetheless.

They were doing so now as she hopped off the bike and headed for the woods. Somehow she knew where to go.

Bang. The first shot rang through the alarmed forest.

She crouched low in reflex and drew her weapons. She had the service revolver out of its holster faster than a blink and a backup she'd kept in a special compartment in her jacket only a second or two later. Even though she was technically on vacation, she had gone through the proper procedures to make it legal to carry concealed in this state. Her badge had helped considerably and she didn't feel quite so naked without her weapons. Over the years, they'd come to symbolize security and independence to her. Armed, she could take on just about any situation. Unarmed, she was much more of a target.

She crept through the bushes, listening intently to the forest and the incongruous sounds of men within, shooting at something. No, wait. They were shooting at some*one*.

Jason was at her side. He nodded when he saw her two weapons, one in each hand. She'd trained to shoot with both hands and found it came in handy every once in a blue moon. Today seemed like one of those days, unfortunately.

"Do you hear that?"

They were quite a distance from where the shot had originated but faintly, coming closer, she could make out the sounds of someone scurrying through the underbrush. Crawling, most likely. She nodded toward the faint sound. Jason took off, still crouched as low as a big man like him could go. Sally followed.

Then she smelled it. The faint copper of freshly spilled

blood. That poor soul she'd sensed through the trees had been hit. Dammit!

"Alpha?" the female voice was barely a whisper, faint with pain and fear. Jason changed course to a dense cluster of bushes set amid a few larger sized tree trunks.

He dove in and Sally followed. Inside the dense cover of the bushes, a young girl lay bleeding from a bullet wound in her thigh. Jason moved quickly to staunch the flow of blood while Sally kept an eye out for the bastards who'd shot the youngster. The kid couldn't be more than fourteen but she was already as tall as Sally.

"You'd better shift, Colleen. The bullet will come out in the shift and you can run to the Pack house while Sally and I take care of these guys." Sally heard his low-voiced words though she knew they wouldn't carry beyond the circle of bushes that surrounded them.

"Give me her jacket," Sally said, thinking fast. "We're about the same size." Sally was already shrugging out of her own leather jacket.

"What have you got in mind?"

"You don't want them to know they actually hit her, do you?" Sally thought not. "I'll keep them busy and hopefully put the fear of God Almighty and the law in them while you mop up and call the sheriff on your cell phone. You do want to report this, don't you?"

"Damn right I want to report this." Jason's face was grim as the teen shed her clothes and began the painful shift to her wolf form.

He handed her the girl's jacket and Sally shrugged into it, transferring a few things from her own pockets into the girl's jacket. Jason's eyebrows rose when her handcuffs jingled as she moved them, but he didn't comment. He rolled up the girl's jeans and shirt, along with Sally's discarded leather jacket. He also collected the bullet when it popped out of the girl's thigh as she shifted form. Colleen stood on four legs, favoring one of her hind legs, but she wasn't bleeding any longer and looked like she could run. Sally was relieved. The sooner the girl got out of here, the better.

Sally checked her own phone. "I don't have any reception up here. Do you?"

"No. I'll have to climb a little higher to get the call out. Will you be okay?"

"I can handle a couple of hunting yahoos, but don't take too long. I'll hold them while you clean up and make the call."

Jason looked uncertain but clearly there was little alternative. "The Pack house is over the ridge. If you need to make a run for it, head due south until you hit a dirt road, then follow that west. The Pack house is off that road. You can't miss it."

"Got it. But I really doubt it'll be necessary. Get her out of here." She gestured toward the trembling wolf. "I'll take care of the perps until you get back."

"There are at least three of them," Jason warned before leading the girl out of the bushes. "Be careful."

Sally only nodded, her mind on the job, her senses open to what the trees were telling her. She didn't want to contradict Jason, but there were four men scouring the woods for the girl. And they were drawing near. It was almost showtime.

Sally ducked out of the bushes, guns in hand and at the ready. She deliberately let herself be seen by the closest goon. Just a flash of jacket, that's all. But it was enough. Five seconds later, a shot rang out, hitting the tree behind which she hid.

"Cease fire!" she yelled. "Cease fire! What the hell do you think you're doing taking potshots at people?" She injected as much righteous outrage as she could into her tone. She'd learned a lot about bullies over the years. Often, if you stood up to them, they backed down. Especially when you were the one carrying the badge. "I'm a police officer," she yelled. "Stand down or I'm going to start shooting back and somebody's going to get hurt. And it ain't going to be me. That I can guarantee."

"She's not a cop," one of the jerks protested to the other.

They'd taken cover when she threatened retaliation, but she knew exactly where each of the bastards was hiding. Three were ranged directly in front of her. One was up a tree but he didn't have a good vantage point to see where she was holed up.

The guy in the tree had been setting up a tree stand. It was a hidden nest that hunters sometimes used to wait for prey without being seen. There was a rope dangling down from the tree with a pack on the end. An idea began to form in Sally's mind about how she might use that to her advantage.

"I am a San Francisco police detective here on vacation. My boyfriend is calling the local sheriff to report this. I doubt he'll take kindly to a bunch of yahoos out in the woods shooting at anything that moves."

"Look, lady," one of them yelled, "we don't want any trouble with the law."

"You should have thought of that before you started shooting at people. Place your firearms on the ground and come out with your hands where I can see them. I won't ask you again. I can't believe you shot at me—twice! What the hell were you thinking?" Outrage, and as much authority as she could manage, rang in her words.

"Thought you were a wolf," the one on the right mumbled as he gave in and followed her instructions.

A rather dull-looking, middle-aged man stepped out from behind the tree and dropped his rifle, raising his hands in surrender. The other two on the ground followed suit. They were quite a bit younger than the guy on the right, but looked like they might be related to him. Perhaps they were his sons or nephews. There was a strong family resemblance.

"Now you in the tree," she called out, allowing her right hand, holding a shiny silver pistol, to be seen around the tree. "Come down and let's talk about this like civilized people."

"Or what? You gonna shoot me, girlie?" The man in the tree yelled down at her. Figured he'd be the holdout. "You're outnumbered. There's four of us and only one of you."

"Maybe so," she admitted. "My boyfriend had to go in search of a signal to make the call way up here on the ridge, but he knows something you don't."

"Yeah, what's that?" tree man taunted.

She took the shot she'd been thinking about since she saw that rope. The bullet left the chamber and sliced the rope in two, dropping the contents of the pack on the ground with a loud clang.

"I don't miss." She'd made her point. "Now get down out of that tree or I'll plug your ass. I've had more than enough provocation, don't you think?"

The man scurried down the tree so fast it was almost comical. Sally stepped from behind her tree only when she was sure all four men had their hands up and weapons on the ground far enough away for comfort. She felt some satisfaction when they saw her jacket—the one the girl had been wearing— and their eyes widened. They'd gotten more than they bargained for on this hunt. Their prey had escaped and filling in was a much more dangerous predator. One with a badge and the skill, and will, to back it up.

She covered them with both handguns, one in each hand, until Jason showed up. He took a hard look at each of the men and she felt a little thrill of elation as they backed down, inch by inch. The tree guy was the most hardheaded of the lot, but he was no match for the Alpha wolf. Even he couldn't hold Jason's gaze for long.

"Are you okay, sweetheart?" Jason was playing his part to perfection. And wonder of wonders, a .357 Magnum had appeared in his hand. A big ass gun for a big son of a gun. It fit him to a T. He added his firepower to hers and she dared the four yahoos to put a toe wrong now.

"I'm good, now that these idiots have stopped shooting at us."

Jason and she knew well and good that the girl had been their true target. They were bewildered now, seeing Sally in the kid's jacket. Colleen and Sally looked enough alike to confuse the issue. They both had medium-length brown hair and a tall build. Hopefully that would be enough to convince these guys they really had shot at Sally and not her lookalike.

They both heard the sound of an engine in the distance. The sheriff must've had someone nearby to get here this fast. Sally heard two sets of footsteps make their way through the underbrush. Jason called out when it was clear to all that somebody was in the woods with them. Luckily, they weren't too far from the road.

The two policemen took over with calm competence. They took the hunters into custody when Sally said she wanted to press charges. One of the deputies asked about her permit to carry concealed in their state and she was able to produce the appropriate paperwork from her wallet. Likewise, they asked about Jason's permit and he did the same. They seemed to know Jason, but the investigation into the incident was carried out with all the professionalism she could ever hope to find.

In short order it was determined that only two of the rifles had been fired. Those belonging to the older guy who'd been on the ground and the tree guy. Both were taken into custody and put in the back of the patrol car so they could be taken down to the station for processing.

As they were being loaded into the car, Sally thought she saw something out of the corner of her eye. It looked like a tattoo on the tree guy's wrist. A tattoo she'd seen before. Once before. And it had gotten her in a heap of trouble and embarrassment at the time. She wasn't about to call attention to it now, and there was no way to discreetly alert Jason so he could take a look. Regardless, it was gone in a flash when the man's long sleeve settled back into place as he sank into his seat.

Sally would to try to get a peek at the police report the next day. That would list any identifying marks on the perps—birthmarks, scars, tats, piercings and the like. That would confirm what she thought she'd seen.

She hoped the local cops threw the book at these two. Assault with a deadly weapon was a likely charge, as was negligence and a few other things the locals might tack on. It wouldn't keep them long, but it was likely the two men would be overnight guests of the county, for which Sally was thankful.

She gave her preliminary statement to one of the deputies and was asked to go to the station the next day to be interviewed in more depth. Fine with her. She wanted this incident on these guys' rap sheets. You couldn't go hunting *people*, for goodness' sake. Even if they were people who could transform into animals.

The two younger men were strongly cautioned to pack up their gear and leave. They hadn't done any shooting so they couldn't be charged, but the deputies made it clear they weren't welcome to camp up on the ridge and would be watched by extra vigilant patrols if they chose to stay. Sally hoped they took the hint and moved on.

Sally and Jason left when the patrol car did, following them down the ridge road until it came to a crossroad. Jason steered his motorcycle onto another country road while the patrol car continued toward town. Sally felt a weight lift off her shoulders as the two jerks in the back of the patrol car drove out of sight. For tonight at least, the woods would be safe for man and beast alike.

Though traumatic, the whole incident took less than two hours. It was nearing dinnertime when Jason pulled the bike to a stop in front of a huge, modern home set back in the woods.

"Welcome to our Pack house," he said as he climbed off the bike after her and unfastened his helmet.

Again, he took hers and stowed them on the side of the bike while she fluffed her hair. It was a mess after all she'd been through today, not to mention the flattening it took from repeated helmet use. She must have looked a fright, but Jason didn't seem to mind. He had a sort of smug pride as he walked with her up the steps to the beautiful home.

A few children played on the wide porch. They all greeted him respectfully as they passed and stared at Sally with wide eyes. She wondered idly if they'd never had a human guest here before.

When he ushered her into the doorway, a trio of shocked faces met her appearance. One was an older woman with gray hair and wrinkles. The other two were younger females, one with a baby on her hip, the other shooting daggers at Sally with her eyes after she saw the possessive hand Jason had around her waist. A rival, then. Sally didn't much care for the woman's obvious attitude but she really shouldn't have worried. Sally was only there for two weeks. After that, the wolf bimbo could have Jason all to herself if she wanted.

Why that thought hurt so much, Sally didn't care to examine at the moment. The old woman overcame her shock first as Jason introduced her.

"Sally, this is Mother Josepha. She's one of our elders and

the backbone of the Pack." It was clear he complimented the woman from the way she beamed. "Mother, this is Detective Sally Decker, the Mistress's friend from San Francisco."

The old woman shook Sally's hand with a sort of cautious welcome, but it was still a welcome, which was more than could be said of the bimbo. The woman with the baby had tempered her response and now watched with nothing but eager curiosity. Jason cut short the introductions by the simple expedience of asking about Colleen.

"She's all right," Josepha assured them. "She came limping in a little while ago and is being coddled by her mother and aunts. She won't have any permanent injury and you can be sure her father will be talking to her later about prowling around alone at her age."

"I think she's learned her lesson." Jason's relief was evident though otherwise, Sally was learning, he kept his emotions very close to his vest. "I need to talk to Detective Decker for a few minutes before we grab some dinner."

So saying, he left the trio of women, Sally following in his wake. There was a tension about him that she hadn't noticed, in the tumult of the situation. Could be he was having a bit of a reaction now that the adrenaline had faded. She'd been through that herself. It happened from time to time. Such was the nature of her occupation. Days and weeks of boredom interspersed with moments of sheer terror.

Somehow, she'd gotten used to it over the years and now she lived for those few moments when life and death were on the line. She wasn't an adrenaline junkie. Not by a long shot. But she no longer appreciated the dull times. There had to be more to life than sitting at a desk or filing papers. Didn't there?

Jason led her through the big house, down a hallway and into a private room that looked like a study. There was a desk filled with papers and a few comfortable chairs ranged in front of it. A long leather couch lined one wall, but that was all she got to see before he closed the door and whirled around, capturing her in his arms.

She found herself the recipient of a bear hug that almost bruised her ribs. He held her so tight, like he would never let go. It felt good. It was also more than a bit overwhelming.

"Jason?"

"I'm sorry, Sally. You were incredible out there. I knew you would be. I could tell you were an Alpha female, but that doesn't mean I enjoyed seeing you in danger. Four men with rifles, Sally. Four! All trained on you."

She could feel the slight tremble of his body against hers. It was anger at those men. His fury came through in every word he spoke, but it wasn't directed at her, thank goodness. No, he was really pissed off at those four jerks she'd captured. She understood. It was hard to go off to take care of business, leaving your partner under the gun. She'd had to do it a time or two herself and she never liked it. Not one bit.

Sally stroked her hands down his back, gentling him.

"It's okay, Jason. It all worked out. And in my job, this wasn't the first time I've had a lot of guns pointed my way. There was a bank robbery last year involving five gunmen and I walked right into their escape path. It was a little tense before my backup showed."

She'd thought her words would calm him; instead, he held her tighter. Damn. She should've realized the man had a protective streak a mile wide.

"If you're trying to make me feel better, it's not working."

She heard the humorous note in his voice that hadn't been there a few seconds ago. Good. He wasn't the type to linger over bad thoughts. She'd had to develop the skill herself.

She smiled up at him as he released her enough to do so.

His arms were looser, but he still wasn't letting her go.

"Then I'd better not tell you about the shootout three years ago."

"Shootout? Damn, woman. You want to get me all worked up, don't you?" His grin told her that might be just the ticket. Getting this man worked up would definitely be her pleasure. All night long.

A flush stole over her body as her thoughts turned lascivious. This man affected her like no other. In his presence—especially in his arms—she had trouble focusing on anything other than sex. With him. Now. On the couch. On the desk. Even on the floor.

Damn. She had it bad.

"If you're good, I might even show you my scar." She was teasing but his eyes narrowed and his armed tightened, just a little.

"Scar? Honey, you got shot?" His gaze was intense.

"Just grazed," she clarified. "Hurt like the dickens at the time, but I only have a tiny scar to show for it. I'm surprised you didn't notice it before."

"Where?" The single word held a multitude of feeling. Caring, concern, desire...it was all mixed up together in his expression and it touched her deeply.

She moved away from him and he let her go. She unbuttoned her jeans and lifted her shirt, displaying the white line that rode along the top of her left hip. Jason dropped to his knees in front of her, surprising her. His fingers traced the four-inch scar almost reverently as his breath wafted over her skin, raising gooseflesh. She would have moved away but he grabbed her hips, holding her in place while his lips touched her flesh, kissing the scar that she never really showed anyone.

To her, it was a mark of stupidity. She'd read the situation wrong and almost got killed for her troubles. It was a mark of experience, of learning. She had never forgotten the lesson of that injury. She had never put herself in the same situation again.

"What happened?" Jason spoke the words against her skin as he continued touching her, moving his hands into the open flap of her jeans. Her stomach clenched as vibrations started deep within her.

"I trusted a perp. I thought we had an understanding and I put myself in the open, expecting no more trouble from her."

"A woman did this to you?" His hands moved lower, taking her jeans down, inch by inch. She locked her knees so they wouldn't give out on her.

"It was a domestic dispute. She'd already shot her husband in the chest. I figured her rage was at him alone and that she wouldn't take it out on another woman. I thought I'd talked her into surrendering. Turns out, I was almost dead wrong. She had nothing left to lose. She had already killed her kids in the other room, before I got there. The husband was the last one she wanted to take out before she committed suicide by cop. She was just waiting until she thought he was good and dead before she took a potshot at me to get the other officers to open fire. I totally misread the situation."

Chapter Five

Jason's hands stilled, one on her belly, under the elastic of her panties, one on her back in almost the same position. He rested his forehead against her hip for a long moment while he took in what she'd told him.

It infuriated him to think of all the close calls she hadn't yet revealed. She alternately fascinated him and made him want to bite. In a big way. Her scent had driven him mad from the first moment he'd smelled her at that damned party. He'd wanted to take her out in the woods right then and there and stake his claim, but he prided himself on being more civilized than his ancestors.

He'd have had her this afternoon in the most idyllic forest glade he knew. It would have been perfect. Except for the cat. Though Steve's presence had brought out a wild side to Sally that Jason hadn't really expected.

He'd been hard for hours, it seemed. He needed to be inside her like he needed to breathe. But his best laid plans seemed to have gone awry this afternoon. Instead, he'd treated her to a day of danger and shotgun blasts. What a charmer.

And now, here he was, listening to her talk about her job—and getting *shot*, for Lady's sake—while he had his hands in her pants. Something was very odd about this whole situation, but somehow, it was also perfect.

This Alpha female would come to him on her terms. If this was the way she wanted it, he'd give it to her. Any *way* she wanted. Any *time* she wanted. Any *place* she wanted. The big, bad Alpha male was well and truly snared.

She wasn't a shifter, but his wolf didn't seem to care. She had a tiny bit of wolf blood, which pleased the beast within him. There was something else too, besides the almost overwhelming scent of human female. Something magical. Something special. It was tantalizing in the extreme. Another mystery for him to solve about this puzzling woman.

"Sally, you shouldn't tell me stuff like that at a time like this," he warned in a gruff voice. "The wolf gets protective and wants to keep you all to himself. If he had his way, you'd be tied to my bed all night and shackled to my arm all day, just to keep you safe."

She surprised him by laughing. "Guess we shouldn't tell him about my handcuffs and zip ties then."

Damn. This woman continued to surprise him.

"I can think of a few hundred good uses for the cuffs, but the zip ties might bite into your delicate skin. The only thing I want biting you from now on is me." He nipped her hip to emphasize his point. Satisfaction filled him when she shivered under his hands.

"That can be arranged." The sexy lilt of her voice made him even harder than he already was. The return of passion was as instantaneous as it was fierce. He'd never been so hot for a woman.

"Are you sure?" They both knew he was asking the big question. Did she really want this? Did she really want him? He thought he knew the answer, but it was only polite to ask.

She moaned as his hand moved downward, under the panties, finding her clit, her opening already slick with her juices. He rubbed and her knees buckled but he was there to catch her. He placed her on the wide couch which was luckily only a foot or two away.

"Sally?" he asked again, wanting her answer in words, not just a physical surrender.

"I've never been surer of anything in my life. Besides, I owe you for this afternoon."

Well, that was good enough for him. He pulled her jeans and panties downward, pausing only when he encountered the difficulty of her shoes. Damn. He'd been too eager to notice he was going to have to stop to get those things off first.

She sat up and helped him, tackling one foot while he handled the other. She giggled and suddenly he didn't feel so clumsy. She made even a tense moment like this fun. What a woman.

She removed her jacket and shoulder holster and gave them to him. He placed the gun, still in its holster, on the end table off to one side. The handcuffs in the pocket of her jacket rattled a bit when he folded it and set it down. He took a moment to place his own ankle holster, with the Magnum in it, alongside hers. They made short work of her footwear.

She then removed her shirt, leaving the bra for him to handle. No way was he leaving her in it this time, though having her slightly immobilized had been fun this afternoon. He hadn't expected her playfulness but liked it. More than he probably should have considering she was mostly human.

But she smelled like his mate. The conundrum had kept him up half the night, thinking, until he finally decided not to think at all and just go with it. The future would take care of itself somehow.

Jason kicked off his boots and slid his jeans down slowly, enjoying the way she licked her lips when she saw him for the first time. No doubt about it, Sally was more than interested in his body. He liked that she didn't hide her appreciation and he hoped she'd be appreciating him in the flesh, so to speak, real soon. But he wouldn't push her. Not anymore than he already had. She had to come to him. She was an Alpha bitch, after all, even if she was only a tiny bit wolf.

When two Alphas mated, fur could fly if one tried too hard to dominate the other. His father had always said it was important to let the woman have the upper hand in sex once in a while when dealing with an Alpha female. Jason hadn't been with any true Alpha bitches—only a handful of younger women with the potential to be Alphas. They hadn't known their own inner strength yet and he'd been able to dominate them easily.

He didn't think he'd have as easy a time with this woman. He'd seen the way she handled herself in the woods with those hunters. He'd seen her glee in a situation that would have sent most women running for cover. Sally knew exactly who she was and what she was capable of. She knew her inner core of strength and had been tested many times in her dangerous job. She was a woman worthy of the title Alpha, whether she could shift form or not. She'd earned it. And she lived it every day.

Jason admired her. That was something new. There were few people in this world he could truly say he admired, but Sally Decker was most definitely one of them. And there she was, lying almost naked on his office couch.

It wasn't the best place for seduction, but he'd tried to plan something idyllic and fate had led them here instead. He needed her too badly to wait any longer. If their first time had to be in less than a perfect setting, he promised himself he'd make it up to her later. Setting could be controlled. Passion couldn't. At least not this kind of passion between two mature Alphas.

She might not understand what that meant, but he certainly did. A mating of equals. Something he'd never experienced before, though he had looked for it all his life. He'd seen the example of his parents, before all hell had broken loose within the Pack. He remembered how it could be when two people shared their lives equally. He wanted that. Had always wanted it. He only regretted his parents hadn't lived long enough to see him find it.

Although, he wasn't sure what they would have said about a human mate for their son. They'd been so proud of their shifter heritage. They'd been almost snobbish about it, never mixing with humans unless they had to. Oh, they didn't despise humans the way some of the old ones did, but they had little use for them, preferring to stay within the Pack for most of their lives.

Jason was different. His worldview had been altered during the clan war that had killed his parents. He'd seen the future and knew that things had to change. Shifters had to be tolerant of those who seemed weaker. In the years since he'd taken control of the Pack, he'd learned many things. Among them was the fact that those *weaker* humans had somehow managed to foment the unrest that had caused the clan war in the first place.

But how could he be thinking of things like that at a time like this? He had the most luscious woman he'd ever met, spread out, naked on his couch. Her scent washed over him like a drug. She wore only that lovely, lacy bra. Her pussy wept for him. Her heat called to him. Daring him to take her, to make her his in the most basic way.

With a growl, he tore his shirt off over his head and joined her. He'd had the couch built long and wide for those nights when Pack business kept him in his office 'til all hours and he could only catch quick naps between crises.

This would be the first time he'd put it to such pleasurable use. He couldn't wait.

Sally made room for him as he lay on one hip beside her. She was up against the back of the couch while he took up the rest of the cushion. It was a tight squeeze, but he wanted to give her pleasure before he sought his own. Crowding her also satisfied his wolf on some basic level. He was so much bigger than she was, it felt good to curl her into him, to surround her with his protective presence. The wolf rumbled low in his chest.

Sally's fingers covered his heart. "I like it when you do that," she whispered.

"Oh, baby. You haven't even heard me growl yet."

He promised her things with his eyes but he couldn't be sure she fully understood. She hadn't been born into shifter society. Who knew what she expected? He only hoped she was ready for him. He'd do his best to temper his animal instincts, but there was only so much holding back he could do.

"I look forward to it." Her fingers traced patterns down his chest and it was his turn to shiver.

"Do you?" He stilled her hand, covering it with his own. "Things might get a little rough."

She tugged her hand free and placed one finger over his lips, her smile still in place.

"I can defend myself, even against you, big boy. Do your worst."

He wasn't completely convinced of her ability to fight him off, if she felt the need, but he would be as gentle as possible. He'd watch her to see how far he could let himself go. If she responded well, he'd push her a little farther, then farther still. Judging by her earlier climaxes, she could handle more than he'd imagined when he'd first met her. He'd been imagining her beneath him almost from the first moment he caught her scent. It was his fondest dream that she could take him all the way—that he wouldn't have to hold back. Time would tell and urgency was riding him.

"Hang on for the ride of your life, Detective."

"Promises, promises," she teased, but he knew it was a challenge. One he would gladly accept.

Jason climbed over her, making more room on the seat of the couch. She slid over so that she lay squarely under him. He insinuated one knee between hers and she eagerly spread her legs. Damn. He liked the way she joined in and took charge.

"This has got to go." He supported his weight on one arm and used one hand to trace the strap of her bra.

"It closes in the front. I think you were moving too fast to notice before." A charming touch of shyness entered her tone while her eyes challenged him to do things he didn't dare try yet. Not with a brand-new lover.

"Do tell?" He reached down and snapped the clasp open, allowing the weight of her breasts to part the cups. She was shapely enough that the cups didn't fall off by themselves. No, that pleasure would be his and his alone.

Jason lowered his head. He had her under him and he hadn't even kissed her yet. Was he a fool? Ah, well, that was soon rectified.

He connected with her lips, sinking his tongue inside her mouth with a groan. He might've growled then. He wasn't sure. She certainly responded with all her might, joining in and tangling her tongue with his. He was quickly becoming addicted to the taste of her. Her soft breaths panting against his face when he let her up for air, then dived back in with reckless abandon. He could kiss her for hours...or years.

But her squirming was getting to him in all too delicious ways. He'd been raw with need most of the day, but he wanted to sample every part of her skin. He wanted to learn the taste of her body from nipples to pussy and everywhere in between.

He dragged himself away from the temptation of her lips to nuzzle her neck. He paused at her earlobe to nip and suck, then trailed his mouth downward to her chest. The cups of the bra teased him. It was like opening presents on Christmas morning, only much, much naughtier. He slid his tongue under the first cup, easing it away from the soft skin of her breast until he could take the fabric between his teeth. Her skin was driving him mad. Never before had he wanted a woman this badly, and never a human.

Sally, bless her adventurous soul, wasn't content to just lie beneath him and await his pleasure. No, she was more a hands on girl—as he learned when she reached down and grabbed his cock.

Then he growled.

Sally shivered when he made the sound that drove her wild. It was deeper this time, throatier and much louder. And it was continuous as she stroked his hard length with her hand. He was growling, but not in anger or aggression. No, this was a growl of pure pleasure.

He paused with the edge of her bra cup between his teeth, his bristly chin resting on the swell of her breast. Mmm. That felt good. She knew something that would feel even better, but while she had a moment to think, she had to ask him some important questions.

"What about protection?" she whispered, hoping he wasn't too distracted to hear her question. She wasn't sure she had the wherewithal to repeat it.

"Weres don't get STDs," he answered in a short burst, his breath coming in rapid pants as she continued to stroke him. "And we're usually only fertile with our mates. That's how our population stays so low."

"Good to know." She was breathing hard too, as if she'd just finished a marathon, but they had hardly even started yet.

She squeezed him hard and reveled in the way his muscles clenched. The man was so beautiful, though he'd probably hate that description. She just couldn't get enough of looking at him, especially now, his taut muscles straining above her. She couldn't wait to see how he looked when he came. Now *that* would be a memory to take home with her.

When she eased off, he took the hint and resumed his position, his teeth on her bra cup, which still hadn't come off. Her nipples wanted some attention and they wanted it now. They ached with the rigidity he had created and needed the relief only he could give.

Jason seemed to understand. He pulled back the cup of her bra with his teeth, rasping his cheek over her sensitive, puckered skin. She moaned. She couldn't help it. That felt so damn *good*.

He paused for a moment to lick her aching nipple before treating the other to the same attention. This time, after uncovering her, he took his time, sucking her inside his hot mouth and nibbling on her sensitive flesh with sharp teeth that stopped just short of pain. Lightning bolts of sensation raced from her nipples to her pussy and back again. After their earlier interlude in the woods, he knew exactly how far to push her, how to touch her, how to please her and make her want to give him everything she had.

He sucked hard for a few moments before moving downward once more. His free hand toyed with the sharp points of her nipples while his mouth explored her waist and belly button. He licked over the scar on her hip, then moved lower still.

Her thighs parted wide as he settled between them. She thanked the powers that be that the couch was extra long and wide enough for this. She didn't think she could wait another second to have him. She'd take him on the bare floor if she had to. The couch would do, though. It was well cushioned and the leather was soft and supple beneath her back.

"Holy hell!" Jason's tongue plunged into her without warning and her muscles went rigid with surprised bliss. He fucked her with strokes of his tongue that seemed impossibly long and somewhat rough.

Then she remembered she was with a shifter. She looked downward, glad to see he was still in human form, but apparently he could selectively shift certain parts of his anatomy. Or maybe it was some sort of special sex thing common to all shifters. She didn't know and didn't really care at the moment. All she wanted right now was *more*.

She tangled her fingers in his hair and pulled gently, urging him on. He began to growl again as her pussy gave up its cream. The vibrations against her clit drove her higher and higher. Rather than move away, her reaction seemed to spur him on. He licked at her opening with broad strokes, moving up to her clit to pause there and suck. His fingers spread her wide for his probing tongue and he began the process all over again until she went wild beneath him.

An orgasm hit her while he continued to lap at her juices, his mouth following her bucking hips as he rode her through the climax. He seemed so intent on her pleasure, it was a bit overwhelming. Finally, she had to push at his head to make him move away. She could hardly breathe, the pleasure had been so intense. She couldn't even imagine what it would feel like when he was finally inside her and they came together.

She couldn't wait to find out.

"Damn, Jason," she spoke between ragged breaths. "That tongue thing is a neat trick."

"Just one of the advantages of being a wolf." He licked his lips as he sat on his haunches between her thighs.

His gaze roved over her spread pussy and the rest of her body before he met her eyes. His grin of anticipation said it all as far as she was concerned. He was enjoying himself, but she knew something that would give him even more pleasure. It was only fair, after he'd given her so many amazing climaxes that day.

"I may not be able to shapeshift..." She sat up and changed positions, urging him into a sitting position on the couch as she leaned over him from the side, "...but I bet I can make you growl again."

She took his hard cock in her hand as she bent down, brushing her hair over him deliberately. She liked the way the muscles in his thighs tensed at the feathery touch. The more she got to know him, the more she liked pretty much everything about him. It was time to learn something new. Something intensely intimate. She was about to learn his taste.

He was long and thick. In every way, he was the best-built man she'd ever had the pleasure to be with. He'd just proven he was a generous lover and she wanted to give him something to remember her by. It worried her a bit that werewolf women could probably do that shapeshifting tongue trick. But she had skills of her own. She eased downward, over him, taking him deep. Focusing on relaxing the muscles of her throat, she tried something she'd only done once before.

Everything about Jason was different. They were from two totally different worlds. He was like some kind of fantasy figure come to life. He made her feel alive again. His confidence in her ability to handle herself and those four assholes this afternoon had gone a long way in endearing him to her. She wanted to try everything with him. And she wanted to give back some of the respect and pleasure he'd already given her.

When she went deeper, he began to growl deep in his chest. Oh, yeah. She'd made him growl and she hadn't even really gotten started yet. Sucking hard, she used her hands and tongue to stroke up and down, over and over, driving him higher and higher. Her goal was to drive him wild.

And she thought she was succeeding too, until the moment he lifted her bodily away and slammed her back onto the soft leather of the couch. She'd driven him wild, all right. Only he didn't seem to want to come in her mouth. He didn't want deep throat. No, he wanted deep penetration.

He gave her little warning before planting his thick cock at the juncture of her thighs. He didn't pause, only meeting her eyes as the tip of him began a strong, steady push into her core. She didn't object. She was primed and ready after that lovely climax he'd given her and the rough handling seemed to have sparked a new round of vibrations in her midsection. She wanted his possession. Had wanted it since almost the first moment she'd met him.

Jason pressed steadily into her, stretching tissues that hadn't been stretched like this in far too long. In fact, they'd never been challenged by a lover so thick and full as Jason, but she was up to it. She'd been anticipating this moment for hours now. Dreaming of it. Waiting for it.

She realized now why he'd pleasured her with those thick fingers of his earlier. He'd been stretching her, preparing her to take the monster he'd had hidden in his pants. Oh, yeah.

And then he was fully inside her, and he paused. His gaze held hers as they were joined fully for the first time. He seemed to breathe easier for a minute before the urgency renewed itself.

"I'm sorry," he said as he began to move. His motions were jerky, out of control, but it didn't matter.

She was as wild for him as he appeared to be for her. She held onto him as his hips plunged between hers, his cock doing amazing things to her insides, touching her in ways no other man had ever achieved. On each stroke he rubbed up against her G spot, driving her to new heights. She was moaning on each thrust, only dimly aware of the deep growling counterpoint coming from his throat.

She came a split second before he did, her body going rigid with the brightest pleasure she'd ever known. He grunted and growled as if he were trying to hold back an even louder response. They were in a house full of people, after all. Anyone could come through the door at anytime, she supposed, which added to the forbidden passion of their joining. His efforts to hold back made her wonder if werewolves howled when they came in human form. Someday soon, she'd dearly like to find out.

The thought made her smile as she floated on the highest high yet, held secure in Jason's strong arms, surrounded by his amazing strength and powerful heat. He was really something and she knew in her heart, she would never forget him, or this time they had together, for as long as she lived. He'd always hold a special place in her heart and a scandalous place in her memories of the hottest sex she'd ever had.

And they'd only just gotten started. She had two weeks here and a hostess who slept all day long. If Jason was willing, they'd probably have more than a few opportunities to try this again. With practice, they might even get better. It was a tantalizing thought. Riding the high he'd just given her, it was hard to imagine this getting any better. He just might blow her mind.

"Oh, sweetheart," he whispered as his hips pushed strongly into hers in the aftermath. "That was intense."

"So you're saying it was good for you?"

Humor in a sexual situation was something new to her. The men she'd been with in the past had been serious, even reserved, in the bedroom but something about Jason invited her to smile. She'd smiled more in the day she'd known him than she had in the past six months. And come harder than she ever had before. The memories made her grin. Although he had a position of authority within his Pack, he didn't take himself too seriously and she felt unaccountably comfortable with him.

"Is there any doubt in your mind?" He eased back and pushed in again, reminding her of the bliss they'd just shared in the most blatant way.

She squirmed under him as aftershocks made themselves known low in her belly. He felt so good there. So right. And his come was thick and warm, heating her from the inside out. It was an odd sensation that she found intensely exciting. Being with a shapeshifter was something out of her experience and everything felt new with him. New and somehow magical.

He made her feel special. And that was the crux of the matter. No matter what Carly had warned about him sleeping around with every girl in his Pack, she still felt special when she was with him. If he made every woman he'd been with feel this way, it was no wonder they were lining up around the block to hop in his bed.

She didn't like the idea of being one in a long line of conquests, but she honestly couldn't hold it against him—or those other women. The idea may make the small part of her ancestry that was werewolf want to challenge the other women to a fight, but she had to remind herself that this wasn't her world. Her existence lay a thousand-something miles to the west. Her apartment, her job, her life were all there, back in San Francisco. This was only an interlude out of time where she could be with a werewolf and learn about his culture. Then she'd go home and resume her normal life...a little wiser, perhaps.

She'd miss him. She realized that even now. But she didn't see any way she could become part of his world. Not now. Certainly not here. If anything, she'd hook up with her newly made vampire friends back in California and give them hell for not telling her about all of this a whole lot sooner. But that was it. She'd go along with being watched and might enjoy some all-nighters hanging out with her fanged friends, but she'd go back to her world when the sun rose and nobody would be the wiser.

Jason rolled in what little room was left for him on the wide couch until she rested on top of his long, lean, muscled body. He was still inside her, pulsing every now and again to remind her of the pleasure they'd just shared. It felt good to laze in the aftermath.

"There. Now I won't crush you." He stroked her hair with one hand. A man who liked to cuddle. Could this guy be any more perfect?

"What about me crushing you? I'm not exactly small."

"Compared to werewolf women you are." His honesty sometimes went a little too far. "Damn. Sorry. That was rude." He sighed heavily. "Honey, you're perfect as you are. You didn't hear me complaining a few minutes ago and you certainly won't hear me complaining now." He resumed stroking her hair and she decided to let it slide. He knew he'd stepped in it and he'd been honest enough to try to fix his mistake.

Nothing would ever fix the fact that she wasn't one of his kind. Or the fact that he was probably the werewolf equivalent of a Don Juan. All that didn't really matter when it came down to it. She was in his bed—well, on his couch—now. She hadn't forced him and he'd given her a memory she would cherish. Hopefully they'd get a chance to make a few more memories before she had to leave, but that was all she could really hope for.

Chapter Six

They lazed together for a while, but eventually sounds from out in the hall intruded. Sally could clearly hear at least two people walk past the door and pause. She'd bet Jason could tell even more about them, with his even more sensitive werewolf hearing.

"As far as seduction scenes go, this wasn't one of my better ideas." He slid his semi-hard cock out of her with obvious reluctance and shifted them around so they could both sit up. "I'm sorry, sweetheart. I should've thought ahead a little better, but all I could focus on was getting inside you as quickly as possible."

The crude admission made her tummy flutter. "It's okay," was all she said. She dared not admit that her own focus had been exactly the same. Nothing else had mattered at the time. Not even thoughts of how awkward the aftermath might be.

"No, you deserve a soft bed and time to enjoy. Not a quickie on the couch. I'm a jerk." He ran one hand through his hair in frustration.

"If so, you're the most sexually talented jerk I've ever had the good luck to meet." Again the humor came easy with this man, which was not her normal style at all. But with him, it worked. She was able to be herself. "Seriously, it's okay, Jason. Maybe next time?" She was putting herself on the line with the question. Maybe he'd gotten what he wanted and there wouldn't be a next time. She sort of thought he was better than that, but the moment of truth had arrived much sooner than expected.

"If you'll allow me to try to make up for this, you're on."

He had a sort of pleased eager puppy look on his face that was totally endearing. Maybe he'd been worried she wouldn't want him again.

"Oh, I definitely want more. As long as you do." Uncertainty was hard to shake.

But his smile widened and he moved in for a quick kiss. "There's no question about my desire for you, sweetheart. It started the moment I first caught your scent and probably won't ever end. If you're breathing, I want to be with you. End of story."

His impassioned tone and the way he spoke the words so close to her mouth as he paused between sweet kisses convinced her like nothing else. They were on the same page. The want and need went both ways. All was right with the world.

Except for those feet pausing outside his office door yet again. She looked over at the door in frustration.

"You can hear that?" he asked with surprise in his tone.

"Yeah. Footsteps. Pausing outside your door. This isn't the first time. I heard two distinct sets before. This is the lighter-stepping set of the two."

"Very good, Detective." He seemed truly impressed. "I bet you'd be able to tell who was who if you hung around here long enough. Our current indecisive visitor is Kathy, who met us at the door with her baby on her hip. She's been living here at the Pack house while her husband is away."

"Who was the other woman? The one who looked like she wanted to roast me over a spit?"

"Ah." He grimaced. "Serena. Watch out for her. She's got enough attitude and cunning to be an Alpha, but it's the wrong kind as far as I'm concerned. She wants to rule and she needs me to do it. She's been stalking me and I want nothing to do with her, but she's having a hard time taking no for an answer."

He grabbed pieces of clothing off the floor and shook them out, frustration clear in his movements. He handed her underwear over after pausing to admire it. The silly smile that graced his features when he fingered the little bows on her panties and bra were enough to make her blush.

"What?" she demanded, snatching the ultra feminine garments out of his hand.

"It's kind of cute that you would choose frilly things when you're Alpha to the core. I didn't expect it. Then again, you continue to amaze me at every turn. I'm going to have a perpetual hard-on wondering what little frills you have on under your clothes."

His words warmed her but something he'd said caught her attention.

"You think I'm Alpha? In what way? Can humans even be that?" She slipped into her bra as she asked the question.

"Definitely. There's a hierarchy in every society. Some are just more subtle than others. If you were a full-blooded werewolf, you'd be an Alpha bitch. There is no doubt in my mind. Even as a human, you're a force to be reckoned with."

He dropped a kiss on her lips before standing and walking across the room to the desk. He grabbed a box of tissues and came back to her. Taking a handful from the box, he slid his hand between her thighs without so much as a by your leave. She jumped, unwittingly giving him just the access he sought to clean up the mess he'd made between her thighs.

He did it so matter-of-factly, as if taking care of her and cleaning her most intimate places was something he'd done for a long time. She couldn't find the words to object, merely watching his face and the little smile of satisfaction there when he had to go back for more tissues.

"Stand up and spread your legs." The tone of command caught her off guard and started a renewed fire in the pit of her stomach.

"What's in it for me?" she challenged.

"A clean pussy, for one thing," he shot back. "More if you're a good girl and obey my orders."

His eyes promised pleasure and she couldn't resist. She stood and spread her legs as far apart as she could while standing before him. His head was on level with her crotch and he wasted no time sliding a clean tissue between her thighs to rub in the renewed flow of his come from inside her as gravity took control.

It was the most intimate thing a man had ever done for her. Somewhat gross if she thought about it in the harsh light of day, but totally hot as his gaze met hers and he discarded the tissue, opting instead to push one of his long, calloused fingers up inside her.

"Just want to make sure it's all out before I go through any more tissues. And we might have time for a bit more if you're willing to live dangerously." His challenging look made her want to take yet another walk on the wild side.

"Do it," was all she could say as her knees began to tremble.

He held her gaze as he began a slow, steady rhythm, pumping his finger in and out of her slick hole. When her breathing grew rapid, he added another finger and slid his free hand around to support her backside as she swayed on her feet.

Her knees bent but somehow she stayed upright, shocks running from his fingers, deep inside her, up her spine and back as his pace increased. When he leaned forward to lick her distended clit, she blew apart in his embrace.

Bianca D'Arc

His mouth guided her climax and his hands supported her as his fingers drove her out of her ever-loving mind. Damn, he was good. His merest touch set her off like a firework on the Fourth of July. She'd never been finger fucked so expertly before today. Jason seemed to enjoy watching her come on his hand and she wasn't objecting. He could do that any time, it felt so damn good.

She drifted down, barely aware of him completing the cleanup job with another wad of tissues. When he was done and she could speak again, he patted the neat curls that barely covered her throbbing clit and grinned.

"You were a very good girl," he rumbled in that deep, sexy voice of his. "And for the record, I like the way you trim your bush. Ever tried shaving?" His gaze rose to meet hers and the devil was in his eyes. The devil who dared her, who pushed her boundaries. She liked that devil and feared she might follow wherever he led.

"No," was all she could get out in reply through a suddenly dry mouth.

"Think about it. I'd be glad to act as your barber." He winked and slid his fingers through her short curls, pressing just enough to make her clit recall the pleasure it had received a few moments earlier.

Able to breathe again, she thought about what he'd said and it made her chuckle.

"What's so funny?" he asked, a smile lingering around the corners of his mouth.

"Don't you think it's a little hypocritical for a werewolf to want me to shave?"

He laughed outright at her words and she joined him.

"You've got me there, sweetheart." He stroked his fingers gently over her abdomen, then lower. "I may be a wolf, but I'm also a man." His gaze turned hot again as he watched his hand rub over her skin. "A man who likes to look at beautiful things. And you're the most beautiful I've seen in a good long while."

Having made his point, he removed his hand and held out her panties so she could step into them.

"It's a shame to cover this up," he said, sliding the fabric up her thighs, his gaze resting on her crotch. "If I had my way, you'd be naked all the time. Ready to take me. Ready for me to lick and taste."

"If you don't cut it out, we'll never leave this room," she mumbled, vaguely aware of the hesitant footsteps pausing outside the door yet again. That made three tries. Who knew how much more patience the woman had?

Jason sighed theatrically. "You're right. Okay, I'll behave." He stood, allowing her to move away, and slid his jeans on sans underwear.

"Commando? Really?" She raised one eyebrow.

"When you have to strip to change shape, the fewer items to remove the better off you are."

She buttoned her pants and reached for her shirt, thinking about it.

"I can see your point, but isn't that a little uncomfortable?" She gestured toward the bulge of his semi-hard erection that was visible under the layer of thick cloth.

"Maybe a little." He shrugged, reaching for his own shirt, which he'd flung on the floor in his earlier haste. "But you get used to it, I suppose."

"I'll take your word for it." She put on her shoes while he finished dressing, then folded her shoulder holster and stowed it in a jacket pocket. She wouldn't put the jacket back on until they left the house, though she'd keep it with her. She was already a little overheated from their recent activity. She didn't need the extra layer of cloth to make it worse.

"Do you want to grab a shower?" he asked belatedly. It was clear the idea had just occurred to him. Men. She had to laugh inwardly. But at least he'd thought of it, if a bit late.

"Now that I'm dressed? Nah. I'll wait 'til I'm back at Carly's where all my clothes are. It's no fun putting on dirty clothes after you've made yourself all clean."

"I might be able to find something you could borrow from one of the girls. Colleen was about your size."

"No, thanks." She held up her hands, palms outward. "I don't want to make a big deal out of this. It's bad enough Kathy's been by here three times now and hasn't had the courage to knock on your door. They all must know I've been in here with you for the past hour."

"They all know what we've been doing too. And if they don't now, they will as soon as they get a whiff of either of us. Our scents are all over each other."

She sniffed the air, well aware of the wafting aroma of sex. Damn. If she could smell it, no doubt the wolves would pick up on it right away. Her panic must've shown on her face.

"Don't worry." Jason placed his hands on her shoulders and drew her against his chest, holding her close for a moment. She loved the feel of his big body next to hers. "Sex is not news to any of the adult wolves in my Pack. The only thing that might make them wonder is the fact that you're human. We don't get outsiders here often." He squeezed her gently as if he didn't want to let her go. "Now, how about some dinner before I take you back to your friends?"

Just like that, she remembered her obligations to Carly and Dmitri. She'd been having fun with Jason all day. Even stepped way out of her normal mode of behavior by having sex with a man she'd only just met. She'd never had a vacation fling before. Never wanted one. But something about Jason made her want to act out her wildest fantasies.

But all good things must come to an end and she had come here to visit Carly. She now had the added task of learning about her friends' new lives and discovering if Carly was really doing as well with all the changes as it seemed. She'd been her friend for a long time and would still be her friend for many, many years to come. Sally's first obligation was to her friend. There'd be time to pet the wolf again the next day, when her vampire friends had to sleep.

"Yeah, dinner sounds good. I doubt Carly has any real food in her house anymore."

Jason laughed and let her go. "The wolves who work for her tend to leave snacks around. We have a higher metabolism than humans and have to eat a lot to compensate for the energy we expend when we shift. If you get the munchies, check the staff kitchenette. There'll probably always be something in there, even if it's just chips and cola. You're welcome to eat here. In fact, I'd enjoy it if you spent your days with us. With me."

He paused near the door as if nervous of her answer.

"I'd like that," she answered, glad to see his triumphant grin as he opened the door and motioned politely for her to precede him.

She hadn't gone two steps before Kathy was there, looking worried. She of the hesitant footsteps sighed in nervous relief when she saw Jason.

"What is it, Kathy?" Jason spoke from just over Sally's shoulder.

Now that it was time to talk, Kathy seemed even more hesitant. "Sorry, Alpha. It's Serena. She's been eager to talk to you."

Jason sighed. "She can wait."

"Yes, Alpha. Dinner is ready when you are."

"Thank you, Kathy."

Chastised, Kathy bustled away down the hall.

She disappeared down the corridor as Jason escorted Sally at a more normal pace into a room she hadn't seen on the way in. It was located toward the rear of the giant house, in a separate wing, almost. It was as if the room had been stuck on to the rest of the house as an afterthought. Or maybe it had been designed that way so this room was set apart from the rest of the place.

It was enormous. More like a great hall than a simple dining room, and it was filled with tables and chairs of various lengths and sizes. As Alpha, Jason had a place reserved for him at a nice table against one wall where he could see all parts of the room. He escorted her to his place and seated her at his side while a number of people looked on with various expressions of surprise, knowing smiles, or envy.

The envy was from the women, of course, who made up the majority of the crowd, though there were quite a few men. Some of them she recognized from the welcome party the night before. A couple of the younger ones waved in greeting and she discretely waved back.

"This is some place you've got here," Sally commented as she sat.

"The hall is open to everyone for meals. And we use it for parties, meetings, and other kinds of get-togethers. Those living at the house share kitchen duties on a rotating schedule. Most of the time, we serve ourselves buffet style. Because you're our special guest tonight, things are a little fancier."

"I'm honored."

Covered trays were already appearing from the kitchen, which she could see through a door on one side of the room. It was an industrial type kitchen with a homey touch from what she could see through the swinging door as tray after tray of

110

steaming hot dishes were brought out.

It looked like there were lots and lots and *lots* of meat dishes of every kind. There were also several casseroles and salad, thank goodness. She'd already had filet mignon for lunch. She was about at her meat quota for the day.

Thankfully there were no long speeches, just a lot of werewolves staring at the newcomer. A sharp look from their Alpha had them looking somewhere else in a hurry. Much to Sally's relief, Josepha sat next to her, with Jason on her right.

When everyone was seated, it was Josepha who said grace over the bounty on the tables. Sally was surprised not only by the unexpected piety, but also by the fact that they gave thanks to the Goddess, not the male God most people of her acquaintance believed in.

Sally didn't have any problem with it. Over the years she'd come to question why God had to be male when it made more sense to her that the supreme being could be just about anything It wanted to be.

As soon as grace was said, everyone started to eat. Jason served her from the steaming platters on the table, watching her cues for what she wanted and how much. She noted the heaping helpings the wolves served themselves and Jason's raised eyebrow when she stopped him at quite a bit less.

"Don't you want more than that?" he finally asked, looking at her plate with dismay.

"No, this is good. Great, in fact. I can't afford two big meals in one day. I don't burn off calories like you do."

"That's right, Jay," Serena's voice purred from farther down the table where she'd managed to finagle a seat. "She's not a wolf, after all. Humans have to be careful or they get fat."

Sally bristled at the woman's tone but decided to be polite and just ignore her. She began to eat, pretending not to notice the cold stare Jason sent Serena until she backed down and looked away. Some Alpha bitch, Sally thought carefully to herself. Serena tucked tail and ran at the first sign of Jason's disapproval. Ha.

The meal progressed quickly, the wolves...well...wolfing their food down with gusto while she picked daintily at the salad and vegetables she'd chosen along with a small portion of roasted chicken. Josepha made polite conversation and even inquired about Carly and Dmitri in a gracious way that didn't send up any alarms in Sally's mind. She was careful to only talk about generalities where Carly was concerned until she knew for certain what kind of information, if leaked, could be detrimental to her friends. She'd do anything to protect Carly, and now, by extension, her new husband.

Serena kept quiet after that initial salvo. Kathy sat at a table a few yards away with her baby and did her best to blend in. She had to be one of the more subordinate Pack members, if Sally guessed correctly about their internal hierarchy.

Jason was attentive and jovial once Serena began behaving herself. Between him and Josepha, the meal passed quickly. A few of the men came over to talk to Jason in hushed tones about business matters. Jason introduced her each time and the men were respectful, though one or two of them seemed nonplussed to find a human at their Alpha's side.

A few knowing looks thrown her way put her in no doubt that the wolves could smell sex on both of them, but nobody was ill mannered enough to mention it. A raised eyebrow here and there was the only fallout, thank goodness.

When the meal was over, Sally stood to help the others bus the empty plates into the kitchen. Jason tried to intervene, but it was only polite to assist after partaking of such a nice meal. Plus, she felt the need to stretch. Her leg muscles weren't quite used to the exercise they'd gotten earlier and walking would help the stiffness that had begun to set in.

Sally also wanted to get a close-up look at the kitchen. Once she stepped inside, she realized it really was as awesome as she'd thought. Most of the wolves just dropped their dishes in the sink and walked out again. Sally stayed, stacking the giant dishwasher, glad for an excuse to examine the finer details of the beautifully equipped kitchen.

Cooking was one of her few hobbies and this kind of kitchen was an unattainable dream for a woman who lived in a small apartment. Especially on a cop's salary. The stainless steel appliances made her mouth water, as did the industrial-sized ovens, range and grill. She could spend some quality time in here. Oh, yeah.

When she looked up from stacking the dishes, she realized she was alone. Except for Serena. The wolf bitch stood off to one side, tapping blood-red fingernails that were long enough to look like claws against her folded arms as if waiting impatiently for an opening. Sally rolled her eyes, not looking forward to the confrontation, but knowing it couldn't be avoided. If this woman was going to pose a problem, it was better to get it out in the open and handle it now than to let it fester.

"You'd better watch yourself, human. Jason is spoken for." The bitch crowded Sally against the counter.

Sally had heard enough. Hip-checking the taller woman away, she gained some space between herself and the kitchen island. She had enough room to maneuver should this turn ugly.

"First of all, he doesn't act like a man who's taken. Second, I seriously doubt he has any interest in you. And third, it really doesn't matter since I'm only here on vacation. In two weeks, I'll be out of your hair and you can resume whatever it is you think you have going on. *Comprende?*"

The bitch growled at her, and it wasn't anything like the

deep, warm, sexy growls Jason had given her when they were intimate. No, this was almost a whine mixed with pure rage and aggression. Serena stepped forward menacingly, one hand upraised as if to strike. It was a human hand, with those red painted, manicured claws. No doubt, she could do some damage with those, even in her human form.

Sally didn't back down. It wouldn't do to show fear in the face of bullying.

"Threaten me again," Sally said with bravado, "and I'll break your arm." Inwardly, she was gauging relative strength, wondering if she had enough leverage, speed, and skill to follow through on her threat. None of that showed on her face though. She was careful to keep her war face on, even as she ran through the various scenarios in her mind.

If she had been facing a human opponent, there would have been no doubt at all about her ability to handle the situation. Werewolves were something new. Something she hadn't dealt with before. Creatures whose natural senses rivaled and surpassed her own. Sally was used to having the upper hand because of her sharpened sense of smell, hearing, eyesight, and agility. If Jason was anything to go by, werewolves were even better. Sally would have to compensate some way. If nothing else, she had more experience in confrontations both armed and unarmed than almost anyone she knew. And that included most of her brethren on the force.

"You and what army? Don't make threats you can't follow through on. You really expect me to believe a skinny little human like you could take on a full-grown Alpha bitch and come out on top?"

Serena made her move even before the last word was out of her mouth, but Sally was ready. She sidestepped the attack, using the other woman's momentum against her. Sally caught Serena's forearm as she stumbled past her, and redirected the flow of energy and movement, using her other hand to grip Serena's upper arm and force the woman downward, into a position where Sally could easily break her arm.

The wolf bitch snarled up at her, well and truly caught. Sally had learned something. Even a werewolf couldn't get out of this hold easily. Especially one that was both surprised and enraged at being bested by a human.

"Simmer down and I'll release you," Sally cautioned, holding tight to the woman's arm. Both of them knew just how vulnerable Serena was at the moment. "And as a bonus, I won't break your arm—even though we both know how easily I could shatter your elbow right now. Somehow I don't think even shifting would heal that. But you called me skinny, so I'm feeling generous. Just don't push me too far."

Serena growled in frustration this time, taking a moment to calm herself.

"I relent," she spit out finally. The word was so formal and spoken with such simmering hatred, Sally believed it was genuine.

Easing her grip on the woman's arm, Sally stepped back and let her go. Serena straightened immediately and stormed out of the room, past the astonished faces of Kathy and Josepha and the hardened mask of disapproval on Jason's normally friendly visage.

Damn. All three of them had been watching from the doorway. They must have come in sometime during the middle of the confrontation, when Sally's attention was focused solely on her opponent. It was bad form to allow someone—much less three individuals—to sneak up on you during a fight, but Sally cut herself some slack considering they were werewolves and had the ability to move silently.

She was somewhat embarrassed they had seen the altercation. She had wanted to settle things quietly between

Serena and herself. There was no reason to embarrass the woman in front of her Pack. She might be a bitch, but all she'd done was growl. She hadn't managed to actually lay a finger on Sally, so it wasn't really a big deal. The audience probably made it into one, at least for Serena. Sally would have spared her that, if possible. It was no fun at all to be a laughingstock, or to lose face in front of your peers.

"I apologize on behalf of the Pack for her behavior," Josepha was quick to say. "You're our guest. She should not have pushed a challenge tonight. It's not polite."

"It's all right," Sally assured her. "I've dealt with worse than her." *But not often,* she added silently to herself.

"You acquitted yourself well." Josepha was hard pressed to hide the surprise in her tone. Sally could almost hear the unspoken *for a human,* tacked on the end of her statement. Sally tried not to let it irritate her. The wolves were clearly unused to having a human in their midst. Especially not a woman who'd just had sex in the office with their beloved Alpha.

"I should be getting you back to the Master's house." Jason stepped in to save her from answering.

The women said their goodbyes and took over the mop-up in the kitchen. Jason led her back through the house on a different route than they'd come in. They passed through a big living room where a familiar teenager was sitting on the couch with one leg elevated on a bunch of pillows.

"How are you feeling, Colleen?" Sally asked as they passed.

The girl's eyes widened and she got to her feet unsteadily. Jason stopped, allowing the girl time to say what she so obviously wanted to say.

"I'll be okay. I wanted to thank you, Detective, for helping me get away. You walked into serious danger in my place and I owe you a debt."

The words and the girl's tone were so serious it made Sally uncomfortable.

"It's my job, kid." She tried to keep her response easy and nonchalant. "I'm just glad I was in the right place at the right time to be able to help."

Colleen responded by touching her arm and moving close for a small hug. It hit home in that moment just how young the girl really was. She may be almost as tall as Sally, but she was more than a decade younger, in that tricky time of life where you weren't quite a child but not quite an adult yet either. Sally returned the hug, putting her arms loosely around the girl's shoulders. She looked up at Jason for guidance, a little surprised that Colleen would turn to her—a relative stranger—for comfort. Jason only nodded, approval in his gaze as he patted Colleen's shoulder.

Sally realized something in that instant. These people were also wolves. No doubt, physical contact meant a great deal in their society. From what little she knew of dogs and wolf Pack behavior, touching was a form of communication that was vital in their society. By giving a youngster a hug of reassurance, the stronger, more dominant members of the Pack surrounded the traumatized teen with their strength and unspoken promise of protection.

Sally was both surprised and honored to be part of that behavior. Colleen stood between her and Jason, no doubt feeling enclosed by his height even though he was at least a foot away from the teen. His presence was undeniable. And his hand on her shoulder was a silent indicator of his support. Sally understood the fear and pain the girl had been through. She'd been shot, for goodness' sake. Only her shifter heritage allowed her to walk away without serious physical injury. Emotionally, the teenager still had to deal with the trauma of strangers in the woods with rifles, trying to kill her. Or maybe worse—capture her.

Colleen had been the victim of a violent crime. It would take time for her to heal on all levels and Sally knew that the internal emotional scars were often the hardest to deal with. It said something for the youngster that she was still able to reach out to a stranger.

When the girl's trembling had eased, she stepped back, out of the hug. "I'll never forget what you did for me."

Sally brushed Colleen's hair out of her eyes. "That's all right. Just promise me you'll be more careful from now on. It was in no way your fault that those idiots were out there, but everyone has some responsibility for their own safety. Idiots exist. We all have to be vigilant to protect ourselves from them. Even strong people like you can get into trouble if you aren't aware of your surroundings and the dangers that might be nearby."

Colleen looked surprised by the advice coming from a human, but nodded seriously. "I wasn't smart about where I was going," she admitted. "I won't let it happen again."

"Good." Sally stepped away from the girl, dropping her hand to her side. Colleen looked as if she were finding her own strength once more. Sally was glad.

As the teen hobbled back to the couch with Jason's assistance, Sally noticed a man and woman watching from the background that she hadn't noticed before. Sally nodded to them cautiously, wanting to be polite and acknowledge their presence. Seeing that they'd been spotted, the woman led the way over to Sally, reaching out her hand. Sally took the offered hand but was a little confused by it until the woman started speaking.

"I'm Colleen's mum, Laura and this is her pa, Jacob. Thank you for helping the Alpha get her to safety."

Now Sally understood. She'd dealt with parents a time or

two in her work. It was good to be able to give them good news whenever possible. The alternative was always heart wrenching for all concerned.

"I'm just glad I was there and able to help," Sally replied quietly. She had always been a little uneasy with expressions of gratitude. She'd just been doing her job. Doing the job well and helping to protect innocent people was satisfaction enough for her.

Jacob moved closer and took her hand when his wife released it. His grip was strong and his gaze was direct.

"We've already spoken to Colleen about going out alone. We're grateful beyond words that you and the Alpha were there to save her from worse injury." Unspoken was the knowledge she saw in his eyes that his little girl could easily have been killed or captured by those jerks in the woods.

Colleen had been in real danger and only Jason's protective instincts that prodded him to check on the cougar's report of hunters in the area had put Sally and him in the right place at the right time. Jason was the real hero here. He was the Alpha who put his Pack's welfare above his own plans. A lesser man would have gone on with his afternoon of seduction and let the reports of possible danger slide until he was done with his personal desires and had spare time to check. Or not check at all and wait until someone was hurt or killed to act.

Not Jason. He'd put aside his own wishes. Sally knew good and well, though he hadn't really spoken of it, that he'd planned to fuck her in the woods earlier that afternoon when he'd taken her to that gorgeous spot by the waterfall. Meeting up with Steve Redstone had altered his plans and he hadn't complained. Even a vague report of possible danger to his Pack had sent him off to check, his own pleasure denied.

Sally had felt the urgency. Her instincts had kicked in too, but she couldn't be certain whether it was Steve's words that had set her on edge or if she was merely picking up on Jason's mood. She was sensitive to him in ways that surprised her. Usually, it took her a while to warm up to people. With Jason, she'd been able to gauge his moods with ease since they'd first met. His open manner hid a deep thinking, deep feeling man. She saw under the devil-may-care façade and had gained insights into the man beneath.

For certain, she'd never slept with anyone she'd only met the day before. Sally wasn't that kind of girl. It took her weeks to get to know a man well enough to want to risk herself that way. Sex was an emotional thing for her and she'd been hurt in the past by trusting the wrong man. With Jason, she'd thrown caution to the wind. She still didn't understand what it was about him that called to her on some basic level. Some cavewoman sort of level that didn't need pretty words or wine and roses. It only needed him. Naked, preferably.

Sally laughed inwardly at her own thoughts. Here she was, faced with thankful parents and her mind was wandering all over the place. Probably because she was incredibly uncomfortable with all the praise and thanks being heaped upon her.

"Like I said, Jacob, I was happy to help. Colleen is a special girl and you can be proud of the way she handled herself. I've never seen someone pop a bullet out of their leg and then manage to get themselves home."

That comment brought the other couple up short. It was as if they suddenly remembered they weren't talking to another werewolf. Laura's eyes widened and Sally could see the sparkle of tears forming in them. Jacob's grip tightened slightly before he released Sally's hand.

Chapter Seven

"That a human would come to the aid of one of our kind is something we never expected," he said gravely. "You've made us think, detective. Frankly, we've grown so fond of thinking we're the next best thing to invincible, that many of us underestimate your people. We don't consider your strength a match for our own—either your fighting abilities or your emotional depth. In one day, you've managed to turn all that conceit on its ear." Jacob grinned at her, showing sharp teeth and a twinkle of respect in his gaze. "I never thought I would ever meet a true female Alpha who wasn't a shifter. I stand corrected." Jacob put his hand over his heart in a small salute that touched Sally deeply.

"You saved our little girl," Laura added. "We can never repay you."

Sally stilled her words by putting one hand on Laura's arm. "I don't do what I do for fame or fortune. Being a cop is who I am. Doing the job and helping people—humans or shifters or whoever—is my reward. It was *my* honor to be able to help. Truly."

"You're a special lady, detective." Colleen's mother was tearful when she leaned in and gave Sally a grateful kiss on the cheek.

The couple turned away and went to their daughter, helping her settle comfortably back on the couch. Jason stood a few feet away, an expression of pride mixed with affection on his handsome face. It made her heart clench a bit to see. She thought she knew him well enough—even on such short acquaintance—that she could read the truth behind his eyes. That he should feel such things about her so quickly, meant more than she could say.

Despite the almost animal lust she felt for him, his opinion mattered. The sex was great and she didn't want to deny its power, but the man himself made her want more. She knew she couldn't have it, of course. She was human. He was the Alpha wolf of his Pack. They came from two totally different worlds and she was scheduled to go back to her regular life in a handful of days. Now was all they had and she planned to make the most of it.

She took his arm when he offered it, and went with him outside, claiming her temporary space behind him on the giant motorcycle. After only a few hours, she felt comfortable there. Almost like she belonged. But she knew that could never be.

He drove slowly down the lane to the road and then back toward Carly and Dmitri's farm. It wasn't far as the crow flies, but by road it took almost half an hour. Night had fallen by the time they arrived and Sally could feel Jason's reluctance to let her go. She felt the same pull toward him, but she had come here to see her friend and get to know Carly's new husband. It would be selfish in the extreme to spend all her time with Jason. She should be glad he would occupy her days while her friends slept.

It had actually worked out pretty well for her. If not for Jason, Sally wouldn't have much to do all day. If not for the fact that her friends were—incredibly—vampires, she probably wouldn't have any daylight hours to herself. A normal human visit usually involved lots of sightseeing, eating out, and talking. There would still be talking and Jason would take care of the sightseeing, but food would no doubt be scarce in a house owned by vampires. There was a lot Sally had to learn about Carly's new life.

Carly met Sally at the door, having heard the motorcycle rumble up the drive. Dmitri was behind her, his gaze scanning the horizon in case of trouble. His vigilance put Sally on edge and the events of the afternoon came rushing back.

"Are you all right?" Carly asked, concern in her voice as Sally walked up to the door. Jason was a warm presence behind her. "We heard about what happened with those hunters."

"I'm fine, Carl. Please remember I do stuff like that for a living." She did her best to make light of the situation. It had been kind of tense for a few moments, but as far as she was concerned, it was part of the job. Even if she wasn't technically working, or even eligible to work as a detective in this state.

"Do you expect further trouble?" Dmitri demanded of Jason in a low voice as they were ushered inside the house.

Jason's expression was hard to read but Sally saw his tension. "Hard to say."

"Come in and sit down. I had some of the kids go out and stock the kitchen, so there's dessert and wine. I heard you were having dinner at the Pack house." Carly winked at her with a sly grin. No doubt she already knew about her tryst in the office with Jason too.

True to her word, there was a pound cake with strawberries and whipped cream set out on the coffee table. A bottle of deep red wine sat beside it, already open and being allowed to breathe. Dmitri poured for all of them while Carly sliced up two servings of cake. One was gigantic, which she set in front of Jason, and one was more normal-sized, created especially for Sally. The disparity brought a smile to her lips as Carly winked again.

Oh yeah, Carly knew all about the afternoon and there'd be hell to pay later. She'd want details. Sally wasn't even sure how she felt about the day herself just yet. Carly would make her talk. And talk. And talk. She'd be lucky if she got any sleep at

123

all.

In a way, she looked forward to it. It had been far too long since she'd shared girl talk about men with one of her best friends. Far too long.

When they'd all been served, Dmitri got down to business. "Now, what can you tell me about these hunters?"

"Two were arrested," Jason reported. "The local cops are going to keep them overnight because of Sally's involvement and willingness to press charges. That's something we never had before."

Sally was confused. "Why wouldn't the police help if your people were being threatened?"

"It's not that they wouldn't. It's more the fact that we've never really asked them," Jason admitted, scratching the back of his neck as if uncomfortable with the idea. "Our society has survived mostly by separating ourselves from humans."

Hmm. She hadn't thought of that.

"I guess I can understand. But in this case, I'm here and I was a witness to a crime. I won't get Colleen or any of your people involved, of course. My testimony should be enough." She looked worried as she realized that Jason had been involved as well. There was no avoiding the fact that he needed to give a statement if her charges were to proceed. "And yours. Sorry, Jason." She bit her lip as she looked at him.

His thumb reached out and released her lower lip gently, lingering for a moment until she remembered that they weren't alone. Clearing her throat, she leaned away from him. His pull was almost magnetic. She had to find the strength of will to resist. At least in public. A knowing smile greeted her when her gaze shifted nervously to Carly. Damn. The interplay hadn't gone unnoticed.

"It's okay. I know those officers. Believe it or not, I joined the Chamber of Commerce in town a few years ago. I thought it would help us expand our businesses so we could keep more of our young people employed locally. The Pack had been losing young members for a long time before I took over. I've been working at changing all of that. Part of my strategy has been to mix more with the local population, whether it be human or vampire or whatever."

"Who were the officers?" Dmitri asked.

"Bell and Horace. Both good men, in my opinion. They'll be on duty tomorrow when I take Sally in to make her formal statement. I asked."

"Good." Dmitri nodded, his expression concerned. "I've met both of them during safety briefings at the university." He turned his attention back to Sally. She felt the impact of his dark gaze as if it were some kind of laser beam, pinning her in place. "What did these hunters look like?"

"There were four of them, but only two actually discharged their weapons." Sally went on to describe the two younger men who hadn't fired, then went into more detail about the two shooters. "There was one funny thing that I saw as they were loading the guy who'd been up in the tree. He had a tattoo on his wrist. I think."

"What kind of tattoo?" Dmitri demanded, his tone eager.

"I can't be certain, but it looked familiar." Sally turned to Carly. "Remember a couple of years ago, I got into trouble for making a mistake on one of my reports? It was back when I was doing a stint with the hate crimes unit."

"I remember. Something about you putting some kind of mark in your report that wasn't on the guy. The other cops hassled you for months, teasing you about seeing things." Trust Carly to remember the hazing that had hurt more than the reprimand.

"Yeah, it was this tattoo. On the inside of the wrist, over the

125

Bianca D'Arc

pulse. A round thing with a design inside. I saw it. I really did. But when the perp died in the hospital and they examined the body, there was no tattoo. I saw him when they admitted him and made my notes from a combination of the doctor's observations and my own. I saw the tattoo and wrote it down along with everything else. But nobody else seemed to be able to see it. Just me."

Both Jason and Dmitri looked alarmed.

"And this is the same thing you saw today? The same design?" Dmitri asked.

"I think so. I only saw it for a split second out of the corner of my eye, but it looked about the same as I remember."

"Can you describe it?" Dmitri leaned forward, pulling a pad of paper off the end table and taking a pen from his shirt pocket.

"It's round, about an inch in diameter. There are two concentric circles about a quarter inch apart with strange symbols inside the ring. In the center, there's an inverted V."

"Can you draw an approximation?" Dmitri handed her the pen and paper.

"Sure. I'll give it a try. It won't be perfect, though." She set to work, noting the frown lines on both men's faces. It didn't take long. She drew what she could remember, mostly from her examination of the guy in San Francisco. As she handed it over, both men bent over the small drawing.

Dmitri's expression hardened and she read recognition in his eyes. He knew something.

"What is it?" Jason asked Dmitri. Sally's ears perked up. She wanted to know too. The damn thing had caused her a lot of trouble.

"In days of old the *Venifucus* used to mark their lower level minions with this kind of symbol. Something like this, anyway.

126

But what you recall, Sally, is close enough to make me worry."

Jason cursed under his breath.

"*Venifucus?*" She'd heard the word from Jason but didn't really know what it meant.

"A group dedicated to destroying all those on the side of light," Dmitri clarified. "Once upon a time, they were led by a sorceress named Elspeth. She was defeated and banished, her power dispersed to the farthest realms, but lately there has been evidence that some of her followers are trying to bring her back."

"Each Pack Alpha or Clan leader is answerable only to the Lords of the Were who set down the overall rules for were behavior," Jason explained. "Every generation, a set of identical twins is born to one of the were Clans or Packs under special circumstances that mark them as the next Lords. They share a single wife between them and she is always a priestess of the Lady. The current Lords are wolves named Tim and Rafe, and they live not too far from here. Their wife's name is Allie."

"A while back, several attempts were made on Allie's life by a magic user who was finally caught and dealt with," he went on. "During the capture, he revealed that the *Venifucus* had not dissolved centuries ago when Elspeth was defeated. The Lords sent out warnings to all Packs and Clans about the possibility that there could be more trouble. Since then, there have been a few incidents around the country. I just didn't expect they would bother my Pack. Especially not this way—hunting children." Jason's lips firmed into angry lines.

Sally felt the weight of his words in the air. This was serious business. Much more serious than just a few jackasses in the woods with guns. She began to think about how she could help.

"Okay. First things first," she began. "Tomorrow when I give my statement to the local cops, I'll try to get a look at the police reports. If either of the perps has a tattoo, it'll be on their sheet. We can get their names too, so we can keep an eye on them. I might be able to call in a few favors to track them through their credit card receipts, cell phones, or anything else that can be traced electronically."

"And I'll talk to the Lords. See what they can tell me. They're coordinating intel on run-ins with the *Venifucus* and *Altor Custodis*."

"Those are the bad guys you mentioned before, right? One of them watches and one of them is actively working against you, if I remember correctly."

"The *Altor Custodis* professes only to watch and record our doings," Dmitri confirmed. "They've been at it for centuries. Until now they've been mostly an irritation, but we've learned that their organization has been compromised at the highest levels. *Venifucus* agents have infiltrated their ranks and we believe they are using the AC's knowledge for their own purposes."

"That sounds bad," Sally said, meeting Dmitri's gaze to see the worry in his eyes.

If he was worried, they were really in trouble. What could worry a centuries-old vampire? Whatever it was, it had to be very bad indeed.

"Let's not get too far ahead of ourselves." Carly was the voice of reason. "Let's make sure about the tattoo first. You guys talk to your contacts and Sally will do her cop thing and we'll go from there. It could just be two idiots shooting at anything that moves."

"You don't really believe that." Sally knew Carly well enough to know her expressions and she was showing an odd mix of hopeful skepticism at the moment.

"No," Carly admitted, folding her hands in her lap with a downcast gaze. "Deep down, I'm afraid this will prove to be
128

something sinister, but let's do what you said and take it one step at a time." Carly looked up to meet Sally's gaze. "For tonight, the jerks are in jail and we're here, safe and sound."

"I'll drink to that." Sally raised her glass in salute, which Carly returned with a grateful smile.

The men were quiet, obviously troubled, but they made polite conversation for a bit before Jason took his leave. He took Sally by surprise with a smoldering kiss that let the cat out of the bag completely—if Carly hadn't figured it out already. But it was worth it. That man could really kiss.

Dmitri excused himself to do some work in his office and left the two women alone soon after.

"He's going to contact the other Masters and find out what he can," Carly said as she watched her husband's retreating back.

"How do you know?"

Carly tapped her temple and grinned. "Sharing a brain, remember?"

"You'd said, but I didn't think..." Sally was at a loss. It seemed so unbelievable. "How does it work, exactly?"

"Most of the time we're just sort of aware of what each other is doing or thinking. I can tune him out if I want to and he's even better at blocking me completely when he feels the need. I don't like that. Now that we're joined mind to mind, I somehow need the connection and start to feel really insecure when he blocks me, but we both have had to adjust. He was alone for longer than either of us have been alive. A *lot* longer." Carly rolled her eyes and they shared a laugh. "He's also a Master and has been one for a long time. He's used to keeping his own counsel. Sharing our thoughts is mostly amusing to him and can be terrifying to me, considering some of the things he remembers. But it can also be really handy. If I want to know something about our new life, all I have to do is think about it and I can access what he knows. It's pretty cool."

"I'll say." Sally thought about the implications but still couldn't really understand what it must be like to share a mind as they did. "There is one thing I've been wondering about. The men have mentioned magic a few times. What's that all about? Are there really witches and wizards roaming around?"

"They call them magic users or mages. The bad ones are sometimes called sorcerers, like Elspeth. She was the baddest of the bad from all accounts."

"And a bunch of wackos want to bring her back?" Sally really didn't like the sound of that at all.

"'Fraid so." Carly looked upset, so Sally didn't push her any farther on that score.

"So there really are werewolves, vampires, and magicians in the world. I've seen some weird stuff from time to time on the job, but I never really expected that legendary beings really existed."

"I know how you feel. When I bought this house, I had no idea a vampire shared my land. Dmitri's home has been under this farmhouse for more than a hundred years." Carly took a sip of her wine, then put the glass down on the coffee table. "Now, what's going on between you and Jason?"

"It's just a fling." Sally tried for nonchalance but failed utterly judging by the look on Carly's face. She had to come clean—a little, at least. She flopped her head back on the couch, giving in. "I have no idea why I'm so attracted to him. Maybe it's a werewolf thing? But none of the other guys in his Pack affect me like this. I wanted him from the moment I saw him."

"And judging by the way you two were cooing at each other when he left, and the scent of him all over you, I'd say the feeling was mutual," Carly accused with a knowing smile.

"Very mutual, if I'm any judge. Of course, he's probably been with half the women in his Pack. So it might just be the temptation of new blood being put in his path."

"I don't think so." Carly looked off into the distance for a moment. "Dmitri has known him since he was a kid and while the wolves like to play around, they never really mix with humans unless..." Carly snapped out of her thoughts, shock on her face.

"Unless what? Were you tapping into Dmitri's memories just now?" That was so cool. She didn't pretend to understand how it all worked, but the concept fascinated her.

"Yeah." Carly rubbed her forehead with one hand. "Did Jason say anything about mating?"

Sally thought back over their day together. "No. Nothing that I recall. Why?"

"Well, Dmitri seems to think Jason's Pack doesn't mess around with humans unless there's a possible mating in the offing."

"Mating? What does that mean exactly?"

Carly got very serious. "Wolves mate for life."

"Life? No divorces? No cheating?"

"Nope." Carly shook her head slowly from side to side. "Once they find their true mate, they are loyal and completely devoted. The only way there could be a problem is if someone is tricked into proclaiming the wrong person as their mate. That's happened a few times in the past, to Dmitri's knowledge, when magic was used by one party to derail the course of nature, and chaos always resulted."

"How does he know all this?" Sally was curious.

"In centuries past, wolves, bloodletters and many Others were allies against Elspeth. Since her banishment, the alliances have broken down and each group went their separate ways.

131

The supernatural races went into hiding as humanity rose to persecute and hunt them. Magic declined and non-magical races took over. The survivors of that purge remained hidden and have managed to recoup some of their numbers only after centuries of living in secret. Some have never recovered."

"That's amazing." Sally was impressed by the knowledge and the way it appeared Carly plucked it directly from the mind of her spouse. She even fell into his old-fashioned speech patterns. It was very cool to witness.

Carly blinked, coming back to herself. "So the bottom line is, wolves play around a lot before they find their true mate, but once that happens, they're loyal to a fault. And though some Packs have different rules, Jason's Pack doesn't mess around with humans unless there is a potential that the human might be a mate."

"How would they know?"

"Scent. Dmitri thinks the wolves know their mates by their scent."

"Gross." Sally made a face and Carly laughed.

"Think about it, Sal. Your nose is human and can't pick up much unless it's really strong." Sally didn't bother correcting her friend. She never talked about her own heightened senses. "A wolf's senses are much more acute. The scent of skin, of arousal, of lust. They can smell it all, and each person's scent is unique to them."

Sally felt warm as she thought about it. While they'd been making love, Jason had spent a lot of time with his nose close to her skin. He seemed to enjoy it, so she hadn't questioned it at the time. Was it possible...?

Nah. He was just being a wolf, no doubt. There wasn't anything special about her except she was human with a tiny bit of wolf blood, if he was to be believed, and she knew about this crazy Other world. That probably made her unique and therefore eligible for fun and games.

"I bet part of the prohibition against getting involved with regular humans is the whole secrecy thing, right?" Sally asked.

"Definitely. They don't mix not because they can't blend in, but because there are Pack rules about keeping their society secret and their Pack protected from humans who might want to kill them just because they're different."

"Like those jerks in the woods." Sally thought about the close call Colleen had earlier. It had been way too close for comfort.

"If they really were simply hunters. If that tattoo exists, and it's what Dmitri thinks it is...well, that's a whole other story."

"Let's hope they're just stupid hunters." Sally grimaced. It was still hard to think about anyone hunting a young girl with a rifle, but it was somehow worse to think they knew what she was and had targeted her specifically because she was different.

"Now, about Jason." Carly's expression turned mischievous. "How is he?"

The question brought back scandalous memories of that afternoon in his office. Sally felt her face heat as she sank back against the sofa cushions.

"He's as good as he looks, if that says anything."

Carly gave a low whistle. "That good, eh? And how does he measure up?"

"Carl! I can't believe you just asked me that." Both women cracked up laughing.

"Well, I saw him once. Remember, I told you, he shifted right in front of me the first time we met? He was pretty impressive even in the, shall we say, *relaxed* state? You can't blame a girl for wondering if there was more to him than met the eye." Carly tried for innocence but her giggles ruined the effect.

Sally felt like a teenager all over again, talking to her best friend about the new and exciting world of boys. Only this time, she had a fully adult appreciation of the male form and they were talking about a magical man who could turn into a wolf at will. It sort of boggled the mind. Or it would have if she hadn't just spent the day with the guy. They'd packed a lot into a day. Danger, passion, companionship, and a great bike ride through the countryside. She'd never had a more interesting or exhilarating day.

"There is definitely more than meets the eye." Sally felt the blush heat her cheeks again as she remembered just how much more.

"I knew it!" Carly crowed in triumph as they both laughed. "Dmitri isn't happy with this discussion," she said a moment later. "If he doesn't like what I'm thinking, I told him to mind his own business."

"Okay, change of subject then—" Sally tried.

"No, I want to hear more about your afternoon with Jason," Carly demanded.

"What's there to tell? He took me up to this really pretty waterfall in the woods, but before he could get his Don Juan on, we ran into this cougar named Steve Redstone. He told us about the hunters and we decided to go check it out."

"Wait. You met Steve Redstone?" Carly looked almost envious.

"Yeah." Sally didn't want to go into too much detail about her first experience with wanton exhibitionism. Luckily, Carly let her one word answer pass.

"The name Redstone didn't ring a bell with you?" Carly seemed frustrated with her.

"No. Should it have?" Sally didn't know what her friend was driving at.

"Don't you remember Christy talking about her good friend, Matt Redstone?" The name clicked into place as Carly said it. "Steve is Matt's older brother. I haven't met him, but I've heard he's been in the area lately. Something to do with their little sister and the eldest brother, Grif. So spill. What's he like?"

"Steve? He's really handsome, but then all these shifters seem to be on the blessed end of the gene pool. He's tall. Around Jason's height and built a bit sleeker. More cat-like, I suppose. His hair is blonde, a little lighter than his fur. More golden, I'd say."

"He shifted in front of you?"

"Yep. And he seemed perfectly comfortable standing there, holding a conversation in the nude." Sally was still a little nonplussed at that. "I guess these guys are used to running around in the buff when they have to. And Lord knows, they've got nothing to be ashamed of when it comes to their physiques."

"I'll bet. I've wanted to meet Steve, but my loving spouse barely lets me out of the house. He's trying to teach me all the stuff I need to know about protecting myself from the various dangers our kind can face. There's a lot to learn, and of course, he does his best to distract me. Several times a night." Carly giggled and Sally almost envied her friend's happiness.

Ultimately she was glad Carly had found someone who had brought joy back to her. Even if she had to become a vampire to do it. Seeing Carly happy once again made it all worthwhile and who was Sally to judge? Carly was her friend, no matter what—or who—she ate for breakfast.

"Now, about tomorrow," Sally had to ask something before she got sidetracked again. "I wanted to ask your permission to work in your garden a bit. I noticed it's a little run down and this place has so much potential. I'd love to putter around in the yard while I'm here, if you don't mind."

"Mind? Heck, no. I remember the gorgeous garden you had

at your last place. You've got a green thumb and I'd be a fool not to take advantage of it. Plus, I know how gardening relaxes you. This is your vacation, after all. Do what you like. I've been meaning to hire a gardener or maybe ask one of the wolf kids to weed the place for me. I've missed the scent of flowers. You'd be doing me a favor."

Sally detected the slight hint of sadness in her friend's voice when she mentioned flowers. Carly had always loved them, even if she wasn't the world's best gardener. She'd loved receiving flowers for special occasions and buying houseplants to bring those fragrances into her dorm room.

This was something Sally could do for her. Something Carly could no longer do for herself.

"Great. I'll start tomorrow. Thanks, Carl."

They talked a bit more before Dmitri made his reappearance and Sally started yawning wide enough to crack her jaw.

"I'll leave you two lovebirds for now. We mere mortals need at least a few hours of sleep and I'm sure newlyweds need their time alone."

Carly would have protested, but Sally knew she was being polite. It was time to turn in. She said her goodnights and made her way to the guest room. It wasn't long before she was fast asleep and dreaming about lush green woodlands, softly scented wildflowers, and a handsome man who could turn into a wolf.

Chapter Eight

Sally had always only needed a few hours of sleep to sustain her. She was outside by about ten a.m., strategically planting the seeds she'd bought the day before. She had a plan in mind for a little patch of land near the back patio that could become a lovely nighttime haven for her friend if it worked out as she hoped.

She made the holes for each seed with precision and dropped one in each, covering it with a fine layer of dirt. The earth here was very rich in nutrients. The seeds should have a good shot at reaching their full potential with little outside help. Sally could read plants. She understood soil. She could hear the whisper of the wind through the trees and listened to its song. It was instinctive and something she'd never questioned though she knew it was different. She'd never met anybody else who could make a seed grow just by whispering to it.

When her pattern was complete, Sally stood in the exact center of her newly planted garden. It was bare earth all around, only the seeds and the disturbed ground marking where she'd put them. Crouching down and balancing on the balls of her feet, she placed her hands on the ground. Sending her will into the earth, she made contact with each tiny seed she had planted and asked it to sprout. Then she talked to the sprout and coaxed it to grow until it reached the surface. Then she cajoled the seedling to take what it needed from the soil and sun to grow large and fast.

When she opened her eyes, the bare earth was gone, covered with lush green foliage and a few daring buds that

Bianca D'Arc

would bloom that night. Every flower in the new garden was of a night-blooming variety. Though it had taken some planning and hard work, this little garden was going to be her gift to her friends. She knew Carly would love it and she hoped Dmitri would appreciate it as well.

They didn't need to know she hadn't bought the plants full grown. That was the ruse she'd used for years when friends asked how she managed to establish such a lovely garden so quickly. She always just told them she knew a good nursery in the area. Nobody needed to know about her weird gift. She didn't understand it herself and she certainly didn't know where it came from. It didn't harm anyone and it certainly wasn't evil, she didn't think, so she kept it to herself.

"How in the hell did you do that?"

Damn. So much for keeping it to herself. Sally turned around to find Jason standing about five yards away, his eyes wide as he looked at the new garden.

She sighed, resigned to her fate.

"Honestly, I don't know. It's just something I've always been able to do."

Jason walked up to her and sniffed rather obviously. "I did scent something else in you, but I still can't quite place it. It doesn't smell like mage, but after what I just saw..." He trailed off, obviously lost in thought. "Are you sure there's no magic user in your family tree?"

"I have no idea. To be honest, I really don't know much about my family. I was raised by a series of foster parents until I was eighteen. I didn't have much of an attachment to any of them, nor they to me, so I don't consider that I ever really had parents. Not the way most people do."

Jason startled her by reaching out and taking her into his arms for a fierce hug. She clung to him out of surprise at first, but after only a moment, she soaked in the comfort of his

138

embrace. There was something to be said for a hug from a friend. And she realized she did consider him a friend, even if they'd only known each other a short time. She was more comfortable with him than she'd been with people she'd known for years. Except the study group. She'd clicked with those girls from the very beginning and their friendship had lasted all this time.

What she had with Jason had a built-in expiration date, but she hoped she could count him among her friends even after she went back home to San Francisco. They wouldn't be close. Not like she and the girls were. But maybe she'd add him to her Christmas card list. Or perhaps she could call him just to chat when she needed a friend.

Nah. Probably not. His wife—make that *mate*—probably wouldn't like it.

"I'm sorry, sweetheart," he whispered near her ear, his touch comforting, not sexual in nature. It felt so right to be held by him. "I wish I could've been there for you. We don't let orphans go to strangers in our society. Every child belongs to the Pack and we all take care of them. With Pack, you always know that you are loved."

"It sounds so beautiful." And a far cry from the way she had grown up.

"It is," he agreed, letting her go by slow degrees. When he looked around at the new garden his gaze softened. "This is beautiful too. A night-flowering garden for your friend. She's going to love it."

It touched her that he understood without being told what she'd done. He was a very intuitive man with a sensitive side, but she knew he was a warrior too. He hadn't become Alpha of a Pack of werewolves without being able to fight.

"I hope so. I wanted it to be a surprise."

"They won't hear about it from me." He let her go and

walked around the small, circular pathway she'd left bare so the blooms could be enjoyed to their fullest. There was a stone bench to one side of the new patch of garden and the patio bordered one edge. "I like the way you planned this out. By the way, I suspect most of the office staff saw your little miracle out the window. They were watching you when I walked in, though they pretended they weren't."

He had a smile on his face, but she was shocked at her own stupidity. She hadn't realized anyone could see her from that far away, but these were werewolves. They could see better than any human. Damn.

She looked up and realized one side of the office wing faced the little patch she'd chosen to work on. No doubt more than a few of them had seen her in action. She'd never been so sloppy before. Then again, she'd never worked on someone else's land before. She'd always been gardening in her own yard, even if it was a rental property. She'd been careful to do it when nobody else was around.

"I guess my secret is well and truly out."

"That it is," Jason agreed. "But it will only add to your mystique. The stories circulating about you already have you at a cross between an Amazon warrior and Bruce Lee's little sister. They figure you must be some kind of ninja to be able to take down Serena so easily. Colleen has done her part too. She thinks you're the bravest woman she's ever known to take her place when those guys were shooting at her. You're causing quite a stir in my Pack, Sally." He moved into her personal space again, his hands on her hips, pulling her close to him as his head dipped. Their foreheads met and he stared into her eyes.

"I didn't mean to cause any trouble," she said softly, as overwhelmed by his physical presence as she had been the day before. His effect on her senses hadn't diminished now that they'd been intimate. If anything, it had gotten even more potent now that she knew how he could make her come.

"You don't start trouble," Jason said, kissing her lightly. "According to growing local legend, you end it. They're beginning to think you're a superhero." He seemed amused by the whole idea.

"And you? What do you think?" Her voice was breathless and low.

"I think you're all of those things, and more. I think you're perfect, Sally. I think you're mine."

He kissed her for real then, hauling her body into his, plundering her mouth with his tongue and making her come alive with need and want. She had never wanted a man so intensely. Jason was a law unto himself.

Before she knew what was happening, one of his hands was up under her T-shirt, the other was reaching down inside her waistband and under her panties to cup her ass. Truth be told, she didn't care if the entire office staff was watching. All that mattered was him in that moment. His touch, his taste, even his scent.

The masculine smell of him—leather and pine and something indefinably attractive—reached deep inside her, wrapping itself around her. She never wanted to let go. She never wanted to *be* let go.

It was Jason who broke the kiss. He was gasping, as was she. He rested his forehead against hers, his lower body rubbing against her in the most sinful way.

"Where's your room?" His demand was rasped in a low growl.

"Follow me." She didn't ask questions. She wanted the same thing he did, that much was obvious.

He let her go, but not far. He kept his arm around her waist and crowded her as she walked over the patio and into the house by the nearest entrance. Her room was only a few yards away, down the corridor. It might as well have been on the moon.

As soon as the patio door slammed closed behind them, his hands went to waistband of her T-shirt, dragging it up and over her head even as she turned into the corridor. He dropped it somewhere along the way. She was in too much of a hurry to wonder much about it. Her bra unhooked at the back today and was dropped on the floor as she opened the door to the guest room she'd been using.

He turned her around, using her hips to guide her motion, and unsnapped her jeans even as he walked her backwards toward the bed. She was glad to see he'd ditched his shirt as well and already had his jeans unbuttoned and unzipped. A quick look told her he'd gone commando again. How convenient. She licked her lips.

He pushed her backward and a moment of slight disorientation later, her butt hit the mattress. He followed her down, whipping the jeans and panties down her legs. She'd already kicked off her sneakers, thank goodness.

Jason paused only to push his own jeans down far enough to free his hard cock, then he pushed between her thighs, sliding home without any preamble. It didn't matter. She was primed and ready for him. She'd been dreaming of him—of this—all night and had woken in a state of arousal. It had only abated while she concentrated on the garden, but even then, he was in the back of her mind, making her body yearn for his.

He felt so damn good inside her. Like he belonged there. Like he was meant to be there, with her, forever.

Dangerous thoughts. Sally pushed them away, concentrating on the slide of him in and out, the way his breathing hitched on each stroke, the way his heat surrounded her, permeated her, branded her as his, indelibly. He was, by far, the best she'd ever had. The best she ever would have, she feared. After him, she'd be ruined for any other man but she didn't care. All that mattered was this moment, this man, this mounting passion that drove her higher and higher.

Sally cried out as his pace increased. This was raw fucking. The kind of animal heat that came along only rarely. At least for her.

She didn't want preliminaries. She didn't want sweet moments. Not now. Maybe later, but definitely not now. She wanted it hard and fast, just the way he was giving it to her.

He seemed to pick up on her needs, pushing in short, hard jerks that brought him into contact with her clit on every pulse. His fingers circled her wrists and held her hands immobile by the sides of her head. He dominated her in every way and she loved it. Loved the feel of him blanketing her, overwhelming her. Hot, fast, hard and long.

It couldn't last. Tornadoes never did. Like that force of nature, his intensity shattered her building passion, sending her into a tailspin that picked up speed as she spun out of control. It culminated in a climax so great, she nearly blacked out as it broke over her. Dimly, she heard a scream and realized it was coming from her.

Damn. She'd never been a screamer before. Leave it to the werewolf to bring out wild side.

Jason followed a few moments behind her, growling as he pushed into her. His muscles clenched as he strained toward his own climax and when it hit, he howled. Not a perfect howl like you heard on a dark summer night, but a broken-voiced howl drawn involuntarily from his throat. It was endearing and shocking and it sent a whole new round of shivers through her midsection.

She could feel the heat of his release flood her. It felt right.

Warm, exciting and intensely satisfying on a level she hadn't expected. She'd rarely let a man come inside her. She hadn't had sex without a condom in a long time. She knew she was out of practice, but Jason's loving sent her to a whole other level of pleasure.

Jason collapsed over her and she reveled in the solidity of him pinning her to the bed. She loved the way he responded to her. He held nothing back. He made her feel like a femme fatale. A sex goddess.

Sally had never in her life felt like a sex goddess before. At best, she'd been a gifted amateur. Jason had changed all that.

"Sorry." His voice was still rough. She loved the sound of it. Knowing she had done that to him. "I must be crushing you."

"It's okay." She was quick to reassure him, enjoying running her fingers through his shaggy hair.

He rolled off her anyway and took a moment to position them both on the bed, spooning her from behind. Oh, yeah. Wolves seemed to like to cuddle. Sally could get used to that real fast.

"Sorry, sweetheart." He nibbled her ear. "I didn't mean to jump you first thing in the morning." Amusement laced his words.

"Really? After dreaming of this all night, I would have been disappointed if you hadn't." She stroked the muscled forearm that circled her waist, enjoying the feel of him and the laziness of satisfaction that stole over her.

"You dreamed of me? Of us?" he asked in a hot whisper.

"Mm-hmm," she answered in the affirmative.

"I think I like that." Smug approval filled his tone.

"What am I going to do about the garden?" She thought aloud, hoping he might have some solution. "Your Pack members will probably tell Carly about my little ability."

"I wouldn't call that little. Besides, I thought she was one of your oldest friends. You mean to say she doesn't know about it already?"

"I've never told anyone before. Nobody's ever seen me do it." Hesitancy filled her voice.

"You never questioned why or how you could make things grow?"

"Yes and no. When I was little, it was just natural. The trees and flowers talked to me. Not in words, but I understood them—better than people most of the time. As I grew older, I began to realize that other people couldn't hear them. The other foster kids in the place I lived from when I was seven to ten years old were pretty mean. I learned not to draw attention to myself. I spent a lot of time in an old tree house, away from the other kids. The place was falling down around my ears. The Frantonis—my foster parents at the time—didn't allow anybody up there, but I went anyway. I knew the tree would hold me up and keep me safe, away from the teasing and bullying."

Jason's arms tightened around her. She felt him place a gentle kiss on her temple. "I'm glad you had someone on your side, even if it was just an old tree. What you've said gives me an idea about what that other blood of yours might be."

She turned in his arms to look at him. "Really?"

"It's a little farfetched, but I think you might have an ancestor who was one of the ancient forest spirits. Not many of them stayed in this realm, but one makes her home on Pack land. In fact, she lives not far from that little waterfall I took you to yesterday. It's funny. My first impulse was to take you to that spot, though I've never taken a woman there before. That patch of forest has always been my solitary refuge. The place I go when I want to think things through on my own. The Pack knows not to bother me there. But when I first saw you, I wanted to share that special place with you. I wonder if your ancestry might have something to do with that impulse?"

"I have no idea." She was really touched by his words. That he'd want to share such a private place with her meant a lot.

"There's one way to find out. We should pay her a visit. Maybe she can tell us for sure if your special abilities stem from that sort of heritage."

"What kind of being is she?" Sally was almost afraid to ask.

Jason grinned. "A nymph."

"You're kidding." Sally was shocked at the idea. "They're real?"

"As real as you or me. From what I understand, there used to be a lot more of them. But like all of the supernatural races, they suffered greatly during the rise of man. They need forests to survive. You only have to look around at the sprawling cities and acre after acre of cleared farmland to realize why many of them may have chosen to leave this realm."

"Are there other...realms?" She wasn't familiar with his usage of the word. It sound is as if there were parallel worlds coexisting alongside each other or something.

"Many," he confirmed. "But like humans, werefolk are pretty much grounded to this earthly realm. There are Others, though. Very magical Others, who can travel between them, and live and thrive in many places. Or so I've heard. I've never actually met a Fey, but I do know they exist. One came to the aid of the High Priestess not long ago. I heard he's been hanging out with a vampire in New York City lately."

"A fairy? In New York City?"

Jason burst out laughing. "He's not a fairy like you're probably imagining. This guy is a Fey warrior. He's more like what you would think of as an elf in the tradition of Tolkien than a Disney fairy, flitting about on tiny little wings." He scooted away from her in the king-sized bed and stood. "I

146

promised to deliver you to the police station today, to make your formal statement. As much as I'd love to stay in bed with you all day, we'd better get moving."

"Yeah," Sally agreed, getting up as well. The Pack and her vampire friends still might be in serious danger. Today was the day for answers.

She dressed quickly, stopping briefly in the attached bathroom to clean up a little while Jason remade the bad. He was very domestic for a man, she thought with a small grin. She could get used to being pampered by the likes of him.

They were out the door a few minutes later. He'd brought a shiny new SUV today. She'd loved riding behind him on the bike, but there was something to be said for the quiet inside the cabin of the SUV. They could talk while they drove into town.

Jason pointed out various sights of interest along their path. Even though he kept the conversation light and flowing, her anxiety began to build as they neared the police station. It was time to get to work. Time to find out if the danger was real or imagined. She hoped for the latter, but feared it was the former. A cold knot of dread formed in the pit of her stomach. She already knew how this was going to turn out. She'd known it from the moment she'd spotted that tattoo.

Putting her game face on, Sally hopped out of the SUV when Jason opened the door for her. They'd been able to park very close to the front door of the police station, so there wasn't much time to get her thoughts in order before they were inside, face to face with the officers who had helped them the day before. The dark-haired one was Officer Bell. The blonde was Officer Horace.

Jason shook hands with both men, and again she got the idea that they knew each other. At least in passing. She went with Officer Horace while Jason went with Bell. Their desks were in the back of the station, where they took Sally and

Jason's official statements.

Sally saw her moment when both officers stood to go make photocopies. With a quick look at Jason, she twirled the official file her guy had left sitting open on his desk and began rifling through it. Jason knew without being told explicitly to act as a lookout.

Sally found what she was looking for on page three. No identifying marks on either of the men who had been arrested. Damn. It was like the last time all over again. Only she had seen the mark.

But why? That question had bothered her for years. Why could only she see the tattoo that was plain as day on the guy's wrist? It still bothered the heck out of her. Was she nuts? Hallucinating? Her mind playing tricks on itself? She still didn't have any answers to those questions.

Jason moved, making deliberate noise and she spun the folder back into place. Just in time. The officers walked back into the room and to their desks. They handed copies of their statements to Jason and Sally respectively. With only a little more fuss, they were out of the police station and on their way. Sally felt both relief and dread as Jason opened the car door for her.

They kept silent until they were both tucked safely inside the SUV.

As he put the truck in gear, he began to talk, keeping an eye on traffic. Nobody could tell looking in from outside that their conversation was tense, their topic of great import.

"Did you get the information?" Jason asked without looking at her.

"Our assailants are named William Sullivan and Bartholomew Samuels. No identifying marks on either wrist." She told him what she'd seen in the police report. "Damn. I really thought I saw it. Just for a split second, but it was there."
148

"If you say you saw it, I believe you." His confidence in her was touching but she'd been through this before.

"Even if nobody else seems to see what I see?"

Jason nodded. "Even then."

"Why?" She couldn't fathom why his faith in her was so strong. Not when she doubted herself.

"Because of what I saw this morning. Whether you believe in it or not, you've got some kind of magic in you, sweetheart. I'm not all that familiar with magic users, but I have heard there are certain things that only they can see. You might have just enough of that special kind of sight to be able to see what you think are tattoos on people marked in a more arcane way."

"You've got to be kidding." The thought had never even occurred to her, though it did explain quite a bit. "So where are we going now?"

"I think it's time we tried to find my friend, Leonora. She might be able to shed some light on the nature of your magic. She's the most magical creature I know around these parts. Well, the friendliest one, at least."

"This is the nymph you mentioned?" Sally wasn't sure how she felt about meeting a nymph. It would be nice to know why she saw tattoos where nobody else seemed to, but she wasn't sure if she really believed there was some magical ancestor in her bloodline that only the werewolves were able to detect.

"One and the same. Don't worry. You'll love her. She's got a way with plants and her place in the woods is breathtaking. I'm glad you've given me an excuse to go visit her. I usually drop by a few times a month when I'm prowling, just to make sure she's okay and has everything she needs. She doesn't get into town much, though she claims the forest provides for her. Judging by what I've learned over the years, I suspect that's all she really needs."

Jason drove them out of town and up into the woods, following the same path they'd taken yesterday. It really was beautiful country and the woods were particularly lush in the area around the small waterfall he'd shown her yesterday. Not dense. There was plenty of room to walk among the trees. But everything was in full bloom, green, growing and healthy.

She had been so enthralled with Jason and the cougar who had visited them, and then worried about the hunters, she'd failed to hear the lilting melody that wafted through the trees. It was beautiful. It got louder and more intense as they passed the place where they'd met Steve Redstone the day before.

Entranced, Sally moved in front of Jason, unaware she'd taken the lead. She only knew she had to follow that sound to its source.

"Leonora's place is back this way," Jason said from behind her.

Sally stopped, only then aware that she'd outpaced him by several yards. Something was drawing her in this direction. She sent out a tentative query to the nearest tree. Not some*thing*, she learned to her joy when it answered back. Some*one*.

"She's not there," Sally told Jason. "But I know where she is."

"How?" Jason caught up to her, his smile quizzical.

"The trees told me." She saw his eyes narrow as though he didn't quite believe her. "You don't hear that?"

"Hear what?" Jason cocked his head as if listening intently, but he shook his head only a moment later.

"How do you find someone in the woods?"

Jason tapped his nose. "By scent."

"Of course." Sally should've realized. He was a wolf, after all. "All right. Well, I suppose it's like that, only I can hear the trees whispering in the wind. The leaves shush a melody all their own. Sometimes, if the trees are active, as they are here, I can even ask them questions. Not in words really, but more like thought impulses, and sometimes they answer back. The birch over there passed my query to the pine who whispered it to the oak and so on. Like a leafy game of telephone." She'd never had a chance to describe this to anyone before and found it hard to put into words exactly how it all worked. "When the answer flew back this way, they told me where we'll find your friend."

"And they told me where to find you," came a feminine voice through the leaves. A woman appeared, her hair blonde as sunlight, her clothes dappled with the greens and golds of the forest.

Jason stepped forward. "Leonora, it is good to see you again."

"And you, Jason." Her smile was angelic but her gaze quickly moved from Jason to Sally, questioningly. "Who is this you bring to my glade? The trees whisper of her magic."

"Sally Decker, a police detective from San Francisco," Jason said formally. "She is a close friend of the new Mistress."

"And a child of the woods," Leonora finished, drawing closer. "At least in part."

"I believe she is part wolf, but only a small part," Jason added as they both turned to look at Sally. She felt a bit like a bug under a microscope. "She can make things grow and I think she sees magical marks. We were hoping you could help shed some light on the nature of her magic."

Leonora giggled. It was a charming sound. Like petals on the wind.

"That's easy," the nymph stated. "Nature *is* her magic. The trees agree. She has a touch of my kind of magic in her, but there are ways to tell how she came by it if you wish to delve deeper."

"Will it hurt?" Sally found herself asking. She didn't know anything about magic. Not really. The thought of anything other than what she did with plants frightened the bejeezus out of her.

Again came the tinkling laugh. "No, my dear. It will not hurt. It won't even require any special preparation. Simply give me your hand and I can call forth your family tree."

Sally looked at Jason, wondering if she should. His encouraging nod decided her. She held out her hand and the nymph touched it. Leonora's hands were warm and dry, full of energy and light. The light reached out to meet her and Sally felt the little spark when their energies met. A spark of recognition, if she wasn't much mistaken. Then again, she didn't know enough about this magic stuff to really know what was happening.

"Watch now," Leonora said softly as between them, a magical, mystical, glimmering sapling rose out of the ground.

It disturbed no earth and it was transparent, though it glowed with life. It had a very specific sequence of branches and as Sally watched, she recognized that each branch terminated in a different member of her extended family. People she'd never known. People she'd always wondered about.

And there, at the top, was her own energy. And it was connected to...

"I have a sister?"

Chapter Nine

"And several cousins you really need to meet. Some of them have rather intriguing abilities. Mostly untapped." Leonora frowned. "That can't be allowed to continue. The forest needs them." She continued tracing downward, following the trunk down to the roots of the tree. "Ah. It is as I suspected. Welcome, granddaughter. I've wanted to meet you—or someone like you— for a very long time."

"You're my..." Sally trailed off, not really sure what was going on. She'd never had family. Not real family, related by blood. She wanted to study the tree and learn all its secrets.

"Great, great, great, great..." Leonora ticked off the rows of branches part way down the glowing tree, then gave up. "Well, you get the idea. It's just easier to say I'm your granny." Leonora stood back to look at Sally, giving her the once over, her eyes glowing with unshed tears as she squeezed Sally's hand. "I've waited a long time for you, Sally."

"Me too," Sally whispered, nearly overcome with the idea that she had a real live blood relative. At last. Maybe Leonora could explain a bit about where Sally had come from.

Leonora let go of her hand and the tree began to disappear. Sally panicked for a split second. She hadn't had nearly enough time to study it.

"Will I ever see the tree again?" Sally asked. Even she could hear the tone of desperation in her voice, but she didn't care.

"Of course, dear. Now that you know the way, you'll be able to call it to you at will. It is *your* tree, after all. The one you will nurture and help grow when the time is right." Leonora sent a speculative look toward Jason and Sally felt the heat of a blush stain her cheeks.

Somehow the nymph—make that Granny Leonora—either knew or had guessed that Sally and Jason were getting it on. Sally's reaction only confirmed any suspicions she might've had. Busted.

Reassured that she could study the tree again later, Sally felt a little better about watching it fade back into the earth. She wasn't all that sure about adding to it. That would mean having kids, and she'd never really contemplated how that would work with her lifestyle.

"How did this happen?" Jason asked as the nymph began leading them through her forest, toward a small clearing.

"The old-fashioned way, of course. Many, many years ago, I fell in love with a human. He was a woodcutter, of all things. After he met me, he found a new profession, of course, but we were married and had a daughter named Marisol who married a werewolf. That is the line from which you branch, Sally." Her grandmother sent her a beatific smile. "Her werewolf took her away to live with his Pack and they were happy for many, many human lifetimes. She returned home exactly once, when we buried her father. My magic had been able to sustain him far beyond a normal human lifetime, but all mortals eventually fade from this world, into the next." Leonora looked so sad for the loss of her love, Sally reached out to her, touching her hand as they walked.

Leonora took it and they walked hand in hand into the clearing. It was a grassy glade dotted here and there with a riot of blooming wildflowers, all bobbing their heads as the nymph passed as if in greeting. To one side was a house of sorts, made entirely of the twining roots and branches of trees, as if the saplings had decided to braid themselves together to protect the one who would live within and beneath their sighing branches.

It was absolutely stunning. Beautiful. Breathtaking.

"This is amazing," Sally whispered as they stepped inside the inverted V-shaped opening. As they entered the dwelling, the tree branches shifted around to close off the door. Sally felt no malice in the trees. They were simply keeping the forest creatures out and the heat in for the comfort of their friend, Leonora. Sally thanked them for their protection and they seemed to recognize her, a few leaves shaking as she passed.

"They like you too," Leonora said with a smile as she led them to a comfortable couch along one wall.

The place was much larger than it looked from outside. And contrary to what Sally had expected, Leonora had a few of the conveniences of modern life in her dwelling. The couch was supported by springy, living tree limbs that had shaped themselves out of the wall to hold lovely, upholstered cushions in shades of green and brown velvet.

A pool gurgled somewhere in the back of the home and Sally caught a glimpse of steam coming from a small pond that was partially hidden behind a screen of young saplings. It was a natural hot spring. Sally guessed that was both the bathing area and the source of moist heat in the home. Another trickle of water flowed downward from a channel made of tree branches into a small, waist high basin that probably served as a sink. It was ingenious.

Leonora motioned for them to be seated on the couch and she took up a chair that was to one side of the couch, also created from the living trees themselves. The walls of the home had an irregular shape with many nooks and crannies like this alcove with the seating area. For all intents and purposes, they were in the living room, but it was like no other living room Sally had ever seen. It took her breath away.

"I am so glad to finally meet one of my grandchildren,"

Leonora began, her gaze focused on Sally with genuine affection. "Tell me all about yourself."

Normally reticent with strangers, Sally felt comfortable with Leonora in a way she never had been before. It made her chatty, but then, she had just met a blood relative and seen for herself, through the magic of the tree, that she wasn't alone. She had family. And now she had a way to find them. A clue about who they were and where.

"I'm a detective. I live in San Francisco. Until a couple of days ago, I didn't know anything about magic, or the fact that one of my best friends had married a vampire. Werewolves were a complete surprise to me." She looked over at Jason with a rueful smile.

"I bet." Leonora seemed delighted, clasping her hands together in front of her heart as she listened eagerly. "Have you always been able to speak to the trees?"

"Since I was a child, but city trees are mostly drowned out by the noise of so many people living together in one place. I grew up in foster homes. I began to realize my way with plants was more than a little unusual when I was about seven or eight. The teasing from the other foster kids protected me in a way. It made me hide my abilities, which was probably the right thing to do at that time. Until this morning, nobody had ever seen the way I could coax things to grow."

"You caught her at it?" Leonora sent Jason a knowing grin.

"Red-handed," he confirmed. "Or maybe that should be green-thumbed," he joked softly, putting his arm along the back of the couch cushion, around her shoulders.

"What were you growing? I felt a little tug on the earth energy, but there's such an abundance here, and the feel of your power is so close to my own, I couldn't really trace it."

"I bought some seeds yesterday," Sally answered, almost afraid she was going to get into trouble for using her skill in
156

such a selfish way. "I grew a night-blooming garden for my friend Carly, as a gift. She only became a vampire recently and I could tell she missed flowers. She used to love my gardens back home."

Leonora's smile reassured her. "A beautiful gesture for a true friend. I'm sure she will love it."

"The thing is, I've never really been in forest this dense." Sally gestured to the saplings surrounding them and the wild woodland beyond. "The trees here are really amazing. They helped me find those hunters yesterday," she admitted, looking at Jason.

"Hunters?" Leonora seemed interested.

"Hunting a teenaged wolf in human form. They shot her before we could get there, but she'll be okay. Sally led the hunters off the scent and managed to capture the two who had fired bullets at both Colleen and Sally." His hand dropped to her shoulder and rubbed in light, comforting circles.

"Where?" Leonora looked incensed.

"Up on Yellowtail Ridge."

Leonora sent a wave of communication that Sally could feel but not hear, through the trees of her home and out into the surrounding forest. It flew toward the site of yesterday's events and back again with lightning speed. This woman had a lot more power and control over it than Sally had, that was for sure.

"I see," Leonora said, her eyes focused beyond the living room. Sally got the feeling the trees were relating the scene for her in vivid detail. "The four who were two are four once more, but they rest for now."

"So I take that to mean the two we had arrested made bail and are back with their buddies?" Sally asked, just to be clear.

"Yeah. That's what it sounds like." Jason squeezed her

shoulder. "I had someone keeping an eye on the police station. They'll stay on the scent."

"It's not safe—" Sally began, but Jason forestalled her words.

"These are adult wolves, trained in ways you couldn't even begin to imagine. Soldiers. Special operators, if you will. The ninjas of the werewolf world. If they can't handle four humans with lousy aim, then nobody can."

Sally hadn't known Jason had those kinds of people in his Pack. There was lots to learn about this new world she'd discovered.

"Now, about the wolf in Sally's ancestry. Do you know who he was?" Jason asked Leonora with keen interest. Sally wasn't sure why it mattered so much to him, but she was interested in hearing more about her ancestors too.

"Certainly. My daughter Marisol was caught and wooed by Ranulf, son of Rothgar the Great and Neveril the Mighty." Leonora sniffed. "Neveril was nice enough, but her mate was an overbearing lout. I had to teach him to respect my power before he would deign to speak with me. That all changed when we allied to fight Elspeth. That's when he really earned his moniker. He united all the wolf Packs and led them into battle. That's what made him great. In his youth, he was a bit of a hothead and didn't respect women until he met Neveril. She changed him for the better, I always thought."

Jason looked at Sally with wide eyes. "You're descended from two of the greatest wolves of all time, Sally. We teach our pups stories about Rothgar and Neveril. Wow."

"Yes, well." Leonora seemed unimpressed. "Their son Ranulf was a jerk, if you'll forgive me for being so blunt. He was truly mated to my Marisol, but he fought against it. He didn't want a non-wolf. He didn't want a non-shifter. He especially didn't want a half-human hybrid nymph. But fate is fate. And

Marisol was his as he was hers. More's the pity. Their children couldn't shift and Ranulf hated that. He kept Marisol away from me and tried to raise his children among wolves who belittled them because they couldn't shift. I think he thought if he beat it into their heads enough, somehow their magic would turn them into wolves. For they were magical. Very magical. But he refused to see it. He wanted wolf pups and he hated me for denying him that honor." Leonora looked bitter. "After her father died, I never saw my Marisol again. And then there was the war with Elspeth and the *Venifucus*. She died honorably, alongside her mate, fighting them. I thought their children had all perished beside them, but now I know at least one survived."

"My ancestor, right?" Sally asked hopefully.

"Yes, dear. Their son Rolf. I don't know about the others because they're not on your tree, but I have hope now, after meeting you, that more of Marisol's children might have survived." Leonora's face glowed with joy. "And here you are, a beautiful acknowledgment of my daughter's life. You look a little like her around the eyes."

"That's amazing." Sally, who'd never known a blood relative before, was touched by the genuine affection she saw in the older woman's gaze.

"You say you live in San Francisco? Are you here only for a visit?"

"Just two weeks. I came to visit Carly but then I found out about her new nocturnal schedule and Jason has been kind enough to take me places during the day. It's hard to believe I only got here the day before yesterday. So I still have the better part of two weeks vacation ahead of me."

"I hope you will find some time to spend with me," Leonora invited. "It has been far too long since I had contact with my family. You'll also want some instruction on how to best utilize your magic. From what I can see, you've done well for a city dweller, but there are certain facets to your abilities that can only be discovered in true woodland, like we have here. I'd be happy to teach you. In fact, it is my duty to both you and the forest. We are its stewards, its caretakers and companions. We act on its behalf and carry out its wishes. We also do for it what it cannot always do for itself." Sally didn't fully understand the nymph's words, but she wanted to learn. She could sense a whole other world out there waiting for her and she wanted a chance to delve into it.

"I'll want to be sure those hunters move on and that the two who fired at me and Colleen are brought to justice, but otherwise, my days are pretty much free and I'd really enjoy spending some time with you. Thank you for the offer."

"Jason, you are welcome too, of course." Leonora winked at him. Sally wasn't quite sure why, but she got the sense that there was something unspoken between them. Jason bowed his head in acknowledgment. "Sally, you need to know that our kind of magic doesn't get passed down genetically. Your mother may not have had an affinity for the forest at all, and then you were born with the natural ability to make things grow and hear the gossip of the trees. The power passes to whomever it wishes—to whomever it thinks will best utilize it for the good of the forest. You were born to a human world but judging by your abilities, you've inherited many of the gifts of my bloodline. It is important to learn how to use that power—especially in this world so dominated by concrete jungles. We are the guardians of the forest. Mankind has begun to wake up and realize that the wild places need to be preserved. There is a desperate need for our kind of magic in this world that is struggling to protect what's left and regrow at least part of what was chopped down in mankind's haste for expansion."

That was a heady thought. All Sally had ever really been able to do was make things grow in her little corner of a neighborhood. She did small gardens. Never anything on a grander scale. If what Leonora said was correct, she might be able to do more. Much more.

"I'd like to learn," Sally affirmed. "We'll have some time over the next two weeks and there's no reason I can't come back. I have a lot of vacation time stacked up that I've never used. I never really had anyone to visit before."

"Well, now you do. You have me, and your friend the Mistress, and Jason here. Something tells me, he'll have something to say about where you spend your time." Leonora winked at her again, a knowing smile on her face.

"How about I bring her by after lunch for the next few days? You two can commune with the trees—or whatever it is you do—while I patrol. I'll come back and pick her up before dinner. You're always more than welcome to join the Pack for dinner, Leonora. You know that."

"I do," she answered graciously. "And I thank you for the reminder. I may take you up on that. I'll let you know. For now, the afternoons would be perfect, if that's all right with you, Sally."

"Sounds great," Sally agreed. "I only need my evenings free to hang out with Carly. She's the one I came to visit in the first place, after all."

"This will work out fine," Leonora assured her. "But now, I think you have to go." Leonora stood quickly, confusing Sally for a moment until she heard it too. The trees spoke of danger. Of horror.

"What is it?" Jason asked, already on his feet.

"A child. A pup," Sally said, not sure how to interpret the song on the wind. "He wandered away from his parents and the four hunters are closing in on him."

"I will ask the trees to intervene but there is only so much they can do," Leonora offered, a frown of worry on her timeless face.

"Where are they?" Jason demanded, all business now as he whipped out his cell phone and started dialing.

"I see the place. I can lead you there," Sally said, still listening to the whispers on the wind.

"Below Yellowtail Ridge between the dry creek and the lightning tree. About a hundred yards north of the bear cave." Leonora pinpointed the location.

Jason placed his call and relayed the location in terse sentences. He hung up and turned to Sally. "Will you know if they move?"

"As long as I can hear the trees," she answered with conviction.

"Great. We'll roll the windows down on the SUV if we have to. Let's go. Sorry, Leonora."

"Don't worry, Jason. Go now and rescue that little boy. He needs you."

They ran through the woods together, back toward the SUV. Sally just barely kept up with Jason's longer strides.

"Throw me the keys. I know where to go," she called out as they broke through the trees.

The keys jangled as they flew through the air toward her. She loved the fact that he hadn't questioned her statement. He took her words at face value, though she was a newcomer to the area.

She saw the phone in his hand as they piled into the SUV. He'd barely shut the door before she threw it in drive. All those years driving in crowded city streets had taught her how to handle a vehicle at speed. The country roads were easy enough to navigate.

Jason exchanged terse words with someone on the phone while Sally followed the map in her mind toward where she knew they had to go. She could clearly see where the abduction had taken place.

She took them as far as the road allowed. While Jason had been talking to his people on the phone, he'd removed his boots and socks. He'd also shrugged out of his jacket. She supposed he was preparing in case he needed to be able to shift forms quickly. All he had left was a T-shirt and his jeans. And the phone, of course. From the level of cursing, she surmised he wasn't getting good news on that end.

The SUV halted in a skid of rocks and pinecones that had built up on the side of the road. Both of them were out of the vehicle before it even stopped rocking. Sally pocketed the keys and began to run. She was fast for a human, but she knew Jason had to hold back to keep pace with her. She did her best to move faster, pouring on speed she didn't know she had as they made their way on foot up the mountain.

Sally saw the first wolf about a hundred yards into the woods. It paced them while Jason made some sort of gestures with his hands. The wolf nodded once and scurried off ahead. Sally realized they must have signals worked out.

"She's going to scout ahead for us," Jason said quietly. He wasn't even breathing hard. Sally was in shape, but the mad dash had her panting a little. That and seeing an enormous wolf running alongside them...well, it had taken her by surprise. She knew intellectually that these people could turn into wolves, but that didn't mean she took it for granted that giant versions of dangerous wild beasts running a few feet away from her didn't make her heart beat faster.

"I'm sorry I'm so slow," she gasped between breaths. She wanted to say more, but time was of the essence. They kept moving, the wolf barely visible in the trees ahead of them.

"You're actually faster than I expected. Faster than any human, certainly. Don't sweat it."

Sweating was exactly what she was doing. Out of breath and dripping, she almost cursed the Alpha at her side who looked as if he were out for a pleasant stroll. No sweat beaded his upper lip. His lungs breathed steadily and at a much slower rate than her own.

A short yip made her jump.

"Damn." Jason's head rose and he seemed to sniff the air.

"What is it?"

"Blood. Lots of blood." He veered to the right, even though she knew the abduction had taken place elsewhere. She paused mentally even as she followed in his footsteps. She had been listening to the trees sing of the child. But there was another song—another story they sang of—a story of death.

"It's a bear. The hunters killed it," she suddenly realized. She had been so preoccupied with the boy, she'd missed it. She mentally kicked herself even as she kicked her heels into high gear to follow Jason. He led the way, but kept his pace slow enough that she could follow.

When he stopped short, she almost ran into his back. A tree steadied her and she felt its presence in her mind. It had witnessed the death of its neighbor. Sally's unprepared mind saw it all as the tree spoke of the events to her.

"The bear lived in that cave over the rise. The hunters shot it and used its scent to disguise their own. This tree saw it all." She spoke aloud to Jason, not really registering the fact that a small ring of wolves had formed around them and the giant bear's carcass.

She was relieved to find that the bear was simply a bear, not one of the bear shifters Jason had pointed out at the restaurant. It was a senseless death of a beautiful animal, but at least the shifters would not be mourning the loss of a member of that family. This old bear had been an aging bachelor, past his prime of life.

"They used his scent to hide their own. Cunning," Jason said with carefully controlled anger. "We know this bear. Jimmy would not have been afraid of his scent. None of our Pack would."

"The boy's name is Jimmy?" It was a nonsensical detail to focus on but she was at a loss.

Jason nodded. "There's been no trace of him yet. The bear's scent is confusing the issue. He's been all over these woods. Tracing him by scent leads us everywhere and nowhere."

She thought she understood. "Follow me. I know where the abduction took place, but..." She hesitated before breaking the news.

"What?" Jason turned to her, his gaze hard.

"They took him in a van and drove away. I lose the trail at the edge of the woods, where the land turns into farmland. No trees." She felt helpless, having listened to the rest of the song. The trees knew only what they could see. Where there were no trees, they had no way to know.

Jason's lips thinned into a tight line. "Show me."

Sally turned and began running again. At least she'd had a moment to steady her breathing. Jason padded along beside her, barefoot. She supposed he was used to the prickly things on the uneven forest floor, but she wouldn't want to do it herself. Her delicate human feet would have been punctured and bleeding within the first few yards.

Sally led the way to a tiny clearing several hundred yards farther up the ridge. She had to slow in places to climb and became aware of the Pack of wolves all around them. They were surrounded on all sides, with several following behind. Sally felt the weight of their presence but no danger from them. Not toward her, at least.

When she arrived at the clearing, she was careful to halt

just outside, cautioning Jason and his people as well. She didn't want to disturb evidence or clues before they'd had the opportunity to study the scene.

"He struggled there," Sally pointed to a patch of forest floor that was freshly turned. "They subdued him."

"Drugged him," Jason confirmed with a sniff. "Strong opiates. And they were messy about it." He strode forward, careful about where he stepped. Sally followed behind when she realized he knew what he was doing. He bent to pick up a leaf that had some sort of fluid congealing on its surface. "They lost some of the drug out of the syringe or dart when he struggled. Could be they only gave him a partial dose."

"It was a syringe," Sally confirmed, spotting a flash of silver near her feet. "Watch where you step, Jason. These guys were sloppy." She bent to retrieve the needle, using a leaf to touch it so she didn't disturb any fingerprints that might be on it.

"They dragged him off this way," Jason observed. "The scent is all confused. I think they were using some kind of scent neutralizer in addition to the bear. They learned from their earlier mistakes." He made some hand gestures to the wolves and a few stayed behind while the rest followed as he led the way toward another, larger clearing.

"They had a four wheeler parked here. One of them drove with the boy in the back while the other three walked." Sally could see the picture painted by the rustling leaves as they walked. "They had a white panel van waiting at the gravel road up ahead. They put him in the back, tied him down with shiny metal cuffs attached to a chain. The trees saw that much. I assume the chain was attached in some way to the inside of the van." Their small group broke through the trees and she could clearly see the skid marks on the gravel road where the van had pealed out in a hurry.

"Hold this," Jason said tersely, handing her his cell phone.

166

She watched in momentary confusion as he stripped off his T-shirt and jeans. A moment later, an absolutely enormous, shaggy wolf stood in his place.

Jason went over the road with his nose to the gravel. His wolf senses must be much more acute than in his human form. He picked up a scent and followed it for some distance in the general area but eventually gave up and shimmered back into his human form. He shrugged into his clothes while she watched and shook his head in disgust.

"Scent blockers. The whole area is lousy with them. They knew we'd hunt them. They know what we are. Which means, they know what they've caught. Lady help us."

Chapter Ten

"I don't know if this is good news or not, but they split up not far down the road." Sally listened intently to the new song in the trees. "The white van stopped in the parking area at the base of a wooded hiking trail. Four men piled out. They argued. Two grabbed their rucksacks and stormed off. Two got back in the van and drove away at high speed." She tried hard to focus on the picture the trees were painting. She'd never seen this much detail before. Then again, she'd never been in such a large, dense or magical forest before. "I think it was the younger two who took off on their own. Looks like they had a pickup truck parked in that lot. They took it and left, going in the opposite direction from the van. That's where the trees end."

"That's more than I could have hoped for," Jason said gratefully. She liked the note of praise in his tone though she hadn't really contributed much. She wouldn't be satisfied until they got the boy back in one piece and the perps had been dealt with.

Jason looked upward and only then did Sally realize the light was fading. They'd spent the early afternoon with Leonora and the rest of the day tracking. Night was falling. Which gave her an idea.

"Dmitri could help." Sally guessed the vampire might have skills beyond theirs. He might be the answer to finding Jimmy alive.

Jason's mouth thinned, but he punched the buttons on his cell phone. Sally wasn't too surprised to find that Jason had the local Master Vampire on speed dial. Jason filled Dmitri in on the situation in a few short sentences. He didn't look happy at whatever Dmitri said in reply. He hung up quickly and turned back to Sally.

"He'll help, but he won't leave home before Carly rises. Damn newlyweds."

"Give me your cell number." Sally was thinking fast, planning and figuring how to best utilize their capabilities. She took out her phone and was punching buttons to set Jason up on speed dial. He dictated the number and it was done. "I'm going to Carly's. I can be of more use where I have computer access. Does anybody you know have a police scanner?"

"One of the cubs has one," Jason said as he dialed another number. "I'll have him bring it to you at Carly's office."

"Good. And leave me a few computer experts. I may need a hacker or two. I'll call when I have news. I'm taking the SUV, okay?"

Jason smiled for the first time in an hour. "I don't need it. Joanna will escort you back to the car. I'd take you myself, but I need to get these guys organized..." He looked around at the wolves, many of whom still had their noses to the ground.

"I understand." And she truly did. She'd be safe enough in the forest. Even the wolf escort wasn't quite necessary, but she'd take it if it made him more comfortable. The blonde wolf he'd called Joanna moved close to them, no doubt having heard her name. "Nice to meet you, Joanna. Ready to go?"

The wolf barked once and waited. Jason moved close to place a quick kiss on Sally's lips, surprising her. "Be careful, sweetheart."

"You too." She set off without further delay, the wolf following along at her side. Sally ran, the wolf keeping pace easily.

Though she'd never spent any time in dense woods, Sally

had no problem finding her way. The trees greeted her as she passed with a flutter of their leaves and a slight change in the pitch of their song. If she'd had time to enjoy the phenomenon she would have, but the circumstances were dire. A child had been abducted and because of the nature of both the child and the abduction, they couldn't involve the human police. Not really. That went without saying.

But Sally might be able to utilize their resources. She'd try her best, at any rate. There were a lot more human cops out there on the roads in the cities and farmland. Maybe she could use that to her advantage.

The SUV came into sight and the wolf bounded ahead to sniff all around the vehicle before she'd let Sally pass. Good idea. The SUV had been left unattended for a while. Anybody could've come by and done anything to it while they'd been occupied elsewhere. The wolf barked the all clear while Sally asked the trees if anyone had been nearby. Both sources confirmed the vehicle was safe.

Sally climbed in and waited to see if the wolf would accompany her farther. When Joanna stayed on the ground, Sally shut the door, rolling down the window again so she could hear the forest song, if needed.

"Thanks, Joanna." She waved to the wolf as she drove off, hearing the yip of acknowledgment as she sped away. She saw Joanna in the rearview mirror for a moment, watching her a bit before fading back into the woods.

Sally made good time back to Carly's. By the time she pulled up in front of the big house, night had fallen fully and Carly was awake. Dmitri and she were waiting at the door for her arrival. Sally filled them in on the bare facts of Jimmy's abduction and she could see from Dmitri's expression that the man was torn. There was no question that he would help search for the boy, but the worried looks he kept throwing at Carly spoke volumes—even to a woman who couldn't read his mind.

Sally put one hand on his arm, stilling him for one key moment.

"You should go. Don't worry. I'll look after Carly. I plan to put her to work with the contingent of wolves in the office. We're going to hack into police databases and do some research." Carly's eyes lit up with excitement, as Sally knew they would. The girl was a geek through and through. "She'll have a dozen werewolves and one very determined, and armed, cop watching over her. We'll be okay. I promise."

Dmitri regarded her steadily for a timeless moment. "Thank you," he finally said, moving toward the door. Carly followed him and they shared a smoldering kiss before he disappeared into the night.

Sally didn't hear a motor start. Her brows lowered in question as Carly turned back to her.

"Is the bat thing true, then?"

Carly laughed. "I suppose he could become a bat if he really wanted to."

"He turns into other things?" Sally began walking toward the office part of the structure, Carly next to her.

"Yeah. It's pretty awesome," Carly admitted. "He can even do mythological creatures like dragons. It's way cool."

"I bet." Sally would ponder that another time. For now, a missing boy occupied her thoughts. "Can you hack into the local police network?"

Carly made a rude noise. "Of course. Ask me something hard."

They entered the office and a dozen eager faces popped up over cubicle dividers. Sally almost laughed, and would have if the situation wasn't so dire. They looked like meerkats popping up out of their burrows. Or maybe prairie dogs, all looking to her, awaiting orders. Maybe there was something to this Alpha stuff after all. She kind of liked being in charge.

Sally wasted no time. She found the kid with the police scanner and had him set it up in Carly's office. She needed a large desk to spread out on and the conference table at one end of Carly's office would do. She set Carly and her favorite geeks to work on the hacking part in computer nirvana at the other end of the spacious office.

"As soon as you get into the network, let me know and I'll take it from there." Carly nodded at Sally's directive.

She assigned tasks to each person. A few were asked to listen to the scanner and write down the calls, even if they didn't know what they meant. One of the computer guys said he could get a list of police codes and Sally let him have at it. The locals might speak a slightly different language than the code Sally was used to. The list would be helpful.

"We're in," Carly reported a few minutes later. She backed away from the computer and let Sally have her seat.

At that point it was going to take some deductive reasoning and there were too many people hanging over her shoulder. She shooed out most of the wolves, asking a few to get some food for the rest of the staff. Sally had hardly eaten all day and her stomach was beginning to growl. They'd need the calories to continue the hunt.

"What are you looking for?" Carly asked quietly from Sally's side. Carly's presence was comforting rather than distracting, like some of the kids who worked for her.

"I'm not exactly sure," Sally admitted, studying the screen. Her fingers whirled over the keys as report after report spilled onto the display.

"Dude," Carly said. "You've really increased your computer skills since college."

"When I made detective, a lot of my job turned to research and desk work. It was either keep up or lose out." Sally didn't stop typing her queries into the police system as she spoke. She'd also become a really great multi-tasker. "Ah. Here we go."

Carly leaned in closer at her side and Sally was vaguely aware that one or two of the wolves were at her back, reading over her shoulder. She didn't mind. As long as they kept quiet so she could think and start to see connections, they were okay.

"How many real estate agents in town?" Sally asked.

It was Seth who answered. "About a dozen different human firms. There's also one shifter who helps us when we want to buy land."

"Okay. One of you call the shifter and ask nicely if they've sold any property to a human in the past two or three weeks. The rest of you—get help from the guys outside." She nodded toward the office proper where a half-dozen wolves waited for further orders. "Each of you take one real estate company and do your best to access their sales records for the past month. Print out a list of the new owners and former addresses if you can, then bring them to me."

Scurrying behind her and out in the office told her the kids were on the case. Carly still sat at her side.

"What are you thinking?" Carly asked quietly.

"I'm thinking that if they abducted the kid instead of just killing him outright, they had to have a motive. I don't think they'd run with him. It feels more personal than that. Like they want to make a point with the local wolves. Therefore, they'd need a place to take him. It would have to be someplace they wouldn't easily be either seen or heard, so that means someplace outside of town most likely, or on the outskirts."

Carly pulled out a laptop computer and fired it up. She didn't speak further, concentrating on inputting commands. It was good to have Carly working on this with her. Sally was competent with computers, but Carly was a genius. She could hack any system but skirted away from doing anything illegal unless absolutely necessary. This was one of those times when the laws of man would prevent them from carrying out true justice. Sally knew she should feel more of a conflict, but after what she had seen over the years, she preferred to carry out justice when possible, even when the rule of law might not approve.

When this was all over, she would have to reexamine whether or not she could continue as a cop. Too often, her hands had been tied when it came to real justice. It had left her feeling frustrated and burnt out. This vacation was supposed to be a reprieve from all of that. Instead, this situation had brought the conflict within her into sharp focus. As soon as they saved Jimmy, she had some hard thinking to do.

"I think I found something," Carly said from beside her while Sally was tracing known associates of the two men who had been arrested the day before.

Sally turned to the smaller screen Carly was working on. There were a few different windows open on a multitude of databases. Carly's genius at work.

"What am I looking at?"

"This is a money transfer from an account Dmitri has been watching. He believes it belongs to a *Venifucus* agent in the local area named Alvin Sanders. Since I became aware of it, only small amounts have been coming and going from that account. Normal living expenses. But this one..." She pointed to an entry on the screen. "This is going into an escrow account at this law firm." She tapped another window open to the side of the first. "This law firm held it for a few days and then transferred it to Hilltop Bank. Hilltop Bank transferred it to another escrow account at another law firm, and they transferred it to Bill Jeremy's real estate agency."

"Who's looking at Bill Jeremy's?" Sally yelled out to the office area. A blonde head popped up from behind a cubicle wall. Seth. Good boy.

"I just got into his system. What do you need?" he asked.

"Do you have a sale on the fourteenth? Or anything that week?" Sally shot back.

"Yeah. There were two on the fourteenth and nothing else that whole week."

"Print out the details—anything you can find—on both transactions, and bring them over please."

Seth nodded and popped back down into his cubicle. In the background, Sally heard a printer power up out in the office a few moments later. She turned back to her screen and pulled up what she could about the name on the bank account that had originated the transaction.

"Dmitri thinks this guy is part of that *Venifucus* group?" Sally asked Carly as she dug up what she could about him in the official law enforcement databases. She sent everything to the printer in Carly's office. If nothing else, Dmitri could look through the information. Maybe it would help in some way.

"Yeah," Carly answered, picking up the pages as they spit out from the printer. "He's suspected based on information from the other Masters in North America and some from a few different were groups. This guy popped up on the radar in our area, so we've been keeping an eye on him and his business dealings as best we can. I think this police data will help us fill out the file we started. Thanks, Sal."

"I can't find a connection to say that he is definitely involved in the immediate case. My gut says the hunters were solely responsible for abducting Jimmy. But the money trail is clear. He bought a place, and it's a good bet, if they're all part of the same club, he's letting them use it. At the very least, it has to be searched in order to be eliminated as a possibility."

Carly nodded. "But you don't know exactly which property it is, right?"

"Well the odds here are much better than they would be in a big city. Only two real estate closings around the date in question. Only two places to check. Believe me, it could've been a lot worse."

Seth loped in with a handful of papers and handed them to Sally. She scanned them, relating the information to what she'd already learned. Unfortunately, there was no way to tell which property was a better choice for the kidnappers. And both sales had been handled by the same attorney and the same bank, so no help there.

"We're going to have to check both of these," Sally said aloud. "Let me call Jason and see if they've found anything that might help narrow down our choices."

She hit the speed dial on her cell and only dimly noted the way Seth's eyebrow rose. Yes, she had the Alpha on speed dial. Why should the kid be so surprised?

Jason answered before the first ring had time to complete. "Have you found anything?"

"I think so. Two possible locations where they might be holding Jimmy."

"Thank the Lady. Because we're turning up big fat zeros here."

"I was afraid of that, considering they knew enough to mask their scent." Sally glanced at the papers and relayed the two addresses.

"We'll have to check both of them," Jason said on a sigh. "We don't have anything that would make me choose one over the other right now. They're almost on opposite sides of the county. Hang on." Jason conferred with someone on his end, then came back on the line. "Dmitri is going to take the property down by the lake. He can get there faster than any of us. We'll head for the closer address on Bush Hollow Road. It'll take us about twenty minutes to get there because of the terrain. It'd be about the same whether we were coming on four feet or two. I'll take those with vehicles by road and the rest will go across country." It sounded like he was issuing the order even as he spoke to her.

"Judging by the map, I can be there in about fifteen minutes," she offered.

"Don't, Sally. Let us handle this." His voice was a growl but she wasn't backing down. She could growl with the best of them.

"I'm a cop, Jason. Don't you dare tell me how to do my job."

"You're not on duty here—" he began, but she was ready for that argument.

"You want to tell that to Jimmy? Sorry, kid. Sally could have saved your life but she was on vacation. I don't think so." She didn't give him a chance to answer that one. "I'll meet you there."

She disconnected the call, knowing he was probably cursing her out wherever he was. Fine. Let him blow off steam. They both needed to be level headed when they confronted the kidnappers.

When Sally stood, slinging her dark jacket over her shoulder, Seth blocked her path out of Carly's office. The look on his face was grim.

"I promised the Master that I would look after you both. I know for a fact the Alpha doesn't want you going. We all heard him on the phone just now."

Damn werewolves and their keen hearing. Sally had just about had enough of this overprotective crap.

"You can look after Carly, but I'm going. Don't you dare

stand in my way."

Seth's eyes met hers for a few moments, but in the end, the kid backed down. He didn't look too happy about it.

"The Alpha will have my hide if anything happens to you," he said glumly.

"And I'll skin you alive if you let anything happen to my friend." The kid perked up. "You promised the Alpha and now I want you to promise me, that you'll keep Carly safe. She's not combat-trained, or even very good at confrontation." Carly rolled her eyes but smiled at Sally's assessment. "You will stay here and if anything nasty comes calling that you can't handle, you phone me or your Alpha right away. Got that?"

"Yes, ma'am," Seth said with renewed conviction. "But shouldn't maybe some of us go with you?"

"Absolutely not. Your job is here. Guarding the Mistress. I'm armed and the rest of your Pack is going to be right on my heels." She spoke as she headed out of the office, the rest of them trailing behind her. "I'll have plenty of help when I need it. I'm just scouting ahead to make sure nothing happens to Jimmy before they get there."

She swung up into the SUV and started the engine. With a quick wave to Carly, she set out as fast as she dared go on the gravel drive. When she hit the pavement of the road, she sped up, pushing past the speed limit on the quickest route to the nearby farmhouse.

It was a good location for bad deeds. There wasn't much cover because the fields were empty, dry stalks from last year's corn popping up at regular intervals. But nothing had been planted this year. Probably because the property had changed hands.

Sally had to leave the SUV parked in the last row of trees before the open pasture. She crept toward the house on foot, crouched low so anybody looking out would have less chance of seeing her approach. The half moon was behind clouds and there were no lights around for miles, so that helped. She wore her dark jacket and blue jeans. Black boots couldn't be seen against the dark ground. Only her face and hands shone in the darkness, but she'd put her hair down to cover what she could, and kept her hands low, one holding one of her handguns. The other gun remained holstered for now, as a backup. She'd taken the ankle holster out of her suitcase that morning and put her backup gun in her boot. Just in case something went sideways.

She'd made good time on the drive over. Better than she had expected. If she calculated correctly, Jason and his Pack were still a good five or ten minutes behind her. Just enough time to take a peek and find out, first of all, if Jimmy was inside the house, and secondly, if he was okay. Discovering where the kidnappers were and how well-armed was another factor. A lot could go wrong in a very short amount of time. She'd seen it before in her years as a cop. Minutes could mean the difference between life and death for Jimmy. She had to find out if her detective work was going to pay off, because if not, they had to come up with another idea very quickly.

She'd set her cell phone to vibrate before leaving the SUV. So far, no news from Dmitri. Both locations were equally likely to be housing the kidnappers. So there was a fifty-fifty chance she would find the house empty. If that was the case, they could concentrate on the other location. Either way, time was of the essence. She crept closer on silent feet, keeping low to the ground, minimizing her silhouette.

There was a barn on the property. It was falling down on one side, but it would offer cover as she approached the house. She'd have to check the barn as well, since they could've stashed the boy just about anywhere. They didn't necessarily have to be using the house.

She eased closer to the barn. No illumination came from

within, but that didn't really mean anything. Sure, it would've been nice if the kidnappers had lit a neon sign telling her where they were, but that didn't happen very frequently in her experience. No lights shone from the house or the barn, from what she could see. She had to be on her toes.

"Well, lookie what I found."

The voice came from behind her and Sally stiffened near the door of the barn. She'd checked the side as she approached, but apparently not well enough. She'd been outflanked by someone who'd come up behind her. With a sinking feeling, she turned to get a look at him.

Damn. It was one of the gunmen. The younger one. She knew his name was Bartholomew Samuels from the police reports she'd seen. She held her gun at her side, hoping he couldn't quite see it in the darkness. The hope was in vain.

"Drop it," he ordered, pointing with his own rifle toward her right hand.

Sally didn't see that she had any choice. She dropped her weapon at her feet. The backup was out of reach for the moment, strapped to her left ankle, under her pant leg.

Jason and the wolves were on the way, only minutes behind her. She had to hold out until they got there, but there was no sign of Jimmy yet. The kidnappers had split up earlier in the day. They might still be operating separately. For all she knew, Mr. Samuels might be on his own here. Sally had to get confirmation that the kid was here. Until she knew for sure—until she had Jimmy away from the bad guys—she wouldn't rest easy.

And she wouldn't let this bozo distract her from her goal. In fact, he might be able to help, though he'd never realize it.

"All I want is the child." Sally knew the guy remembered her from their earlier run-in. She'd seen the flash of recognition in his eyes, even in the dark.

180

"And all we want is to rid the world of their filth," he spat, gesturing with the gun barrel for her to move into the barn. "Devil-worshipping werewolves." Each of his words was dripping with hatred. There would be no reasoning with a mindset like that.

Sally went into the barn, scanning what she could see of the interior quickly as Samuels crowded her inside with the muzzle of the gun in her back. It was a small structure with no walls inside, only open box stalls that had probably once housed horses. There was a giant hole in one corner of the structure where the roof sagged almost to the ground. She might be able to get out that way, if she could get away from this jerk.

The barn was empty. Disappointment warred with relief. Given the opportunity, she could subdue Samuels without putting Jimmy in further danger. Samuels had already fired at her once. She knew he wouldn't hesitate to shoot her if provoked.

"Werewolves? Are you nuts?" She wanted to keep him talking. If he began to rant, she might be able to use his distraction to her advantage.

"Don't pretend you don't know what I'm talking about. You're one of them."

He backhanded her and then she saw it. The tattoo on his wrist. It glowed evilly with dark energy now that she could see it close up. It made her shiver.

"No," she said with deliberate calmness. "I'm a police detective from San Francisco, here on vacation, visiting friends. I've seen a lot of weird stuff living in San Fran and all, but I've never even heard of people thinking werewolves were real before. What kind of drugs are you on?"

"If you're not one of them, you're fucking one. Moore is their leader, or didn't you realize it? We've seen you with him.

We know you're involved. He moves fast. Or maybe you're just easy. I want to find out for myself. Get some of what he had."

He maneuvered her toward one of the stalls that was mostly sound. If he got her in there, she'd be more or less trapped. But he didn't know about her backup weapon. If it came down to it, she might have a chance to draw on him. She'd kill him if she had to. She'd killed twice before in the line of duty. She didn't enjoy it, but if it came down to her life or his, she'd choose herself every time over a criminal. Especially a lowlife who would kidnap children and shoot at young girls in the woods.

"Jason Moore is an upstanding member of the community," she protested loudly, hoping that Jason or one of his Pack members would hear her if they were near enough. "There's no way he's involved in anything occult."

"He's in it up to his eyeballs, missy. He was born to it. The worst kind of werewolf. But we'll get him. Just like we'll get all the other wolf filth he calls a Pack."

He was gloating, and that's when a terrible suspicion formed in her mind.

"Kidnapping the boy to lure him out, are you? Not smart, Mr. Samuels. He's got to realize what you've planned. He's smarter than you are."

"He's not smarter than a couple pounds of C-4," he retorted with an evil laugh.

Oh, no.

Chapter Eleven

The rifle barrel smacked her in the face, causing stars to swim before her eyes for a moment as he pushed her into the stall. Outmaneuvered. Damn.

When the ringing in her ears subsided, she was flat on her back in the dirt, Samuels above her. He'd switched out his rifle for a wicked-looking blade. The rifle was out of reach, slung across his back. Double damn. And the knife was headed for her.

She breathed a small sigh of relief when the blade sliced through fabric instead of skin. He was undressing her with the knife, not murdering her. Not yet, at least.

Shit. Where the hell was Jason? She had to warn him! And she had to get free of this moron before he raped her.

She had to make noise. Jason would be here any minute. She had to give him a clue as to where to find her.

She struggled and screamed as Samuels cut her T-shirt and bra down the middle. He dropped the knife momentarily to fondle her and she tried to grab for it in the dirt at her side, but he retrieved it with a laughing sneer.

"You're not getting away from me this time, girlie. I'm gonna fuck you before I kill you and then I'm going to enjoy watching the fireworks as we barbeque the rest of those filthy wolves." He applied the knife further down, working on her pants.

She had to do something quick or she really was going to be on the menu for this lunatic, and that was completely unacceptable. Where the hell was Jason? The one time she needed backup in a big way and he was late. Dammit.

Fear crept into her thoughts. Might he have already found Jimmy and the explosives? Could he be dead or dying at this very moment? No. She would've heard a boom that loud even if it were twenty miles away. Jason had been on his way here. He had to be on course. She just had to wait it out and alert him when he showed up.

But she still didn't know where the kid, and the bomb, was.

"C-4? You're going to use military-grade explosives to kill a harmless teenage boy and whoever shows up to try to rescue him? You're not just high, you're insane!" she screamed, hoping someone would hear her.

He backhanded her again and her head swam for a moment. Her jeans were giving him trouble and she felt that hunting blade slice through her skin a few times, but they were shallow cuts. Nothing too serious. He was cursing as he concentrated on undressing her uncooperative body. She cursed right back at him, calling him every filthy name she'd ever heard on the streets.

And then a hand reached out from the darkness above him. A huge, hairy, clawed hand that grabbed him by the scruff of the neck and hauled him off her.

Samuels flew through the air backwards, sailing into the opposite wall of the barn and making his own private doorway with his body. She heard snarling and realized Jason's wolf Pack must have him. Thank God.

Sally sat up, confronted by the biggest werewolf she'd ever seen.

"Jason?"

It had to be. And he was in that scary, half-human battle form.

He moved closer, picking up her trembling body in those giant clawed hands and cradling her against his furry chest. Her arms went around his neck and he loped out of the dilapidated barn, taking her away from the scene, back toward the road.

"Wait! Jason, there's a bomb." She had to warn him before others died. "Taking Jimmy was to lure you out. Samuels said they had a pound of C-4 wired to blow when you found the boy." He wasn't slowing down. She wasn't even sure if he was listening to her. She tugged at his shoulders. "You have to warn your Pack, Jason. They're trying to kill your Pack!"

That seemed to get through. Jason halted in the field, near the tree line and raised his head, letting out a short howl that seemed to communicate to the other wolves. She could see some of them in the distance raise their heads and begin to follow Jason.

He moved her into the trees and stopped, thankfully.

Some of his Pack members approached in both human and wolf form. One of the men reached for her, as if to take her from Jason's arms, but he pulled away almost violently. He refused to let her go.

"Let me take care of her, Alpha," the man tried to reason with him but Jason was having none of it.

"My mate," he growled back at the man. A shocked silence greeted those words and though Sally didn't fully understand werewolf customs, she thought maybe Jason had just drawn some kind of line in the sand.

"There's a bomb," she said quickly, to distract the men. It worked. All eyes went to her and she sort of wished she'd had time to tie the loose ends of her shirt together. They couldn't see much the way Jason was holding her and she supposed werewolves were used to nudity, but she wasn't. "Jimmy was taken to lure Jason and the rest of you out. Samuels knew you're werewolves and that Jason's your leader. He had that tattoo on his wrist. I saw it close up this time. The one Dmitri said marked the *Venifucus*."

As she spoke, she felt stronger. The trembling in her limbs had stopped and she was ready to rejoin the action. She would've been okay before, had Jason not picked her up bodily and taken her away. They'd have to talk about that later. She wasn't some fainting damsel. Not usually. Of course, Samuels had gotten closer to causing her real harm than anyone had in a long time.

"Warn the Pack," he ordered in that growly voice that seemed the norm for this form. Some of the men pulled out cell phones. A few of the wolves bounded away, vocalizing in yips. More came in from the fields and gathered under cover of the trees, surrounding them.

She pushed at Jason's shoulders, liking the feel of him, even in this half-man half-beast state. He had to be one powerful shapeshifter to hold that form for so long without any sign of strain.

"Let me down, Jason. Please," she whispered.

"You're hurt," he growled, arguing.

"No. Only cut a little from the knife he was using to try to get my pants off." Jason growled at that, and it wasn't a friendly sound. "Just shallow cuts."

He dropped to the ground then, in a move so quick it felt like freefall, but he laid her gently on the loamy earth, his fingers tender as he examined the shallow cuts on her midsection.

"I'm okay, Jason. Really." She sat up and gathered the ends of her shirt together, tying them in a knot under her breasts. She felt better already. Covered up with a certain bimbonic flair. It would almost have been funny if the situation weren't so dire.

He shifted to his human form while he examined the bruises on her head from where Samuels had struck her with the gun and his hand. Her lip was split. She knew that much. And from the tenderness of her cheek she'd probably have a black eye tomorrow too. Oh, joy.

"I'm okay," she repeated, taking his hand in hers. She met his gaze and there was a great deal of emotion in the depths of his eyes that she hadn't expected. She felt the answering feelings welling up inside her, but this was neither the time nor the place. "Your people are in danger, Jason."

He blinked, releasing her from his gaze as they both came back to the present moment.

"We'll talk about this later, sweetheart," he promised.

His serious tone indicated it might not be an altogether pleasant conversation. She knew he'd have something to say about the fact that she hadn't waited for him to arrive. She'd put herself in danger, and she knew he didn't like that. Still, danger had been her job for the past decade. She'd never had a Pack to call on for help and protection. She often didn't even have a partner, since the budget cuts. And few human policemen were able to keep up with her on the street. She was used to being on her own in dangerous situations. It was a hard habit to break.

"Now, what's this about a bomb?" Jason's gaze sharpened. Someone threw him a small knapsack and he began dressing as she made her report, the gathered Pack members listening in.

"Samuels said there was a pound of C-4 wired to explode when you find Jimmy. He's the bait. The real target is the rest of you—your Pack. These guys want to kill as many of you at one time as they can. They know you're werewolves and that Jason was *born to it*, whatever that means. They know he's your leader," she addressed the gathering.

"If they know that much, what about the women and

children back at the Pack house?" one of the men asked.

"Make the call," Jason said shortly. "Tell them to scatter." Jason stood as he pulled on black pants that had been in the knapsack. "Who here knows the smell of C-4?"

A few hands shot up, mostly from men decked out in black or camo fatigues that had a well-worn look. Several of them held military grade weapons casually in their hands, aimed at the ground. Former soldiers. Had to be.

"Len, I want you to take point on the main group. Arlo, you've got Team 2. Jesse, I want you with me. Teams 1 and 2 will focus on finding bombs and clearing the house. With that much C-4, they probably spread it around a bit. My group will get Jimmy out."

"You know where he is?" That was news to Sally.

Jason nodded. "He's under the house. There's a small basement."

"It's more of a storm shelter, actually," the man called Jesse added, coming up alongside Sally. He handed a small headset to Jason while he spoke. "If the bomb is down there, all those cinder blocks and cement will focus the blast upward toward whoever might be in the house at the time."

"Good to know." Sally looked the newcomer up and down.

Yeah, he was definitely a soldier—or had been before rejoining his Pack. He'd seen battle. Everything about him said competence and power. If he'd had a mind to, she thought maybe he could've given Jason a run for his money in claiming the Alpha role in the Pack, but he seemed to have his own reasons for staying in the background. He was a ghost in the woods and that seemed to suit him just fine.

"Sally, this is my brother, Jesse," Jason introduced them.

She saw it then, the family resemblance. The men were very alike, though Jesse seemed to have a lot of sadness hanging around his shoulders. War could do that to a man. She'd seen it in the vets who found their way onto the police force.

"And here I thought you crawled out from under a rock," she joked, trying to lighten the mood. She offered her hand to Jesse and gave him a smile, which he returned.

"Nah, little brother there was the apple of our mama's eye. She spoiled him when we were pups. Don't you make the same mistake, Detective Decker."

"I'll try to remember that." She shook his hand, marveling at the similarities and differences in the two men.

Jesse's words had confirmed that Jason was the younger of the two. She hadn't been sure if her perception of Jesse as being older was really years or just mileage. She knew now it was both. That he hadn't wanted the Alpha role in the Pack was interesting and something she'd ask Jason about later, if she had a chance. The Pack dynamics fascinated her, though she really understood very little.

The first two groups were beginning to move out stealthily across the landscape. They were staggering their movements, one or two going at a time. Some were in wolf form, some in human form. Sally had a hard time spotting them, even though she knew where they were supposed to be. Even in human form, werewolves knew how to blend into the scenery. Their stealth was amazing.

Jason caught her elbow and tugged her gently around to face him. "I'd ask you to stay here, but I know you won't." He seemed resigned to that fact, which unaccountably warmed her. "I'd rather have you with me, where I can keep an eye on you. All right?" As he talked he placed the super-tiny earpiece Jesse had given him in his ear. It was almost invisible. Definitely high tech gear she had never seen before. Some kind of tactical radio setup.

"That suits me fine." She really wasn't as stealthy as these wolves, but she could contribute. And she didn't want to be left on the sidelines.

"Jesse's got the lead until the bombs are accounted for." Jason addressed the small group left in the woods. There were two wolves beside Jesse. A small team of five to retrieve the kid. Only Jason and Jesse were wired for sound. She assumed that the other men dressed as soldiers were keeping them informed of their progress.

They set out a moment later, Jesse in the lead with one of the wolves, then she and Jason in the middle, followed by the final wolf. Jason kept her tucked low next to him as they moved through the empty field. He seemed pleased with the way she moved and after a while he stopped hovering quite so much. She breathed a sigh of relief. She might not be a werewolf, but she did have some skills.

They stopped at irregular intervals along the path toward the house. At one point, Jason whispered to her, giving her an update from his radio connection.

"Team 2 found about a quarter-pound of C-4 on the west side of the house, rigged to a trigger from within. My guess is the perimeter charges are meant to go when the main charge does to cover the broadest surface area. Get the most of us they can with one blow. It was packed with silver shrapnel."

"It's disarmed?"

"Already done."

Sally was appalled by the brutality of the hunters. An explosive wrapped in shrapnel was the purview of terrorists who wanted to harm as many people as possible with one bomb. The little sharp fragments—whether they be nails or other kinds of harmful metal objects—were meant to become projectiles when the charge they were attached to went off. And she already knew silver was poison to the werewolves.

"Team 1 is working their side of the perimeter," Jason went on. "I'd lay odds they'll find the same kind of thing." Silently, Sally agreed.

They moved along at a quicker pace after that, knowing the two teams had already cleared the area they were moving through toward the house. That, and having Jesse up front, leading the way. He knew the scent of C-4. He could lead them safely and quickly to their objective.

The team halted in the shadow of the barn, within visual distance of their objective. The way into the storm cellar was clear. It made sense if the intent was to lure Pack members down into the cellar and then blow them up. They were about ten yards away from the outdoor entrance to the cellar and Jesse moved closer to Jason for a quick consult.

"Taking the main path inside is a little too obvious for me," Jesse said, motioning toward the double doors that led down into the cellar.

"Agreed." Jason nodded. "What other options do we have?"

Jesse scratched the back of his neck with one hand. His body language said he really didn't want to reveal what he was going to say next.

"There is only one other quick way in, but you're not going to like it." He pointed to the tiny window just visible above the foundation line of the house. "None of us will fit in that window."

"I will." All eyes turned to Sally.

"No," came Jason's adamant reply. "No way."

Sally just looked at him. "Seriously? You know I'm the only option unless you all want to get blown up together. Let me at least reconnoiter. I'll stick my head in the window, take a look around, and let you know what I find. It could save us all a lot of trouble in the long run."

Jason's mouth thinned to a tight line. "I don't like this. Not one bit," he ground out.

"I know." She placed her open palm above his heart. "And don't think I'm not touched by your concern for my well being, but this is the kind of thing I was born for, Jason. This is the kind of thing I do every day. You can't protect me from myself, or my calling. I can do this. I can help you, your Pack, and that boy in there." She nodded toward the basement and his eyes followed her gesture. She could read the pain in his gaze, the worry, the way he was torn. It touched something deep down inside her.

She realized in that moment that she didn't want to see him go down those steps either. Into certain danger. Into a blast zone. But he would. And she'd be right there with him. Walking into peril because somebody else—somebody weaker and dependent on them for protection—needed their help. It was what they'd both been born to do.

She reached up and gave him a quick kiss. "I'll be all right. Let's do this together," she cajoled. "Admit it, you need me."

He squeezed her hand as his gaze met hers. The ghost of a smile moved around his lips. "That I do," he agreed quietly.

The moment held for a heartbeat. Two. And then he was all business once more. A man in fatigues materialized at their side. It was the one he'd called Len.

"The perimeter is secure. We found another quarter-pound of charges on our side, near the foundation. That leaves about a half-pound unaccounted for, which I assume is with Jimmy in the basement."

Sally heard the low-voiced report and saw the interest in Len's eyes as he took in how close she stood to his leader. He wasn't unprofessional enough to mention it now, but she was pretty sure gossip would be running rampant once again as soon as everyone was safe.

"All right," Jason sighed heavily. "Sally will peek in the window but only after Jesse sniffs around to be sure it's not wired too." He nodded toward his brother as the others listened to the plan. "She'll relay what she sees so that we can enter the more obvious way." He held his hand out to Len and the man gave up his earpiece with obvious reluctance. Jason handed it to Sally. "You know how to operate a tactical radio?"

"Of course, though I've never seen one this small." She took the equipment from Jason and though she would've preferred a new earpiece, beggars couldn't be choosers. She inserted the little device into her ear and learned the controls.

Jason explained briefly how it worked, though the mic would remain in the *on* position for the time being. Jason wanted to hear every breath she took while she was out of his sight apparently.

"I can't get more than my arm in there." Jesse spoke in a low tone, looking from the small window to Sally. "But you're tiny enough to fit. See the way it juts out from the foundation? I put a snake camera through there earlier and spotted Jimmy tied to a chair to the right. Stairs to the left where we'll enter once we have your intel. Jim won't be able to see you unless you stick your head past the foundation, about a foot inside. Talk to him. Tell him to hang tight and not to move until we say it's okay. Tell him we're coming to get him."

"Roger that." She nodded. "What if they have ears on in there?" she asked, knowing the kidnappers might've left a microphone or camera in the basement with the kid so they could hear or see when help arrived.

Jesse held up a small black box. "Jammer goes on the minute you go in, just in case."

The plan was sound though there was always the possibility the bad guys could blow the charges remotely at the first sign of snow on their monitors. It was a chance they'd have to take.

Jesse went ahead to check the window and pop it open. If it was wired in any way, he would be taking the brunt of it. Sally didn't like it, but she knew Jason's overprotective instincts were being pushed to their limit as it was. When Jesse gave the all clear, Sally made her move. Jason let her go with only a last lingering look and an admonition to be careful.

Sally crept up to the window where Jesse waited. She kept her eye on the house. There were windows in the house above. She didn't think any of the other kidnappers would be foolish enough to stay in the house after they'd wired it to blow, but who could tell. So far, she wasn't impressed by their intelligence.

"Perimeter's clear. Best I could tell, the basement is clear, but I can't be absolute on that. We're keeping everyone back from the house, just in case they're watching. They want to take out as many of us as they can in one shot," Jesse reminded her. "Better to keep us scattered instead of congregating in one big group. Tell us what you see when you get inside. The Alpha and my men will hear you. We only have a couple of these tac radios to go around." A ghost of a smile graced his lips as she nodded and he moved away to give her room to work her way inside the small opening.

It was a tight squeeze, but she managed to get her head and shoulders inside the tiny window, her hands braced on the sill beneath her. The light was dim inside the dusty basement. Even darker than it was outside, with no moon. Her eyes were sharp though and they adjusted. Turning her head to the left, she could make out the old wooden steps leading down into the cellar. To the right, she could see the outline of a human-shaped figure, tied to a chair. A quick look around didn't reveal anyone else.

"Jimmy?" she whispered, just loud enough for the boy's

enhanced senses to pick up. She saw his head lift and the glistening reflections that had to be his eyes turned toward her. "I'm Sally. Nod if you understand."

A slight movement in the darkness answered her question. They had established contact.

"Are you alone down there?"

Again came the brief nod. He was alone, but why didn't he answer in words?

"Can you talk?"

He shook his head and she tried to peer through the darkness to see what might be preventing him from speaking. She thought she detected a faint line of what could be duct tape over the kid's mouth. Damn.

"Is that tape over your mouth, Jimmy?"

He nodded again. Mindful of the microphone attached to her earpiece, she reported what she saw.

"There appears to be duct tape over his mouth and he says he's alone." She made a decision. "I can't see enough from here. I'm going in."

She wiggled her way into the window, ignoring the curses and admonitions that sounded in her ear. Jason wasn't pleased and he made it well known.

"Give it a rest, Alpha," she said finally as she hit the dirt floor on the other side of the window. "Clear the channel so we can get some work done. I'm in."

"We're going to discuss this later, Sally," Jason promised in a tense tone. "What do you see?"

Good. He was back on target. They needed to get this job done. The quicker, the better.

She moved carefully through the darkness to Jimmy's side, mindful of where she stepped. The whole place had the potential for being booby-trapped but she didn't see any signs so far. Only when she got close to the kid did she realize what they had done.

"Jimmy is okay, but there's a vest strapped to him. I think I just found the other half of that stuff we were looking for." She didn't want to alarm the boy if he didn't yet realize he was wearing a bomb.

"Son of a bitch," Jason cursed.

"It's okay. Keep him calm," Jesse said in that quiet, steady voice of his. "Tell him not to move."

"I'm going to remove the duct tape," she said quietly as she bent over the youngster. "Try not to move, Jimmy. This might hurt your face a bit, but you'll be able to talk to me and I want you to know that I am talking to some people that can help. See in my ear? That's a little headset. They can hear us." She talked while she worked the duct tape free as gently as she could, hoping to distract him from the pain. It seemed to be working. Jimmy held perfectly still, the little trouper.

"Okay. Duct tape is almost off. How are you doing, Jim?" She tried to sound positive though, truth be told, she was scared of the bomb this poor kid wore strapped to his chest.

"I'm okay. The vest is a bomb," he whispered, surprising her. He had known and still kept his cool. Maybe werewolf kids were tougher than others. Or maybe it was just this one.

"I know." She met his gaze, amazed by the courage the youngster demonstrated. "But it's okay. Just sit tight and we'll figure out how to get it off you without blowing us all up."

"We're coming in," Jason warned in her ear. She spun to examine the entryway.

"Hold that thought," she cautioned him over the radio. "Something's funny with the stairs."

"Those two men were wiring something under the stairs for

hours today," Jimmy confirmed. "And something's buried at the bottom, under the dirt."

"Thanks, Jim. That's really good to know. Sit tight and don't move. I'm going to get a closer look," Sally praised the boy as she moved closer to examine what might be under the dirt. Probing cautiously, she found the edges of a metal plate.

"I think it's a pressure plate of some kind. Same on the stairs. I don't want to touch anything but I can find the outline of the edges under the dirt. The doors look clear from what I can see. I think they wanted to catch you on the stairs." She looked for wires or other kinds of triggers on the doors and didn't see anything that looked suspicious.

"I'm going to open the door to your left. That would be the one on the south side," Jesse clarified. "I'll do it slowly. Tell me if you see anything inside like a trip wire or magnetic trigger or anything."

"Roger. Anytime you're ready." She gave him the go ahead. A second later, the left side of the double door lifted a fraction of an inch.

"I don't see anything. Keep going." They were on the clock and the agonizing slowness with which they had to move was making her antsy. "I hope one of your guys knows explosives really well."

She didn't say exactly why, but the implication was clear enough. That bomb vest was unlike anything she'd ever seen. Of course, she'd never dealt with a bomb of any kind before. Luckily, that kind of thing had gone beyond her purview for most of her career.

"Don't worry." Jesse's tone was reassuring. It spoke of experience. "I've seen bomb vests before. Just keep him calm."

She glanced back over her shoulder. "Jim's doing okay. He knows not to move. You guys should be proud of him. He's a credit to his Pack." Nothing like a little positive reinforcement to help a kid keep his cool. But from the quick glance at Jimmy, he was holding his calm remarkably well. He really was a smart kid.

The door rose an inch or so in painstaking slow motion. She examined every centimeter of the surface but didn't see any kind of booby trap.

"You're okay. Nothing's attached to the door either on the edges or on the surface of the panel."

"How about the hinges?" Jason asked sharply in her ear.

"Hinges are good too. I'd say you can open it all the way. The stairs are the problem and the pressure plate at the bottom." She didn't know how the guys were going to get around that.

The door opened more quickly, but with deliberation. She continued to watch for any sign of a trap. She found nothing obvious on the door. It seemed like forever but was probably less than half a minute before she could see Jesse's face through the widening crack in the door. Jason was right behind him. It was a relief to see Jason's worried face, but she didn't like knowing he was walking into a basement with a bomb anymore than he probably had liked her going down there.

Well, if the worst happened, at least they'd be together.

That thought made her brain stop working for a split second. When had this man—this werewolf—come to mean so much to her?

When, exactly, had she fallen in love with him?

She didn't know for sure, but she definitely felt the emotion welling deep in her heart. She loved him. There was no denying it now.

But the situation was hopeless. He was a werewolf. She was some kind of human-nymph hybrid, with a life of her own back in San Francisco.

And a live bomb not more than ten feet away.

That thought sort of put things back in perspective. First things first. They had to deal with the bomb and save the boy. Then they had some so-called *hunters* to track down. Safety and justice had to come first. Her problematic love life could wait a bit.

The door was fully open. It was wide enough for the men to come through one at a time. These old cellars had been built strong and tough, with doors wide enough for farm equipment to come through. Originally, this room had probably been a root cellar where crops like potatoes and onions were stored through the winter. It had been reinforced to act as a storm cellar at some point, but the wide doors remained.

"Is that the edge of the pressure plate?" Jesse asked, peering in and looking at her handiwork.

She'd drawn a line in the dirt around the edges of the plate with her finger, leaving at least an inch of margin to avoid touching the plate. She wasn't sure how sensitive it was, though chances were it would require a person's full weight on it to go off. No sense taking a chance that a stray mouse or rat scurrying through the cellar would set it off.

"Yeah," she confirmed. "Can you see the line I drew around it?"

"Got it. Stand back." Jesse stood, hefted his gun and simply jumped.

Holy shit. She'd never seen a human being jump that far without even taking a moment to back up and start at a run. He made it look like he was just hopping over a line, when in fact, he'd covered a good fifteen feet horizontally. Sally was impressed.

And he'd done it while holding onto his assault rifle. He wasn't even off balance. He'd landed on both feet, happy as a clam. He moved forward and a moment later, Jason landed in exactly the same spot. Same way. Damn. It wasn't just a soldier thing. Jason was every bit as nimble as his older, more worldly brother.

"You guys don't mess around, do you?" Sally stood off to one side as Jesse busied himself examining Jimmy and the vest. He didn't touch, just gave a visual inspection that was very detailed and competent. Jesse didn't give a hint to his thoughts until a tiny smile quirked one corner of his mouth.

While she watched Jimmy and the soldier, Jason sniffed out every inch of the cellar, returning to her to stand close behind her. He didn't put his arms around her. He didn't impede either of their abilities to move quickly. He just surrounded her with his warmth, letting her know he was there, strong and tall behind her. His head dipped to place a quick kiss on her temple, but that was it. When she glanced over her shoulder, he was watching Jimmy and Jesse with an intense expression.

Jesse looked up and signaled with one hand to his brother. Jason moved out from behind her.

"What do you need?"

"A steady hand and small fingers." Both men turned their gazes on Sally. Jason didn't look happy, but he was already resigned to her involvement in this. Jesse, by contrast, seemed slightly amused.

She stepped closer to them. "How can I help?"

Chapter Twelve

"I'm going to be disconnecting these wires in the pocket of the vest. See?" He showed her what he meant. It was a tight squeeze for his big hands. "It's vital that none of the bare ends touch each other or anything conductive while I do this. That's where your dainty digits come in. I want you to get your fingers inside that little flap and keep the wires apart as I disconnect each one in sequence."

She examined the pocket again and tried to memorize the layout. "Okay. I'm ready." She steeled herself mentally. She looked up at Jimmy and took one of his hands in her free hand. She wasn't sure if she was reassuring him or herself. Either way, the contact helped steady her. This youngster, and his Pack, was what she was fighting for here. It did good to remember that.

In the background, she could dimly hear Jason giving orders over his headset and his cell phone as he kept his eyes trained on them. She knew there were others outside the cellar, keeping watch over the grounds. And still others in the trees, guarding the perimeter.

But where were the other hunters? They'd dealt with one. There were three more to find once they had the boy safe. Plus the guy who'd purchased this property for them. He had to be dealt with too.

"Here goes. I'm going to put the first one between your pinky and ring finger," Jesse warned a moment before he acted. Her hand sat in the pocket, alongside his two fingers that manipulated the deadly wires. It was a tight fit, but it was safer this way. His hands were just too big to do both the disconnecting and separating.

He passed the first wire to her and she closed her fingers on it, feeling the sharp ends of the metal stick into the soft skin between her fingers. It hurt a bit, but the pain was nothing compared to being blown up. She grit her teeth and nodded at Jesse when he started on the second wire.

"I'll put this one between your ring finger and middle," he told her. "One more to go for you, then the last connection and it'll be disarmed. We're almost there."

"How are you doing, Jim?" Sally asked the boy. He barely seemed to be breathing and his eyes were as wide as saucers as he did his best not to move.

"I'm okay," he squeaked. Jesse spared him a quick glance and a lopsided smile.

"You're doing great, kid. Just two more and you're home free. Concentrate now."

"Yes, sir, major," the boy replied.

Now that was interesting. Jimmy referred to Jesse Moore by rank. Very interesting, indeed.

"Third one coming at you, detective. It'll go between your index and middle fingers."

He suited actions to words and she did her best not to move a muscle. The wires were separated by her fingers. One false move before he got that last connection severed and there'd be hell to pay.

Jesse moved slowly but with confidence. Their hands brushed in an impersonal way as he reached for the last of the wires. She caught her breath when the motion of his fingers inside the pocket threatened her grip. Jason hovered, having shut his phone and narrowed his eyes. She met his gaze and held it while his brother finished the nerve-wracking work of disarming the bomb.

She felt the fourth and final wire come free against the tips of her fingers but she waited for Jesse to give her the all clear before relaxing her grip on the other three. He removed his hand from the pocket, pulling the wire he still held out with him.

"Hang tight, detective. Just to be certain..."

He pulled a roll of black electrical tape out of one of the many pockets on his fatigues and ripped off a small piece with his teeth. He wrapped the bare end of the wire so that no bare metal was showing anywhere along its length. It was fully insulated when he asked for each of the wires she held in turn. One by one, he taped those up too. There was no way they could even accidentally touch by the time he was done.

She retrieved her hand from the pocket, but Jimmy had a death grip on her the other hand. She examined the vest to see how it was closed over his chest. It had plastic clips that could be undone with a simple snap.

"Can we take this off him now?" she asked Jesse, just to be sure.

"Allow me," he said, only half jokingly.

Jesse went slowly, examining each step before he took it, removing the nylon webbing that was packed with high explosives. She didn't breathe easy until the repulsive thing had been slipped off Jimmy's shoulders. Jesse stood, putting the vest aside for a moment while he took a close look at the way Jimmy was bound to the chair.

"No more pressure plates, thank the Lady," Jesse commented, cutting through the cable ties that attached Jimmy's legs to the legs of the chair with a knife he'd taken from another pocket. "Can you stand, kiddo?" he asked Jimmy gently when he'd been cut free.

Jimmy tried his best, but his legs were a little wobbly from sitting in one position for so long. The poor kid must've been down there for hours, Sally realized. Jesse took pity on him and hoisted the kid into his arms, taking him over to the window through which Sally had entered. Jimmy was still small enough to fit through there easily. It was the safest way out considering the pressure plates by the stairs might still trigger something else besides the bomb in the vest.

Jason moved closer, taking her in his arms for a quick, brutal kiss that had her breathing hard before he lifted his lips from hers. It was a kiss of relief, of passion, of possession. It made her hot.

"I know this isn't the right time or place..."

"It's also an open channel," Jesse's voice in their ears reminded them. "Unless you want the rest of us privy to your private affairs."

"Damn, bro," Jason groused. "Give me a break."

Jesse's chuckle prefaced his words. "Get out of the danger zone, Jase, then I'll cut you some slack."

Jason sighed. "Good point."

Sally found herself on the verge of a giggle. She liked the camaraderie between the brothers.

"Can you go out the way you came in, sweetheart?" Jason asked her gently, his finger stroking her cheek with a tenderness that almost stole her breath.

"Yeah, just give me a boost."

They moved together toward the tiny window. His big palms shaped her ass as he boosted her upward. If his hands lingered just a little too long, she wouldn't complain. She crawled her way out of the little hole, surprised to find Jason's hands waiting to help her when she was most of the way through. He must've leapt out of the basement the same way his brother had. Being a werewolf certainly had its advantages at times.

Jason pulled her the rest of the way clear and then they were loping off together into the darkness, away from potential danger.

They met Jesse by the wall of the barn. By now, the wolves had been all over the property. Only that one hunter had been found and dealt with. She didn't want to ask too many questions about what they'd done with him, but she figured he would never be bothering anyone ever again.

"Good work in there, detective," Jesse complimented her as he came up beside them in the darkness.

Arlo and Len were right behind him, appearing as if out of the mist that began to coat the bare ground in the darkness. Fog would be rolling in before the night was through, if she didn't miss her guess. She could see a few wolves prowling through the low hanging mist and a shiver went up her spine. Jason's phone vibrated and he moved only slightly away to answer it.

"Thanks. You weren't so shabby yourself. I'm just glad you knew how to disarm that thing."

"Any of us could do it." He gestured toward the other two men who were dressed much the same was he was—as professional soldiers with well-worn gear.

"Can I ask a personal question? You don't have to answer if you don't want to." Jason was still busy with his call and her curiosity was getting the better of her.

"Fair enough," he agreed to her terms.

"You three are obviously soldiers. Is that why you stay in human form? Before tonight I would've thought werewolves would choose the sharper senses, not to mention claws, of your wolf form for hunting."

Jesse shrugged. "You spend enough time fighting as a

Bianca D'Arc

human, you get used to the dulled senses. They're still much sharper than other people's. And having opposable thumbs has its compensations, not to mention my beloved MP-5." He caressed his assault rifle lovingly and she grinned as the other men chuckled.

"Yeah, I thought it might be something like that. Thanks for answering my nosy question. Being a cop, I'm sort of used to giving interrogations. It's one of my biggest faults—wanting to know the *why* of everything." Jason seemed tense beside her as he drew his call to an end. Something was going on. "Here..." she returned the tactical radio to its owner, "...you probably need this back. Thanks for the loan."

Jason's phone snapped shut and all eyes turned to him.

"The Master checked the other location. It was clean. He then caught scent of the hunters. The two younger men have fled. They're already out of the county, heading east on the interstate. Jess, do you think you and your team are up for a manhunt?"

"We'll handle it." Jesse didn't even have to look at his guys, though Arlo and Len were both nodding. A cold look came into Jesse's eyes that sent a chill down Sally's spine.

"Good." Jason nodded at his brother. "Call Dmitri for his intel. He's expecting your call. And Jesse?" Jason paused, his expression grim. "If they're *Venifucus*, they'll have to die. Get on the road, but stay in touch by phone. I want frequent updates. Let's see if we can follow them to their source. I'll have to report all this to the Lords."

"What about the missing man? There were four hunters. We've only accounted for three," Sally reminded him as Jesse and his guys prepared to leave.

"Dmitri spotted him in the woods about a mile from the Pack house." That news brought the other men up short. "Don't worry. The house is empty. I'll handle it."

206

"I'm leaving Freddy here to dismantle the devices and save the C-4. You never know when it might come in handy." Jesse threw her a wink and she pretended not to listen as they discussed keeping the highly illegal fireworks.

She also wondered who the heck Freddy was. She'd only seen the three men in fatigues, but there could've been more. Arlo and Len had only made themselves visible when Jason tapped them to head the two other strike teams. Before that, they'd been ghosts in the background. Come to think of it, there could've been quite a few men with them who'd been dressed the same way. They were so good at camouflage, they were just barely noticeable. Scary. And reassuring too.

"Good. Check-ins on the hour. Leave a message if I don't pick up. And Jesse..." he grabbed his brother's forearm, "...be careful."

"You too, bro."

With nods all around, the three soldiers faded into the darkness. In the blink of an eye, they were no longer visible. Damn. Sally was glad she was on their side.

Jason knew what he had to do. It wasn't going to be pretty, but he had an intruder on Pack land. An intruder who had already shot a young girl and had managed to capture Jimmy and wire him and a house with explosives. Not to mention the fact that he had pointed a rifle at Sally. His mate.

Jason knew for certain now that what he'd suspected all along was true. Sally was the one for him. The only woman who could be his perfect match, his partner, his love. She was his mate. The wolf in him stood up and howled when he'd first caught her scent. When she had been in danger, the wolf's rage had been off the charts. Even when he had her in his arms—in the half-wolf fighting form—he'd refused to relinquish her to anyone. Not even trusted members of his Pack.

Bianca D'Arc

She was too important to him. Too vital to his continued happiness. Without her, he didn't think he would be able to go on. She was quickly becoming the center of his universe.

He'd tried to fight against it. She was human. Weak. Her wolf genes were too far back to really make a difference. Then he'd discovered her magic. He'd begun to feel better about their involvement. She had some protections of her own. She might be able to hold her own among his Pack.

He hadn't even declared himself, and she'd been threatened and forced into a confrontation at the Pack house. The way she handled it made him proud. An Alpha wolf female couldn't have done better. Only then did he start to think she might be able to earn the respect of the Pack. That was essential if he planned to continue as Alpha.

If the Pack wouldn't accept her, he had already decided to step down. Jesse—no matter how much he complained about it—could have the job. He should've had it from the beginning. But something had changed him—damaged him—in the wars he'd fought. Something inside had curled in upon itself to the point where only his fellow soldiers could understand him.

Jason would've handed the leadership over to his brother with no dispute. No contest. The sad truth was, Jesse didn't want it.

If push came to shove and the Pack refused to accept Sally, Jesse would find himself in a position Jason had been protecting him from. He'd have to take on the role of Alpha. He was the only male strong enough both physically and mentally to handle the responsibility. The Pack loved him. They respected him. They would take to him easily as Alpha. Screw him if he didn't want it. He'd have to take it for the good of the Pack if they didn't like Jason's choice in a mate.

The Fates had spoken. Sally was it for him. She didn't know it yet, but wherever she went, he would go too. If she

208

didn't agree to be with him here, he'd follow her—to the ends of the earth if necessary—and do his best to convince her to marry him, live with him wherever she chose, and be his mate for the rest of their naturally long lives.

He hadn't figured out how to broach the subject yet, but his decision was made. He just had to find the right time to tell her how he felt and ask her that all important question. The mere thought of it made his mouth go dry with nerves. Did she feel the same? Could she? She only had a little wolf in her and he had no idea how humans, or nymphs for that matter, chose their mates.

With wolves, it was instinctual. Her scent, her form, her voice and the things she said and did, the way she moved...all of it combined to let him know that she was his perfect match. He supposed, if he had to think about it, her scent had captured him first. He'd known when he breathed her in for the first time that she was special. So very special. He'd been entranced from that moment on and as he got to know her, he only liked her more. Her allure was undeniable. Her intellect matched his own. She was smart, funny, sexy as hell, and all his. Whether she knew it yet or not.

She looked at him now expectantly and it was all he could do not to drag her into his arms. What a time to realize he was hopelessly in love.

Jason settled for a quick, hard kiss before he settled down to business. There was still at least one more dangerous man out there, in the woods, gunning for his people. That old bastard who'd been setting up the tree stand had to be stopped before Jason could turn his full attention to matters of the heart.

"What was that for?" she asked breathlessly when he released her.

"For not getting us all blown up," he answered flippantly.

He wasn't about to reveal the deeper thoughts in his mind at the moment. For one thing, there were too many witnesses. When he declared himself, he wanted them to be alone. Preferably in bed, with hours free before them to explore their love—if she did, indeed, love him back. If she didn't, it would be better to have privacy in which to lick his wounds, and try desperately to convince her otherwise.

"I'll have to not get us all blown up more often then." She smiled at him, not knowing the thoughts racing through his mind. She would soon. That he promised himself. "Now, what about that fourth hunter? How do you want to do this?" she prompted him.

"Alone, preferably," he answered bluntly. He really didn't want to put her in danger any more than he already had.

"Sorry. As the song goes, you can't always get what you want. That man is armed, dangerous, and completely off his rocker. You know I can handle the armed part. Seems to me, you just sent your best weapons experts away. I think you'll need me. To watch your back, if nothing else."

Though he'd rather see her well away from danger, he also perversely wanted her with him. At his side. Fighting together. Where he could keep an eye on her. Where he could protect her. It didn't make a lot of sense, but sometimes the wolf's instincts went contrary to the man's intellect.

"All right." He made his decision and gave the signal for the rest of the Pack's fighters who were present to move closer for instruction.

They formed a loose circle around him and Sally. Interesting. They saw her as separate from them, otherwise they would have included her in the circle around him. Whether that was because she was not a wolf, or because they perceived her as being equal in rank, or perhaps part of his authority as Alpha, remained to be seen. Still, it was an intriguing development. One he hadn't anticipated.

"The last man we need to deal with tonight is closing in on the Pack house. He doesn't know it's empty. He's hunting werewolves and he knows a lot about our Pack. He may even know some of you on sight. He's been stalking us for a while and we honestly don't know how much he knows. I can guarantee it's more than he should. He knows what we are and where we live. He knows I'm your Alpha and he knows how to kill us."

"What do you mean?" Sally asked, looking up at him with those big brown eyes of hers that made him want to kiss her. Not the right place or time, but he still felt the undeniable pull of her attraction.

"Samuels had silver bullets in his rifle tonight." A murmur of anger went through the Pack members gathered all around.

"But the bullet that hit Colleen wasn't silver, right?"

"No, thank the Lady," he confirmed. "When we get hit with silver, it's like a human getting hit by a regular bullet. It hurts and it doesn't heal the way we're used to healing. In fact, it's a little worse. You've got a bullet wound that can't be easily healed, plus the poison. It's not a good combination."

"Wow." She looked like she was thinking hard. "So the fact that they were using normal ammunition when they went after Colleen means they were just trying to slow her down, not necessarily kill her outright."

"She was probably their first choice for a kidnapping victim. When she escaped, they went after Jimmy instead. Either way, they intended to kill a child. And as many Pack members as they could lure in. A bomb works just as well at killing werewolves as normal people. Rip us into enough pieces and even our healing powers won't be able to put Humpty Dumpty back together again."

A few of the men snickered at his graveyard humor. He had

to get the plan in motion. Every moment delayed was another moment that bastard had alive. Jason firmed his resolve.

"I want to push him away from the Pack house, if possible. Without putting yourselves in the line of fire, I want you all to herd him toward the bear den. Blood has already been spilled there. I don't want to foul our home woods with this bastard's blood if we don't have to."

Murmurs of assent went around the group. The scent of blood was one of the most powerful to their kind. And the enemy's blood would be spilled that night. Oh, yes, it definitely would.

Chapter Thirteen

"All right, same teams as before. Team 1 will spread out from north to west. Team 2 will do the same from north to east. Start above the ridgeline and work your way down toward the bear den. We don't want him slipping past. Sally and I will come up from the south with you all either herding or leading him toward us. The Master will meet us there. He's hunting with us tonight." Murmurs of interest rose around them.

Jason continued to give orders as Sally watched. Looking at the circle that had formed around them she saw mostly men, but there were a couple women too. She liked that. The protective instinct ran very strong in females of most species. It was only right they be part of the group protecting their own.

They all scattered when Jason gave the word. He led her back toward the road where he'd parked his pickup truck out of sight. A few other vehicles were nearby so it wasn't until they were both sealed in the cab that they were truly alone.

Jason started the truck and headed down the road in the opposite direction from the majority of the vehicles. As he drove, he began to speak.

"You took about ten years off my life when you went through that window." He didn't look at her in the darkness, staring intently at the road, but she could see his tension in the way he gripped the steering wheel. She didn't know what to say.

"I was the only one who fit."

"I know." He banged one fist on the steering wheel. "If there was any other way, I would've taken it. As it is..." he trailed off.

"As it is, I'm still alive. So is Jimmy. So is everyone who took part in his rescue. I think it was a win all around. Though I will admit, it was a little hairy there for a few minutes."

"You mean when that bastard was trying to rape you?" His tone was harsh. Raw. As if it hurt him to remember that moment.

"Yeah," she agreed quietly. "That was probably the worst moment of the night, if truth be told."

"So far." He seemed to bite off each word.

"Thank you for saving me from him, Jason." Her voice trembled and she did her best to firm her backbone.

It looked like he swallowed a few times before he could speak again.

"We'll talk about it more later. For now, I'm just glad I was there." He cleared his throat and continued to watch the road with a strange intensity as he drove fast down the mountain road. "Be careful of Dmitri." His change of topic caught her off guard.

"How do you mean?"

"Vampires can get a little...difficult...when the bloodlust is upon them. I've never hunted human prey with him and I don't know how he'll react. He's one of the older ones, so I assume he knows how to behave himself. I don't think he would have lasted this long if he hadn't. Still, be wary. Stay close to me when he's around and blood has been shed. Once a bloodletter gets the scent, things can get dangerous real fast."

"You mean Carly could...?" She couldn't bring herself to finish the thought.

"Any of your newly turned friends. You have to be cautious around them all. They're too new at this to really know how to handle all the impulses and instincts coursing through their bodies. I'd hope their link to their partners grounds them enough to shorten the learning curve, but I don't know for sure. For now, just be careful around Dmitri. I don't know how he's going to act when the hunt is on."

"Okay." It was a lot to think about. Not only were they going to be hunting a man who had no compunction about shooting anybody he came across in the woods, but now she'd have to worry that the vampire hunting with them might turn against them when he caught the scent of blood.

She wasn't sure how justice worked in this new world she'd been introduced to, but she had a feeling it was more...um...Biblical...than in her world. More eye for an eye, tooth for a tooth kind of stuff.

Nothing had been said about the man who'd tried to rape her and she hadn't seen any evidence of him since Jason pulled him off her. There'd been some smears of blood on Jason's hands, but nothing to indicate he'd actually killed the man. Yet, the feeling persisted that he had.

Sally didn't mind. A bastard who would commit those kinds of acts against innocent people deserved to die, to her mind. She'd hated the way the human justice system had all too often allowed violent criminals back out on the streets to do it again. Yet she'd sworn to uphold that law and she did so every day when she went to work.

But those laws never took into account things like vampires and werewolves. There was no consideration of penalties for those who could control magic. It was a square peg and round hole kind of situation. She assumed Jason and his people had their own laws and code of ethics. While operating in their world, she'd have to trust them to adhere to them.

"What are you going to do with the hunters once you find them all?"

"The two who kidnapped Jimmy have already decided their own fate." His voice was grim. "The other two? We might let them run for a bit. See where they go. Try to find the source of the danger, if there is one. It'll be up to Jesse. He's better at dealing with covert operations than I am." He turned the vehicle down another road she hadn't been on before. Thirty seconds later, he stopped.

"Where are we going to meet up with Dmitri?"

"Just up ahead." Jason grimaced, scanning the area with annoyance. "I'm going to park the car down here and we'll hike up, okay? Belakov's late. We'll go ahead. He'll have to catch up."

She agreed and hopped out of the truck. The moment her feet touched the ground, she could tell something was wrong. The song in the trees was off. Way off.

"The forest doesn't like him," she said absently, listening hard as Jason came around to her side of the truck, closest to the tree line. "The hunter is back. Oh, God—" She took off running, pausing only to draw her weapon.

Jason easily kept pace with her, touching her arm to get her attention. "What's wrong?"

"He's got Leonora." She paused, turning to him.

"How the hell did he manage that?" Jason seemed astounded by the news.

"She let him capture her. She's got the trees working with her, but I don't think she realizes just how dangerous this really is."

Jason's lips thinned in anger. "Lead the way."

They began running again, slowing only to hide the sounds of their movements. The trees warned her to be quiet and she listened to them. She listened to the voices on the wind too. Leonora's and the man's as well. Leonora sounded remarkably calm. No doubt the trees had told her rescue was on its way.

Sally and Jason slowed to a crawl as they drew near. Leonora and her captor—the eldest of the hunters, Sullivan, who had been in the tree stand—were uphill from their position. Large boulders sticking out from the side of the hill provided cover. Sally understood why Jason had chosen to come up from the south. The terrain was in their favor.

She stopped behind a rock to take a look around. Jason did the same a few yards away. Her gaze met his and she realized how much he was adapting to her ways. He nodded, knowing without words what she had in mind—and vice versa. She'd never had a partner so in tune with her. Probably never would again. It would hurt to leave Jason for so many reasons.

Best not to think about it now. She listened to the song of the leaves. Leonora was just ahead on the side of a small clearing. Sullivan was tying her to a tree. Silly man. Sally almost laughed aloud. Trees were her friends. Leonora would be in good hands bound to one of them.

Sally concentrated and tried to send a message through the saplings above the rock where she hid. *"We're here, grandmother. Help has arrived."*

A moment later, the answer came back from the trees. *"She knows. She will assist. She has a plan."* Sally got the idea that mere rope couldn't keep her bound when there were small branches within reach that could untie knots or saw through bindings.

It was up to Sally and Jason to capture Sullivan's attention to give Leonora time to work her magic on the trees. Sally looked at Jason and he nodded toward the right. She'd take the left. His hand gestures were adamant that she hold back and cover him while he forced the needed confrontation. It was clear to her what he had in mind. He'd distract the man while the women got to safety.

She'd go along with that as far as it went. Sullivan was going down and Sally vowed to be there if Jason needed her help in making that happen. She was all for Leonora getting out

217

of the line of fire, but Sally would watch Jason's back, whether he wanted her there or not. They were a team. The sooner he got that figured out, the better.

Counting down via hand signals, Sally judged their moment to spring their trap by what the trees told her. Jason probably had his own methods of detection—his sensitive werewolf nose and acute hearing were the most likely candidates. When this was all over, she'd like to learn more about how he saw the world. And she wanted to learn all she could from Leonora. That went without saying. They only had to make sure Leonora was still around when all this was said and done so Sally could continue to get to know her magical ancestress.

With a final nod, they were off. Sally felt more than saw Leonora take off into the leafy canopy with an assist from some helpful branches.

Jason went right while Sally went left. Jason would confront the hunter first and if all went well, Sally wouldn't have to intercede at all.

It didn't go well.

Sullivan seemed to be ready for them. He began shooting the moment Jason ran into the clearing. Only superior reflexes and a nearby rock saved Jason from being hit on the initial charge.

Sally fired above the man's head to keep him off balance but Sullivan had his own plans. He was in a niche between two boulders that provided him an annoying amount of cover. Leonora, thank goodness, was nowhere to be seen. Sally knew she watched from above, safe in the tree canopy.

Jason was pinned down opposite her, stuck behind a rock with no other cover nearby.

"I got lots more where those silver beauties came from," Sullivan chided. Silver bullets. Damn.

"Not enough, Sullivan," Sally said from behind the wide old conifer that shielded her and brought her the news on the wind.

The wolves were gathering in a circle around them. They'd stay out of sight unless they were needed, but no matter how many of them it took, Sullivan would not be escaping this night. The Pack was out in force.

"I'll shoot you too, bitch. Just give me a chance," Sullivan yelled.

"Shoot me and you'll go down for shooting a cop. That's serious prison time."

Sullivan laughed at her. "You think I'll do time? You have no idea who you're dealing with. We have connections all over the place, in normal human society and among Others. I'd never spend a day in jail, even if you could catch me before I killed you. One bullet. That's all I need."

"Silver doesn't harm me," she replied, willing him to come out into the open where she could get a clear shot at him.

"I bet bullets will. Step out here and let me see for myself."

"Fat chance. By the way, good work on keeping your prisoner under control. Where'd she go, I wonder?"

For a moment, nothing but curses floated on the wind as Sullivan realized his prisoner was gone. Sally would have laughed if the situation wasn't so dire. The wolves were in true danger from the silver bullets this crazy jerk was firing indiscriminately. She was in danger from the bullets themselves and this guy had what looked like an endless supply in easy reach.

Another thing she noticed. The trees cried out when bullets hit them. Not loud enough for anyone but her—and Leonora, no doubt—to hear, but they were definitely injured by the silver bullets. Sally couldn't let the forest suffer too. The madman had to be stopped as quickly as possible for all concerned.

"Use the power of the forest. Use your magic, granddaughter." Leonora's voice came to her in a whisper of wind that only she could hear.

"How?" she whispered back.

"Bind him," came the simple reply. The trees whispered of their abilities and desires. They instructed her in what she should do.

She placed one hand on the wide trunk of the conifer, connecting herself to the forest. It probably would have been easier for her to touch the tree she wanted to take action, but this would have to do. The maniac could kill her, or Jason, or a member of his Pack at any time. And his silver ammunition was seriously injuring the trees. He had to be stopped.

Murmuring her desire and injecting her own special power into the bark of the tree she touched, she watched with her mind's eye as it was passed along from pine needle to pine needle and leaf to leaf until it arrived at her target. A lovely, pliable willow tree that was right behind the outcropping of rocks where danger hid.

It moved slowly at first, sinuously reaching downward from above and outward from behind. The branches swayed in an invisible wind, guided by Sally's magic into useable shapes. The power gathered and struck without warning, plucking the rifle from Sullivan's hands and hoisting it high up into the tree.

Sullivan went next. Bound at each limb, he was spread-eagled as he was lifted into the air, held in place by a myriad of twined tendrils. A leafy set of manacles that he could not escape. He would not be released until everyone was safe. Only when Sally—or Leonora—wished it.

Sullivan screamed obscenities as Sally stepped into the open. Jason rose from behind the rock and took in the scene, whistling between his teeth. At the low signal, a few of the wolves came into the clearing.

"Damn you to the farthest hell, bitch!" Sullivan ranted. "You and the filthy dog. You'll both burn!"

Sally diverted a small bit of energy to cover Sullivan's mouth, gagging him with another tendril of pliable tree branch. A moment later, Leonora descended from her leafy hiding place to drop gently to the ground, a broad grin on her face.

"Well done, granddaughter." She gave Sally a hug.

"You could have done that at any time. Why'd you wait for me to do it?"

"I wanted to see if you could, for one thing. For another, the Pack needed to see your capabilities. They need to know that you truly are an Alpha female worthy of their respect."

A shot rang out and Leonora clutched her chest. Chaos reigned as wolves scattered and Jason ran at full speed toward where the bullet had originated. Sally grabbed Leonora as she sank to the ground, dragging her to cover as best she could.

Stupid! She'd been stupid to let her guard down. She'd never considered Sullivan might not be alone.

With her concentration blown, Sullivan tumbled from the tree, but she didn't care. Her only concern was for Leonora.

But Sullivan had a new target. Dmitri swooped in from above in time to stop the man from rushing Sally and Leonora with the knife he'd drawn from his boot. It gleamed silver in the night. Sullivan rushed the vampire and the blade slashed downward, missing Dmitri by a mile as time seemed to slow.

Dmitri moved so fast, he was a blur. But he found his target with unerring capacity, dropping Sullivan to the ground several yards away. Sally looked away as Dmitri's fangs ripped into Sullivan's flesh. Wet sounds followed a gurgle, and that was the end of Sullivan's evil.

Sally felt the violence on the air but refused to allow it to distract her again. The immediate threat was gone. Dmitri was finishing him off as Sally cradled Leonora in her arms. Jason was off somewhere with his Pack taking care of the shooter—whoever that was. The bastard. He'd shot her grandmother.

"Leonora. Talk to me. Tell me what to do." She tried to stop the flow of blood, but Leonora's blood was like nothing Sally had ever seen before. It wasn't red. The wound spilled sparkling, clear, sap-like fluid onto the ground as it bled. It smelled of chlorophyll and growing things. Leaves and light. The scent wafted to her, subtle on the night breeze.

"Silver may not harm you, granddaughter, but it doesn't agree with my magic at all," Leonora grumbled in a low voice.

"I lied before. I don't wear silver jewelry. It turns my skin black." Sally babbled as she tried her best to take care of Leonora's wound.

Leonora smiled. "Believe it or not, that's good to hear. It means you have more magic than I thought."

"What can I do for you?"

"You must remove the bullet." Dmitri's voice came from over Sally's shoulder. He'd snuck up on her so silently, she jumped when he spoke. He had a tiny smear of blood on his chin and his eyes were dilated just the slightest bit. Probably signs of the bloodlust Jason had warned her about. "You're the only one among us who is not poisoned by the silver. It might singe you a bit, but I don't believe it will poison you the way it would the wolves or myself."

"I see your point." Sally searched her mind for what little first aid she knew. She dug a small pocketknife out of her pocket. "What about germs? Should I sterilize this?"

"Infection is not a worry. The silver poison that is already spreading through her body is. Time is of the essence." Dmitri sounded worried, which spurred Sally into action.

She pulled the fabric away that she'd used to try to stop the flow of the nymph's sap-like blood. The ground soaked it up like rainwater. Sally could see the silver of the bullet, not too far down inside her flesh.

Gritting her teeth, she dug into the wound as gently as she could, coaxing the bullet out as quickly as her fingers would allow.

"I'm sorry," she mumbled as Leonora's body went rigid on the forest floor. With only a little more effort, the bullet came out.

Leonora's relief was evident almost immediately, but her blood still flowed.

"Put the bullet in your pocket. Best not to litter the forest with something that could harm our furry friends," Dmitri advised. Sally saw the merit in his words and put the dully gleaming bullet away.

"Such a small thing to cause so much harm." She looked from Leonora to Dmitri. "What now? She's still bleeding and I can't seem to get it to stop."

Dmitri crouched on Leonora's other side, across from Sally. He took her hand and smiled gently at the bleeding nymph.

"So it is true that dryads bleed tree sap. I've always wondered." His teasing words brought a faint smile to Leonora's face, though her energy was fading.

"Of course you have, old friend. But it is too magical for the likes of you. If you're tempted to taste, go slow. It could change you for all time."

"What can we do for you now, sweetling?" Dmitri was so tender with Leonora, it brought a tear to Sally's eye. Could Leonora be dying? Is that why the ancient vampire was being so kind to her?

Sally wouldn't stand for it. Not when she'd finally found her. Sally had lost enough people in her life. She wasn't about to lose the only grandmother she'd ever known.

Sally called on her power as she'd never done before.

Wind sang through the leaves, whipping the forest into action. The branches of the willow under which they sat closed in around them, forming a canopy. A living, breathing, leafy green canopy in the night that blocked out almost everything. Only Dmitri and Sally hovered within, Leonora between them.

"I think your granddaughter is unwilling to let you travel beyond this realm just yet, my friend." Dmitri's eyes blazed encouragement in the night. An unearthly light surrounded them, painting each living thing within the dome of the tree in a hazy glow. Dmitri was outlined in red, Leonora in the purest golden green, while Sally's light was more toward the muddy end of the spectrum, a sort of olive green that leaned heavily toward brown. It was darker than Leonora's golden light, but it was no less powerful.

"Her light is that of the earth itself," Leonora whispered, her gaze taking in the magic Sally had called with what looked like pride. "It can heal me, but not quickly and not alone."

"Tell me what else I need to keep you here, grandmother," Sally pleaded. "I'll do everything I can. Just tell me how. I know so little of my heritage."

"And yet you've learned so much," Leonora said. Her gaze was calmer now as the bleeding began to slow. "This willow will protect me while you gather the necessary people."

"People?" Sally was confused.

"Your tree, my dear. You must find your sister and cousins. It will take a blending of all their magics with yours to bring me back. I can heal with help of the forest alone, but it would take many decades. If you can find your relatives and bring them here, together you could augment the power of this wood many times over. For now, you must put me in the care of the forest. The willow will anchor my body to this realm while it heals. My spirit will float on the edge of this realm and the next while you fulfill your quest."

"Will you take the gift of my blood to help sustain you while you rest, Leonora?" Dmitri asked in a gentle voice. "Fair warning though—it could change you for all time as well." He winked at Leonora, bringing a faint smile to her face. One of her eyebrows quirked upward.

"An even exchange then? It's probably about time we expanded the bounds of our friendship to include that kind of trust."

Dmitri nodded gravely, the smile still touching his lips. "As you say, my old friend. I have long valued your presence in the woods near where I have made my home."

"And your empire," Leonora added with a weak grin. She was losing energy. Whatever they were going to do, they had to do it now.

Sally's power flared along with her worry. That seemed to get Dmitri's attention.

"Right. Let's get on with this so you can rest more easily," he said, his gaze moving from Leonora's to Sally's.

Lifting one hand, he shifted the shape of just one finger into a wickedly sharp claw. Sally felt the rush of magic in a way she'd never before experienced and saw the glow of red increase around his hand as he willed it to change. Before she knew what he intended, he used the claw to slash a fine line over his other wrist. Blood welled and he was careful to drip it directly into the hole in Leonora's shoulder.

From about twelve inches above, he dripped his dark red blood into the wound as Sally watched, dumbfounded by his actions. Leonora wasn't complaining, other than an initial hiss as the first drop found its way into the wound and sent up a sizzle as it began to react with her own chemistry. Sally had to trust that these two magical creatures knew what they were doing. She was totally out of her depth where vampire blood was concerned.

Dmitri stopped at exactly thirteen drops. He removed his hand from over Leonora's body and licked at the remainder of blood on his wrist. When Sally looked at his wrist, the wound was gone. Not even a faint scar remained. Amazing.

Leonora looked a little better too. Her wound was bubbling with pinkish light as her magical blood met and was aided by Dmitri's. She stopped fading though she was quite obviously still in bad shape. Still, the effects of the poison seemed to have stopped in their tracks. She wasn't getting any worse, which was a huge relief.

"You'll understand my inclination to wait until you are completely healed of the poison to complete our exchange." Dmitri bowed his head in a formal manner.

Leonora nodded slightly, a faint smile hovering over her lips. "I look forward to the day I can fulfill my promise. For now, I must rest in the wildwood."

"And I will guard over your resting place by night, my old friend."

"The wolves will watch by day," Sally said without thinking.

"Already you speak on behalf of your mate?" Leonora seemed amused.

"I—"

"Don't worry. I approve wholeheartedly of Jason Moore. He's nothing like the creature my Marisol chose to wed. He's a good and honest man and you will do well with him. He will also support you on your quest, which could be useful. It's a good match."

Sally was speechless. She and Jason...well, it didn't bear thinking about at the moment. It was too complicated.

"You will find your way," Leonora assured her. The woman

amazed her. She was at death's door and here she was reassuring Sally. Leonora was a trooper, that was for sure.

A tear tracked down Sally's face to splash onto the leaves that were hovering close. It sparked silver off the leaf. Only then did Sally realize the willow was weeping. It rained dew from its leaves onto Leonora, though none of the three within the circle of the willow's embrace were wet.

The silver sparkling dew was life. The tree's life force. Perhaps the whole forest's life force, being given to the nymph who loved and sustained this portion of the wildwood. The dew landed on Leonora and her body soaked it in. The dew seemed to be somehow preparing her body for what would come next, if Sally understood what it was Leonora wanted her to do.

"It's nearly time." Leonora's voice was fading as her own power ebbed. "You must deliver me into the willow. It will hold my body safe for as long as it takes."

Dmitri pressed a quick kiss to Leonora's hand, then retreated a short distance, not touching her. He nodded toward Sally and she took his signal to mean that it was show time. Now if only she knew what it was she was supposed to do.

"Speak the willow's name in your heart," Leonora coached. Sally held tight to her hand, disliking the way her skin had cooled. Leonora was in bad shape. "Ask for its help. Send it your power to help it do what it must."

Sally tried to do as Leonora instructed. She searched for and found the willow's name. How? She had no idea. She only knew that when she sent her thoughts spiraling toward the tree, she knew exactly what to say. It was as if some ancient instinct kicked in and took her by the hand, showing her what to do.

Sally kissed Leonora's hand much as Dmitri had done, then moved back a few inches to let the willow do what it would. It was in the tree's hands—or limbs, rather—now. As she

227

watched, feeding her power to the pliable branches of the willow tree, small tendrils snaked down from above and wove a complex pattern under Leonora's pale body. In no time at all, it had woven a sort of basket around her. Sally and Dmitri stood as one when the branches lifted Leonora off the ground, raising her to a standing position before pulling her into the heart of the tree.

She blended with the trunk in a flash of golden, green and pulsing brown light. A blend of her magic and Sally's, along with a hint of the blood red essence that Sally now recognized as Dmitri. The power flared to a high intensity. It was so bright, Sally had to look away. When she turned back, Leonora was inside the tree, standing in the trunk as it slowly faded from crystal clear, to translucent, then to opaque.

Before she lost sight of her completely, Leonora smiled. She looked stronger. Happy in the embrace of the tree's ancient wisdom. Sally had touched its heart, its mind, and knew it would hold her safe for as long as it took, sustaining Leonora's life with its own. With the life of the very forest around it, if necessary. It was her guardian now, and honored to be so.

"I'll miss you, Leonora," she whispered tearfully.

"I'll be with you in spirit, granddaughter." Sally shook her head, surprised to hear the voice in her mind. *"Now go settle things with your mate. I'll be around, but not often. It's taxing to communicate this way, so don't expect me to be here all the time. Just know that if you need me, I can be with you in your thoughts."*

"Wow."

Leonora's tinkling laughter faded as did the touch on Sally's mind as the willow returned to its normal appearance. With a last word of thanks to the tree that would give its life for Leonora's if necessary, she drew her newfound power back. The glow of magic faded and the forest returned to normal. The leaves parted as if driven by the wind, and a circle of wolves was waiting for her.

Dmitri faded into nothingness, mist evaporating before anyone could see him. Leaving her to face the music all alone. Nice.

Chapter Fourteen

"Where is she?" Jason stepped forward, facing Sally, his gaze speaking of his fear that Leonora had indeed died.

"She rests inside this willow until I can gather her granddaughters and bring her back."

"Then our Pack will guard her resting place." Jason didn't let her down.

"Good. Because I already sort of promised her you would." Sally tried to brazen it out but ended up smiling sheepishly, wondering if she'd overstepped some sort of magical boundary.

Jason surprised her by yanking her into his arms for a fierce kiss. It was a possessive kiss. In front of the toughest wolves in his Pack.

Instead of jeering and complaints, Sally was shocked to hear wolf howls in the night. Joyous wolf howls.

When Jason let her up for air, he turned her in his arms to meet the gazes of the main fighting force in his Pack. Some were in human form. Many were wolves. Quite a few of them were bloodstained, but it didn't seem to be their blood. Why that sent a rush of relief through her, she'd question later.

"They all saw your power, sweetheart," Jason whispered in her ear. "They'll accept you as their Alpha female." She turned in his arms to look at him. He looked suddenly uncertain. "If you'll accept me, that is."

"Accept you?"

"As your mate. Your husband. For as many years as the Lady grants us. After all, wolves mate for life." He went down on one knee and the howls stopped as the whole forest seemed to hold its breath. "Will you be mine, Sally?"

Her heart felt like it would burst with joy. The emotional roller coaster of the day had just taken her to an all-new height.

"Are you sure?"

"Surer than I've ever been about anything. I love you, Sally."

"Oh, Jason." She choked up. Reaching down with one hand, she cupped his cheek. He was so tall, even kneeling he was close to her eye level. "I love you too."

She closed the space between them and kissed him with all the love blossoming inside her. The howls resumed at an even louder volume. She heard it only dimly as Jason stood, lifting her into his arms as he continued to dominate her mouth in the most thrilling kiss she'd ever received. She'd instigated it, but he'd taken control in a big way.

The earth fell away beneath her as Jason began to move. He continued to kiss her as he walked and before she knew where they were, he was placing her on the softly cushioned passenger seat of the truck. He broke the kiss, taking time to fasten her seatbelt before bolting around to the driver's side.

The ride passed in a blur through country she hadn't seen before on roads she'd never been down.

"Where are we going? Not the Pack house." Nothing looked familiar at all.

"Not the Pack house," he agreed, pulling into a driveway that led through the dark heart of the forest.

She couldn't see where it led for all the trees. Wherever he was taking her, it was well hidden in the woods.

They rounded another bend and there it was before her. A lovely, rustic log home that blended beautifully with its surroundings. It added to the forest, not invaded.

"This is my home. Yours now too, if you agree." He stopped the car, turned off the engine and sat there for a moment, his hands tense on the steering wheel. "If you don't like it, we can build somewhere else. Anywhere you want, Sally."

She liked that he was willing to sacrifice this beautiful place for her, but she would never dream of asking that of him. It was clear he belonged in the wild places. This house suited him.

"It's beautiful, Jason."

"Come on, I'll show you around." Relief filled his voice as he opened the door and came around to her side to help her out of the truck.

He surprised her by lifting her into his arms again. He wasn't letting her walk. Not one foot. He marched her right up the steps and paused only when he came to the threshold. It was a significant moment. She felt like a bride, even if they hadn't had an official ceremony.

"Do werewolves have weddings?" She spoke the words as she thought them.

Jason paused. "Not like the shindigs in the human world. In the eyes of my Pack, we're already mated. They'll probably throw us a party at some point, when we have time to celebrate."

"Okay, but I'm human." She placed one hand on his chest.

"And part dryad," he went along with the spirit of her teasing.

"I thought it was nymph."

"Dryads are a kind of nymph. The ones who look after trees," he confirmed as he walked through the house. She wasn't able to see much of it. He seemed to have a singular destination in mind.

"There are other kinds of nymphs?"

"A few. But we can talk about that later. What does the human part of you require, my love?" Oh, she liked the sound of that. His love. Part of her wanted to bask in that for a little while, but he dipped to open a door and jostled her.

It was the door to his bedroom. He carried her over that threshold too and walked right up to a massive, wood framed bed.

"I want a wedding. One I can invite my friends to, like normal people." He placed her on her feet, only inches away from the edge of the mattress.

"Might I point out that most of your friends are vampires?"

"Details, details," she teased as he began to undress her and she returned the favor.

He removed her weapons first, placing them on the nightstand alongside his own. He then made short work of his shirt and hers, throwing them to the floor somewhere behind him. She'd have to pick up after him later, but for the moment, all she wanted to do was feel his bare skin against hers.

He reached around her to release the clasp of her bra, dragging out the motions, making the act an embrace in itself. She rested her head on his deeply muscled shoulder while he unhooked the bra one tiny hook at a time. When all were free, he held her for a long, timeless moment, rubbing circles on the skin of her back, rocking her slightly within the circle of his arms.

When he finally stepped back, he took the straps of the bra with him, revealing her breasts to his gaze. His hands rose to cup her, fingering her nipples with his large, work-roughened hands. The dark tan of his skin made a tempting contrast with the parts of her body that never saw the tanning rays of the sun. He stood, less than a foot away from her, his hands laying claim to her bounty as his gaze met hers.

"You're mine, Sally. For the rest of our lives."

The moment was charged with a delicious electric tension. He seemed to be waiting for her reply, though she'd already told him she loved him in front of his Pack. What more validation could he want?

"For the rest of our lives," she repeated. "So don't you get any ideas about chasing any other tails but mine," she teased. Which brought up another question in her mind.

Jason's hands moved from her breasts upward, to cup her face. "Sweetheart, wolves mate for life. There will never be anyone but you ever again."

"Good. Because I have a gun and I'm not shy about using it." She tried to deflect the tension with humor, but failed. "Do you mind that I can't become a wolf?" There. It was out in the open. Her biggest concern now that she'd committed to him.

It worried her. Would he grow tired of always having to run alone? Would he see her as too weak or too human to be his equal? She knew his sex drive was urging him on now—as was hers—but what about later, when their passion cooled to a more manageable level?

He lowered his head to stare deep into her eyes.

"Get this straight. I love you. No matter what form you come in. I love *you*. Nothing can ever change that. The only thing we can't do is mate while furry and frankly, I lost my taste for that kind of pastime soon after puberty."

"Really?" She was intrigued by how being a werewolf really worked. She hadn't thought about them having sex in that form.

"Mating in our fur is all about the animal." He pulled away and began working on her jeans. He talked while he continued to undress her. "It's about dominance and control. It's not something I ever really enjoyed, to be honest." He shrugged as he helped her step out of her boots. His fingers went to her waistband and he tugged down on the jeans and panties at the same time, pausing only when he revealed her neat curls.

He let the fabric fall the rest of the way and she kicked out of it while he sat on his haunches in front of her, his gaze fixed between her thighs. Gently, he pushed downward on her hips until she sat on the edge of the bed. He spread her thighs and made a place for himself between, petting her curls as he continued the conversation.

"Some men like the primal rush, from what I understand, but I prefer the nuances of making love in human form. For instance, in wolf form, I couldn't do this..." He pushed one finger deep inside her, using his other hand to spread her wide for his inspection. "Beautiful," he murmured, sliding his finger in the slick juices her body produced for him. He watched with rapt attention as he added a second finger, stretching her, preparing her, though in truth she was already primed and ready for anything.

"Jason," she panted his name as his fingers began a steady rhythm within her. She clutched his shoulders for dear life.

He gave her a small climax before retreating to remove his jeans. She licked her lips as his hard cock bobbed in front of her. She wanted to taste him but he moved out of reach.

"Later, sweetheart. I'm too close to the edge right now and I want nothing more than to be inside you." His voice was ragged as he moved around the edge of the bed, encouraging her without words to slide into the middle of the huge expanse.

If it meant having him sooner, she was all for it. Sally scooted backward, hoping he would follow. His gaze was centered on her pussy as she spread eagerly for him. It didn't take long for him to join her, climbing over her in the most primitive, exciting way.

"Don't wait, Jason. I want you now," she whispered in his ear, rising up to nip his earlobe. Her instinctive action seemed to drive him over the edge.

Jason found his place between her thighs and slid home in one long, forceful stroke. Her body welcomed him and she felt complete as she hadn't since the last time they'd been together. No other man had ever made her feel this way. No other man had ever claimed her so totally—body, heart and soul. It was all his. All for him.

She let go of his earlobe and licked the place she'd bitten. "I love you, Jason."

Her whisper seemed to ignite him. His hips began to move in a primal rhythm, thrusting and retreating, pushing her up the bed with his force. She dug in her heels and matched him as best she could. Her body strained, her passion rising with his as he powered into her. They were a matched set, each reaching for something only the other could provide.

When the crisis came, it came upon them both at the same time. She screamed his name as he went rigid inside her, his head thrown back as his muscles strained. The pleasure blinded her and she knew he felt the same. On some basic level, her newly discovered magic reached out and intertwined with his.

She would never be the same again.

Jason breathed hard as he collapsed half on top of her. He'd tried to roll away, but neither of them had much strength left after the cataclysm that had rocked them both.

"What was that?" he asked, wonder in his voice along with a bit of concern.

"I don't think it's anything to worry about. I sort of expanded my abilities a little when I had to help Leonora. Putting her into that tree opened something up within my mind. At least, that's how it felt. I can't really describe it."

"You put her in the tree?" Jason found the strength to roll away until he was facing her, one hand propped under his head so he could meet her gaze.

"Yeah. What did you think?"

"I figured she did it somehow, with her last little bit of energy."

"No, she was too far gone. It was all I could do to get her into the tree. She showed me how. She spoke into my mind." Sally squinted, searching for the right words to describe what had happened. It was so out of the realm of her prior experience, it was hard to come up with accurate descriptions.

"Telepathy," Jason nodded as if it were commonplace. They'd have to have a long talk about what was considered normal in this altered world of his. She definitely had a lot to learn.

"I guess," she continued. "Dmitri gave her a few drops of his blood to help counteract the poison and she stopped fading, thank goodness. She had enough strength to show me what to do and I followed her instructions and my own instincts. She connected me with the forest in a way that I'd never experienced before." Her voice trailed off as she recalled the wonder of those moments. They'd been fraught with fear for Leonora and a myriad of other strong emotions, but they had also been magnificently magical.

"Dmitri gave her his blood?" Jason seemed more interested in that than her experience, which drew her back to the moment and made her look at him.

"Yeah. Is that a big deal?"

"A very big deal. Vampire blood is potently magical and can heal mortal wounds. But ingesting it forms a bond. Considering how long they live, most bloodletters don't form those bonds easily or often."

"Leonora agreed to reciprocate once she was better," Sally offered.

"Curiouser and curiouser. I'm not sure what nymph blood

would do to a bloodletter." Jason looked pensive. "It could probably kill a young one, but someone of Dmitri's age and power..." He paused for a moment. "I guess he can probably handle it. It might give him a boost in magic too. Quite a bit for Leonora to trust him with."

"They talked about that, I think, and moving their friendship to a new level of trust. Something like that."

"Interesting." Jason rolled over onto his back.

"You know, with everything that happened, I never did find out who shot Leonora."

"A guy named Alvin Sanders. At least that's what his driver's license said."

"That's the man who bought the house where Jimmy was kept. Dmitri had Carly watching his bank account for possible *Venifucus* ties." Sally's mind spun as she sorted through the various tendrils of information.

"Looks like we found them. He won't be a problem anymore." Jason's voice was very definite.

"I saw Dmitri kill Sullivan. How can you hide something like that from the police?"

"Simple. We don't." He sighed. "Much as I dislike it, we'll have to blame their deaths on the bear they killed and present it to the local cops as *fait accompli*. That way, the cops won't go on a bear hunt in our woods. The killer has already been dealt with and we have a convenient explanation for two mauling deaths."

"Won't the coroner look more closely? Any good forensic specialist should be able to tell the wounds weren't made by a bear."

"You'd be surprised. But, if anyone starts asking questions, Dmitri has spent a lot of time building relationships with certain key people in the area. So have we. We just don't mix with humans as much as the bloodletters do. But if we need help, we have enough friends in high places to make this work."

"I'll take your word on that. If we want Leonora back anytime soon, I have to find her other grandchildren. Leonora claims they all have magic and that together, we can bring her back. I promised her I'd try."

"We'll do more than try. We'll make it happen, sweetheart. Leonora's my friend too." He rolled toward her and pulled her back into his arms. She hugged him, loving the fact that she was free to do so and would be for the rest of their lives.

"I never thought I'd have someone of my own. Someone who loved me and that I loved in return." Her words were full of the wonder she felt.

"I dreamed of it, but never really expected it to happen. I've looked for you for a long time, sweetheart." Jason kissed her, reigniting the fire that had been banked in her blood, then pulled back to place little kisses all over her face and neck, working his way downward. "I never expected you to be so magical."

"I didn't either," she agreed breathlessly. Then a thought occurred to her. "Does it bother you?"

Jason's head rose and his gaze met hers. "Never. You're perfect just the way you are and whatever you become as you learn more about your heritage, I will love you for the rest of my days."

"Oh, Jason." Tears sparkled in her eyes as the love within her welled up and overflowed.

He rolled with her so that she ended up on top of him. Her legs spread for balance and her mood changed in an instant as she discovered his renewed interest.

"Really, Jason?" One eyebrow rose in teasing question. "So soon?"

His smile warmed her from within. "There are many advantages to being a werewolf."

"I think I'm going to enjoy learning all about it." She didn't resist as his hands cupped her shoulders and guided her downward.

Her breasts were in perfect line with his mouth and he took full advantage. He started out gentle, licking and nibbling, but as his caresses grew progressively more demanding, her body began to sing above his, demanding more. He knew just how to touch, just how to tantalize, just how to drive her wild.

"Jason," she gasped as one of his hands found its way between their bodies to touch between her thighs. Just a light touch—at first. Like he'd done above, he gradually increased the contact. What started as light petting of her curls grew into the slick slide of his fingers deep inside her until she couldn't stop squirming above him. She needed him again. Now.

His name became a litany as he teased her into a state of acute sensitivity and need. For him...and him alone.

"Are you ready for me, sweetheart?" His tone said he already knew the answer, but he wanted to hear her say it just the same.

She didn't mind. At this point, she'd do just about anything he asked. As long as he'd give her what she wanted. What she needed.

"Please..." Her voice trailed off as he drove her higher. He really did know just how to touch to send her passions soaring.

"What do you need, sweetheart?" His fingers slowed, then withdrew. She wanted to whine at the loss. Only sheer force of will kept her from begging.

"I need you, Jason. Inside me. Now." She was demanding in her need but he didn't seem to mind. In fact, he gave every appearance of liking it.

Emboldened by his response, she took matters into her own hands, reaching between them to wrap her hand around him. She squeezed, tantalizing him as she held his gaze, but she couldn't wait too long. Promising herself she'd play more later, she guided him into her opening and sank downward.

Oh, yeah. That's was it. That was what she needed. That...and more. She began to move on him, slowly at first, drawing out each sensation, but then the need spiked and she began to lose control. Her movements weren't as fluid, her muscles quivered under the strain.

Jason was there to help. His hands framed her hips, supporting her as her pace became frantic, aiding her movements, thrusting upward with his hips to meet her. Oh, yeah. He knew exactly what to do.

"Just like that, sweetheart," he whispered as his breathing increased yet again. They strained together upward, toward some goal only they knew. Together.

Pleasure broke over them in unison and for that moment out of time they were truly one. Sharing one skin, one being in the face of the tempest. Sally screamed his name as the warm essence of him filled her, bathing her senses in the greatest pleasure she'd ever known. Only with him.

Of all the men in the universe, this one had been designed with her in mind. As she had been made for him. Together they were unstoppable. Unbeatable. Invincible.

And their passion was one for the ages.

And then, inevitably, it was time to let go of nirvana. Time to come back down to live among the mortals once again. But that glimpse of heaven remained and would be reachable again in the not too distant future.

That's what life with Jason would hold. Moments of perfection followed by other moments of laughter, love, joy and, of course, some pain. But he'd be there to catch her when she fell as she'd be there for him. And he would comfort her as she would comfort him. They were a team now. A partnership never to be broken.

Sally liked that. She liked belonging to someone and having someone so incredibly special belong to her for the first time in her life. She liked being a part of Jason's life. She only feared one thing...that the rest of the Pack wouldn't be as welcoming.

She knew she had a hurdle to jump there. The soldiers in the field with them had accepted her and a few others at the Pack house. But the Pack was made up of many individuals. Some had already taken a dislike to her based purely on genetics. There could be others who would make her life difficult—and Jason's by extension—because of her.

Jason rolled them to their sides and made her comfortable in the aftermath. She was glad he had the strength and presence of mind to take care of them both because she was useless. Limp as a wet rag and completely wrung out.

"You okay?" Jason panted, his breathing still affected by their exertions.

"Never better." She tried to be nonchalant but he didn't seem to be buying it. His hand came around her waist and squeezed gently, forcing her to meet his gaze.

"What's with that little frown between your eyes? Can't be what we just did because that seemed just about perfect in every way." A little sliver of doubt crept into his expression and she was quick to reassure him.

"You know it's not that. Every time we're together it only gets better."

"Then what is it?" His hand smoothed over the skin of her waist and back, soothing her.

"I've been thinking..."

"Well, that's your problem right there," he joked. She

smiled, but she wanted to talk to him about this. She just didn't want to sound like a scaredy cat. He sobered when her tension didn't ease. "Seriously, how can you think after that? My brain is fried."

"Yeah, mine pretty well short-circuited there for a while too, but then the little doubt came back."

"Doubt?" He seemed appalled, shocked and a little scared, though hid it for the most part. "Doubt about what? Can't be about us."

"No, not about us." She stroked his shoulder, reassuring him again with her touch. "But about how your Pack is going to accept me. I don't want to cause you trouble. I know I'm not what they expected. Not what *you* expected, for that matter."

"Sweetheart, you're you and that's all that matters. You've already proved yourself to the toughest badasses in the Pack. The soldiers are the ones who would give you the most trouble if you weren't strong enough to be their Alpha's mate. If you weren't an Alpha female in your own right. But you've already proved that to them. The rest of the Pack will get the message and fall in line. If the soldiers support you—and after last night, every last one of them thinks you walk on water—then you've got no problems. Believe me."

She tried. She really did. She wanted to believe what he said was true, but a niggling little doubt remained. Her first experience at the Pack house hadn't been exactly peaceful. And women could be a lot cattier than men. Or maybe that should be wolfier, in this case? She laughed at the thought and he seemed to relax.

He pulled her back into his arms and they cuddled for a bit, dozing as the events of the past day and night caught up with them again.

It was around lunchtime before they finally got up for the

day. It seemed werewolves ran on only a few hours of sleep—something that had been characteristic of Sally all her life. She and Jason were well-matched in that respect. They showered together, sharing a quickie that involved a lot of slipping, sliding and soap bubbles, not to mention laughter and incredible passion.

Sally had to borrow some of Jason's giant sweats, but it was way better than putting on her dirty, torn and ruined blouse. Her jeans went in the wash with some of his clothes and they left his house for a companionable stroll through the woods.

She knew they were heading for the Pack house, which was just over the hill as the crow flies, but with Jason's arm around her shoulders, she found it hard to be apprehensive. Still, when the big structure came into view, she felt her heart sink and a bit of the fear return. How would they receive her? Would she be welcome among them? Would they accept her as Jason's mate?

They mounted the steps to the big house together. Each step she took closer to the doorway saw uneasiness build in Sally's mind. When they reached the door, Jason turned to her and put his hands on her shoulders, looking deep into her eyes.

"It'll be okay. I promise you." He dipped his head for a quick, reassuring kiss and turned to open the door. He wasn't giving her any more time to stew.

He stepped across the threshold to the back part of the house where the giant dining hall was and the noise level within dropped like a stone. Oh, boy. Sally followed him, expecting the worst.

Instead, when they saw her, the gathered wolves sent up a cheer that rocked the rafters. Howls, whistles and the stomping of feet welcomed them as Jason took her hand in his and raised it as if in victory. They were a couple and the smiling faces of the werewolves all around made it clear that most of the Pack was happy about it.

Out of the corner of her eye, Sally saw Jimmy moving through the cheering crowd. When he made it to the front, he stepped right up to her and dropped to one knee, his gaze holding hers. The room's exuberance died down as they watched the youngster's actions.

"I pledge my fealty to you, Alpha, and to your mate." It wasn't precisely clear whether he was addressing Sally or Jason, but either would work. It was a major step for her and one she hadn't expected. "Thank you for saving my life," Jimmy added as he knelt before her, his heart in his eyes, his neck bared in submission.

Sally wasn't exactly sure what to do, but she couldn't leave him on the floor like that. She took his raised hand and tugged upward. Jimmy rose with a grin splitting his face.

"I'm glad I was able to help, Jim. Thank you." She didn't know what else to say, but it seemed she was on the right track.

"Everyone," Jason addressed the gathered wolves. "As you probably have already heard, Sally is my mate. She's agreed to live here, among us, if you will have her."

The cheering renewed at an even higher volume. Sally was overwhelmed by the response. They really did seem to want her here. With Jason. Wow. They were welcoming her when she'd expected to be challenged at every turn.

Jason leaned in to put his arm around her shoulders, tugging her to his side.

"I think they like you," he said just loud enough for her to hear over the crowd.

Tears sprang to her eyes then. Tears for the unfailing confidence in his voice and the warm acceptance of the Pack.

Not only had she found a man that was her perfect match in every way, but he had introduced her to a new world and a Pack full of amazing people who were willing to accept her the way she was and take her in among them. Would wonders never cease?

Sally had gone from having no family and only a handful of friends that she saw less and less frequently, to finding a new home with a man she loved and the surprising acceptance of a werewolf Pack.

They had lunch with the Pack that turned into a celebratory feast that lasted for hours. Everyone in the Pack seemed to have turned out for the impromptu party. It was like a welcome home bash to a place she had never been before. Almost everyone found a minute or two to spend congratulating them. Some of the older couples teased her and Jason about the delights of being mated and Sally found herself laughing more in a few hours with Jason and his Pack than she had the whole previous year on her own.

Her life had changed in a big way and so far, it seemed all for the good. They excused themselves toward sunset when the party showed no signs of winding down. Sally's bags were still at Carly's, with all her clothes. Carly greeted her with a giant hug and Dmitri gave her a small bow of respect. It seemed she'd managed to impress not only the werewolves, but the Master Vampire as well, last night.

Carly demanded details about the action of the night before while Jason and Dmitri shared information about the ongoing hunt. Sally was surprised to learn that sometime during the afternoon of feasting and laughing, Jason had heard from his brother, Jesse, who was on the road following the two hunters they'd let escape. Jason and Dmitri compared notes about the three who had been killed and how the police were reacting to the supposed bear maulings.

One of Jason's older Pack members had made the report earlier in the day, bringing proof to the police department in town of the bear's demise and leading the local cops to the bodies. So far, no further questions had been raised. Dmitri would keep an eye on the police reports with Carly's help and together the Master and the Alpha would make sure no inappropriate questions were asked. They both had a vested interest in keeping things quiet—and their existence hidden from the general human population.

Carly was sad to see Sally pack up and leave her house but she was supportive and helped with the folding and packing. Sally took only a few minutes for a quick change of clothes so she didn't have to wear Jason's giant sweats any longer. She'd felt a little odd all day, surrounded first by the wolves and then at Carly's, dressed like a hobo, but nobody seemed to mind.

She felt a little more human after she'd changed and Sally took a few minutes to reassure her friend that she was making the right decision. So much had happened that Sally hadn't had time to tell Carly about.

"Let's take a little walk outside. I want to show you something." Sally tugged Carly through the French doors to the patio while the men watched from the living room. Dmitri was vigilant with Carly's safety, but he seemed okay with Sally taking her outside without a chaperone.

"What is that heavenly smell?" Carly's eyes searched for the origin of the flowery scent even as Sally knew she would. A smile broke over her face and Sally knew the exact moment Carly became aware of the night-blooming garden Sally had planted as a gift what seemed like eons ago but was really only a day or so ago.

"This is my gift to you," Sally said, leading Carly on a small tour of the little garden. "I can add to it if you like it, but I wanted to be certain before I made it too big."

"How did you do this, Sal?" Tears formed in Carly's eyes as she looked in awe at the garden. It was going over as well as Sally could have hoped. Carly seemed truly touched by the gesture and Sally was on the verge of happy tears herself as she watched her friend enjoy the scents and shapes of the blooms under the light of a pale moon.

"Did Dmitri fill you in on Leonora? Turns out she's my many-times-great-grandmother. I'm part dryad. That's why I've always been able to make things grow." Sally shrugged, not knowing what to expect from such an admission.

"All those beautiful gardens," Carly said, seeming to think back, remembering the earlier landscaping Sally had done with fondness. "I should have known you had some kind of magic. But where did you buy all these? I didn't know there was a nursery that had this kind of stock around here."

Might as well come clean, Sally thought. She reached into her pocket where she'd placed a single seed, for just this purpose. Pulling it out, she held it up between her thumb and forefinger for Carly's inspection.

"I didn't buy the plants. I never bought fully grown plants. All I got were seeds. Like this one here. Now, watch." Sally bent to place the seed into the soil, then put her hand over the spot, closing her eyes and calling her power.

It was easier than it ever had been before. The magic was closer to the surface of her soul and much more accessible. The seed sprouted in no time at all, then broke through the ground to twine upward, around a small trellis that already held a few other vines like this one. The new plant happily joined its fellows, filling in a small gap with its dark green leaves a few seconds before sprouting flowers that bloomed a moment later. The rich smell of the blossoms filled the garden, blending with the other heavenly scents.

Sally watched her friend's face, glad she could bring such a beatific smile to it.

"That's awesome, Sal," Carly said with surprise and wonder in her tone.

"That's just the tip of the iceberg, my dear," Dmitri said, coming up behind his mate. He pulled her back into his embrace as Jason moved to stand next to Sally. Dmitri looked around the new garden and even he seemed to be impressed with its beauty. "I see in this garden your true friendship and love for my mate, and I thank you for its beauty, Sally. I'm glad you are here. Glad your friendship with Carly can continue despite her change. Glad we are allies."

That was a lot to be glad about and Sally was impressed with the Master Vampire's formal tone.

"And I'm glad," Carly added, "that you've found someone to love, Sal. You deserve happiness."

"Back at'cha, kiddo." The tears threatened to start again, so Sally tried to defuse the situation.

If anyone had told her a week ago that she'd be standing in the middle of a vampire's garden with the man she loved, who also happened to be a werewolf, she would have sent them to a psychiatrist. As it turned out, she'd never been happier in her life, or felt more safe. Or more loved.

Epilogue

The next day, just after sunrise, Sally crept from Jason's bedroom and found her way onto the wooden porch. It was so peaceful here, yet so full of life. The trees sang their morning song. The wind whispered of many things. And she was beginning to be able to understand so much more than she ever had about her power and the world of the forest.

She knew a werewolf family skirted the edge of the wood, out for an early hunt. Mother, father, and two youngsters—both just learning the ways of their wolf form. The parents were supervising their hunting efforts with great amusement and a whole lot of love. The forest approved and watched their passing as they kept a respectful distance from their Alpha's home. But the trees knew.

They also knew their new magical friend and guardian was living there now, among the wildwood, where she had always belonged. She was young, the leaves whispered, but powerful. And she would learn how to use the full extent of her power in the fullness of time...to awaken the one the willow kept safe within its heart.

Sally thought about Leonora and how much she missed the woman she'd only just met. They were alike, yet so very different. Leonora's power seemed to be that of the trees itself. Sally's was more grounded to the earth that fed their roots and the branches and leaves that reached toward the sun. Leonora was the center. Sally was more above and below, but she could still have an impact on the forest as a whole. She could still help. She was still connected in a way she was only just beginning to understand.

To understand better, she'd need Leonora's teaching and guidance. And the only way to get that was to free her and heal her by finding the other part-dryads running around out there who were related by blood to Leonora.

It wasn't such a bad task, really. Sally was good at uncovering secrets and finding people. She'd use her detective skills to find her lost family. And she might just gain a sister and some cousins at the same time. Not to mention rescuing a grandmother she had come to love dearly in only a short amount of time.

"I'll find them for you, Leonora. I'll find them and bring them here to help you. I promise," she thought hard toward the place where Leonora rested in the willow, but no answer came back to her. Leonora was there. She knew it for a fact. But communication was difficult, she had been warned.

Behind her, the screen door opened and bare feet padded outward from the house, toward her. Jason sat down behind her, pulling her backward into his arms. He was so warm. He felt good on this crisp morning.

"What are you doing out here when you should be snuggled up in my bed?" He kissed her cheek from behind, nuzzling her hair and neck as he rocked her back against him. He was in a playful, cuddly sort of mood.

"I'm having a hard time believing this is really real." She decided to go with candor over joking.

"I'm real all right. So are you." He kissed her again.

"I feel so lucky. So blessed. I never thought my life would turn out this way. I never thought I'd find true happiness."

"So then you're happy with me?" He seemed almost uncertain.

She turned in his arms. "Are you kidding?"

Relief flooded his features as he drew her in for a kiss that was all the answer she needed. When he let her up for air, the light of passion had flickered to life in his eyes. He let it simmer for a moment when she put one palm on his bare chest. His jeans rubbed against hers as he shifted them into a more comfortable position. She had things she wanted to talk about, plans to make and a morning to enjoy before they resumed their passion play.

"I'll phone my boss on Monday and tell him I'm quitting."

"You'll miss being a cop, won't you?" Jason's eyes narrowed. "You could try for the department out here if you want. They might have an opening."

"You wouldn't mind?" This was really important to her. She wasn't sure what was expected of her as the Alpha's wife, but she'd never been very good at being ornamental.

"Mind?" Jason looked surprised. "Sally, you have a profession that you seem to enjoy. As your mate, I won't keep you from it if you want to continue. I could wish you were a professional basket weaver or something else that would keep you away from guns and violence, but you're my mate. You're also a dedicated police officer. I respect that."

Relief surged through her. "I'm not sure yet, but I'm glad to hear you say that. When I came out here, I was completely burnt out on police work, but working with you and helping Colleen and Jimmy—that reminded me why I became a cop in the first place. We made a difference and I was glad to be a part of it. For now though, I'll just take this one step at a time. First, I need to settle things in San Francisco. I've got to quit my job there, pack up my things and make the move out here."

"I'm glad you're willing to move. I do want you to know that I'd have given up the Pack to be with you wherever you wanted to live, but it's not something I'd do lightly. It's a relief to know you want to be part of it."

"I wouldn't ask that of you, Jason. I have no particular attachment to San Francisco, other than my friends and a fondness for sourdough bread. But Carly's here and the others are tied up in their own adjustment to their new lives right now. I only see them once a month and for the past few, they've been keeping their changes from me. It'll be good to have it all out in the open and it'll be good to be near Carly. She was marooned out here when she married Dmitri. I've missed her. And I can be a cop anywhere. I might look into joining the local force after I've settled in. I like this house." She looked around at the magnificent wood structure that was so much a part of its surroundings. It really was beautiful.

"I'm glad. I had a mate in mind when I built it, but I never dreamed she'd be part human and part nymph." He looked at the log home with pride. "It's a fitting place for someone of your background."

"It's perfect," she agreed. "And if, in the future, you want an addition or any improvements, I can work with the living trees to help out. At least, I think I can. Leonora can teach me the right way to go about it, once we free her."

"Then that will be our first order of business," he said with finality. "I miss her already and the forest feels different without her in it." He looked around, seeming a tad uncomfortable. "It's like the trees miss her."

"They do. I'm a poor substitute—a newcomer and not nearly as powerful as a full-blood dryad. Plus, my energy is on a different spectrum than hers. Mine is more brown and olive green. Hers is the purest green-gold I've ever seen."

"You can see that kind of thing?" Jason seemed impressed.

"Well, I couldn't before, but I did for a few minutes there when Leonora got shot and I had to call on magic I didn't even know I had, to do something for her. Dmitri helped. His—aura, I guess you would call it—is blood red, by the way. No big surprise there."

"Really? And do I have one of these auras?"

"I'd have to see you shift, but I'd lay odds the color of your magic is more golden brown. We have that in common at least, the brown part."

"Oh, we have a lot more than that in common, sweetheart." He stood with her in his arms. He really was incredibly strong. Turning her, he bent for a quick kiss as he kicked the screen door open and carried her inside. Talk would wait. For now.

They'd settled the most important issues and the rest would come in time.

As he took her into the wooden house she heard the song of the trees change and turn joyous. The daughter of the dryad had found her mate and in time, there would be more daughters of her line to carry on the magic of the trees and plants, and protect the forest. The wildwood rejoiced.

About the Author

Bianca D'Arc has run a laboratory, climbed the corporate ladder in the shark-infested streets of lower Manhattan, studied and taught martial arts, and earned the right to put a whole bunch of letters after her name, but she's always enjoyed writing more than any of her other pursuits. She grew up and still lives on Long Island, where she keeps busy with an extensive garden, several aquariums full of very demanding fish, and writing her favorite genres of paranormal, fantasy and sci fi romance.

You can learn more about Bianca and her work by visiting her website at: www.biancadarc.com. You can also friend her on Facebook at: http://www.facebook.com/biancadarc and follow her on Twitter at: http://twitter.com/biancadarc.

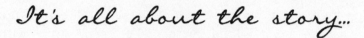

CPSIA information can be obtained at www.ICGtesting.com
Printed in the USA
BVOW041414160413

318326BV00002B/16/P